BACK, TO HER FUTURE

THE GENX SERIES

CARY J HANSSON

ABOUT THE AUTHOR

Cary is a fifty something mum of three, an ex-dancer, actress, waitress, cleaner, TV presenter, double-glazing sales rep, fax machine operator ... You name it and she's cleaned it, served it, sent it or sold it.

She writes stories about ordinary people, living lives of extraordinary courage and indestructible humour. She promises only two things: no knights in shining armour and no flying cars. Her characters save themselves, as in the end we all must do.

She is also a certified practitioner of Writing for Wellness.

To learn more visit: https://www.caryjhansson.com/

All characters in this publication are fictitious and any resemblance to real persons, living or dead, is purely coincidental.

Cover design and art direction by JoJo Ford, of JoJo Ford Illustration

❀ Created with Vellum

For all the Meryems of this world.

PROLOGUE

F*lat 3, Sydney House*
5 Layton Rd
Enfield, London

TUESDAY 14TH JANUARY 1986

DEAR MERY,

I'm writing this letter even though I haven't got your address. Mum says she's sure we'll get one soon. I thought I'd write because otherwise I'm going to forget all the things I need to tell you. It's been twenty-four days already and I miss you.

PART ONE

1

FATHER FIGURE

Turkey, present day

THE TAXI SPED across the red dust of the Anatolian plain, Meryem's hair streaming through the open window like black flames. The driver balanced the stub of a Marlboro between yellow fingers, the sun had an hour left and the car's suspension creaked like a restless skeleton. Ahead, huddled in the fold of the mountain, the village crouched.

'Ankara,' she said as she lifted her arm and waved it at the plain. 'All that is in front, or below, is Ankara.'

The driver watched her in his mirror, a beetle of a man.

Meryem smiled, her teeth polished pearls. 'My father's words. He always said everything outside of the village was Ankara.'

'You are coming home?'

She looked up at the fast-approaching cluster of buildings, at the slender grey tower of the minaret soaring higher than anything else. 'I wouldn't say that,' she murmured.

'To your father?'

'He is dying.'

The driver nodded. 'You are a good daughter,' he said and showed his own teeth, brown stubs.

'I wouldn't say that either,' Meryem said, and pulled her sunglasses over her eyes.

HER FATHER'S VILLAGE.

In all the years since she had left, one hand would suffice to count the number of times she had been back. The single pail of water in the toilet – no roof and no paper. The wheeling storks her aunties had insisted were good omens, as if she should have been grateful... And dust clouds, always dust clouds on the horizon signalling every arrival and every departure. Yes, one hand would suffice.

She looked down and straightened the square-cut emerald on her middle finger. The road across the plain was paved now; too little dust for tell-tale clouds. Whoever was already here wouldn't have seen the taxi arriving. Her grown children? Back for one last visit to their grandfather? Unlikely if they knew there was a possibility of running into their mother. Her brother? Of course. She leaned back in her seat, her skin melding through the expensive silk of her blouse to the warm sweat-stained upholstery. Ahead the driver's hair was sparse; patches of nut-brown skull peeped through, like speckled eggs.

Her father could no longer sit, so, cloud or no cloud, he wouldn't have seen – not as he had seen her leave. Then, he might have watched an hour or more, a swirl of red cloud marking every mile she travelled away from him.

Did he?

The emerald glittered like a dew-crowned leaf as she brought her hand to her chest and took a deep breath. If there was one rule she had learned to live by, it was that she did not dwell on questions she couldn't answer. It was better to concentrate on what she knew – the hard dried patches of sugar still flaking between her legs from when they ripped her hair away in preparation for the wedding. Laughing because she cried. *If you think this hurts,* the women had teased. And they had been right. The heavy jangle of gold at her slack wrists, the flabby weight of her new husband's middle-age girth and the scorching dry pain as he took her virginity – *that* was what was known about the day she left this village. Hand trembling, she pushed her glasses up and stared out of the window.

A grove of oleaster trees, silver-grey against the burned earth, shimmered so close as they passed she could almost reach and touch them. Old Ali Solak's trees, still alive long after Old Ali Solak had died. Leaning out, she scooped her hair back and stretched her neck and breathed deeply. She was trying to catch the scent that as a child she remembered her mother trying to catch. But it was the wrong season, and perhaps, although again this was something she could not answer, it had been the wrong season for her mother too.

Turning away from the trees she unfolded her palm and saw the angry crescents her nails had gouged. No roof on the toilet? No paper? Now she had a toilet that flushed jets of water and blew warm air to dry her bottom, and if she still waxed, she did so for her own pleasure and, at this thought, her lips turned up in a small and secret smile.

When she saw that the driver was watching, she laughed again, just for him.

. . .

THEY CAME to a stop by a cobbled square, in the middle of which a small stone fountain bubbled silver water. The square was empty. Electricity and plumbing had come to the village; no one collected water anymore. She took out a gold compact and a pearl-pink lipstick and worked slowly. Blotting, pouting, reapplying. When she was done, she snapped the compact shut and pulled out several clean, crisp notes, double what was expected.

'I won't be long. Wait, if you want the return fare.' She handed the driver the money and stepped out of the taxi. Her blouse was cut deep, revealing skin polished as the inside of an oyster shell. She straightened her jeans, removed her sunglasses and looked up. There it was, marking the edge of the village, her father's house. Still the largest, the same black gates, the same black fencing, the same shutters at his bedroom window. She felt the scratch of dust at her neck and turned, a half-forgotten sound floating towards her. Meryem smiled, her hand at her eyes, shielding the sun as she looked across at the low grey hills. Sheep. How patient they had been with her. A terrified fourteen-year-old, she hadn't known one end of the animal from the other, but how silent and still they had stood as she'd learned to milk them. Not the goats. The goats had kicked and struggled. And the cows... Her eyes smarted, with tears as sudden as they were unexpected. The memory, so long buried, still burned. They had understood. The cows had sensed her pain, their eyes, black pools of reflected sadness. Blinking the heat away, pinching her palms, once again she pulled her glasses over her eyes and began picking her way across the sun-baked earth towards her father's land. Every stone stabbing at the slender soles of her stilettos, painful as red-hot coals.

'*Kiz kardes*, Meryem.' As if she were contagious, Emin stood with his back pressed stiffly against the door. His mouth had twisted so tightly, she wondered how he got the words out. 'Why can't you show some respect?' he hissed, staring at her blouse.

Meryem didn't answer as she offered her cheek for the customary greeting. When it came, his kiss was hard and dry and more uncomfortable for him, she knew, than for her. '*Abi,* Emin,' she murmured and almost pitied him this forced ritual, his inability, always, to do anything other than what was expected of him.

'If it was my decision I would not let you over the threshold. You look like the slut you are.'

She took her glasses off. 'But it's not,' she smiled and when he said nothing, added. 'He is upstairs?'

Balling his fists, Emin nodded.

Meryem put her head to one side as she looked at him. She would *not* ask. She would not ask if her son and daughter were also upstairs. Instead she reached out, put her hand on his arm and felt him flinch.

Her father's bedroom. Broad as it was long, shaded from the sun by tall shuttered windows. Sparsely furnished. For his feet, hand-spun wool from Istanbul, sessile oak to hold his hand-stitched shirts. Her husband had been rich, and she had been valuable. A virgin, with a British passport. He had paid generously; the evidence was all around her.

And her children? They were not here. Her mouth hardened. She hadn't expected to find them, of course not. But she had hoped. That was clear, as always, by the leaden disappointment she felt, and as she looked across the room towards the bed, she wondered if it would ever leave, this torch she carried, that they would come to understand, or at least try to understand.

On the bedside table stood a jug of water, white pill bottles lined alongside. She took a step closer, stopping as a small pebble-shape emerged from the pillows, brown against the crumpled white of Egyptian cotton. At first she didn't understand... She didn't see that this pebble was her father's head. And when she did, when she saw his yellow face and the skin hanging from his bones like poured butter, the shock winded her. She stepped back, her hand at her mouth.

His breath was shallow and ragged, every snatch of air a struggle. Meryem breathed herself, long and deep, hearing in the ringing silence how her heart pulsed.

So, this was her father. The richest man in the village. The boy who ran up mountains, the first to go to Europe – this is what he had become. Her hand began to tremble and she looked down at it as if it were not a part of her. As if it belonged to the teenager she once was. *He can't hurt you,* she whispered, *you are richer than him now.* And the truth of this, calmed her. Twenty-four hours ago, she was in her Dubai apartment, sipping champagne, watching another sun set over the Persian Gulf when Emin's text had arrived.

Baba is dying. You need to come.

She hadn't responded. And it wasn't until she had stood to re-fill her glass that she saw the second text.

He has something he wants to tell us. About Mamma. He is waiting for you to arrive.

She held her hand over her heart, hearing as it settled, feeling the tremors at her fingertips still. And then she was ready. She walked across the marble floor, took a chair, sat down and waited to hear whatever it was her father had called her there to say.

MANY MINUTES PASSED. The sun slipped lower. The housekeeper brought tea and opened the shutters, a delta of cool air spilling across the room. Emin came in, positioning himself on the opposite side of the bed. At first he didn't speak and then, when he did, he did not look at her.

'Ayla was here. She's gone back.'

Meryem kept her voice light. 'To Singapore?'

'Ask her yourself. She is your daughter.'

'I would. If she would talk to me.'

Emin leaned over the bed. 'Why *should* she talk to you, Meryem,' he whispered. 'She is disgusted with you. We all are.'

Meryem held her chin high as she turned away to look out of the window. With the sun so low, the village had once again been swallowed by the shadow of its mountain host, only a lone oleaster tree far out on the plain still caught the light, a silver-grey glittering. But that wouldn't last. Soon enough, she thought, even this last tree would be swallowed by shadow.

A hand touched her arm. Startled, she turned. Her father had gone from sleeping, to waking, in an instant and she watched as his long jointed fingers scrabbled and failed to find a grip on her sleeve.

The exertion of his attempt had him coughing. He pulled his hand back and tried to push himself upright, his thin arms trembling as they buckled under the weight.

Emin was on his feet, calling for the housekeeper.

She came instantly and together they eased him up,

propping his back and head with pillows, coaxing him to take a mouthful of water. He spluttered it back into the glass and waved a hand at the woman to dismiss her.

'Sit down. Sit down,' he said to Emin, and to Meryem he said nothing, for she hadn't stood.

'Sit down,' he rasped again, as Emin hovered. 'I have something to say.'

IT WAS dark when he finished speaking. He closed his eyes. And although the death rattle of his lungs was loud in the quietened room, it was not as loud as the blood that rushed her ears, nor his laboured words, destined to live long after the tongue that had spoken them was silent. Destined to live as long as she did, because it was not so. It was not as she had taught herself to believe. *Her mother had written.* The mother he had taken them from, the mother he said had abandoned them. Years of letters. All returned, unopened.

The corners of her mouth turned down as she watched a spittle of foam leak from her father's slack lips. He would not speak again, and what she was wishing was that his speech had failed earlier. For what was the point of those words now? What was she, or Emin, supposed to do with them? They should have stayed buried in the blackness of her father's soul, in the red dust of this village, until she was dust herself and her children's children were dust. Through the semi-darkness, she looked across the bed, to Emin. The room was so gloomy now, he was almost a silhouette and because she couldn't see the features of the man he had become, she was able to picture the boy he once was. Always clutching her hand, her waist, holding onto her, those first weeks, as if she were life itself. Life, or their mother. What was he thinking? It hurt too much to even imagine, so she didn't try, she folded her hands in her lap and did the only thing she could. She sat and waited for her father to die.

'BENI AFFET.'

At first the sound was a thin whistle that didn't separate into words. Another struggle for breath. But then it came again.

'*Beni affet.*'

And this time, she heard. Despite herself, she leaned in close to his face, her cheek against his. She wanted to hear what she couldn't believe he was trying to say.

Emin had leaned in too, and now their heads touched. Meryem glanced up at him. They had not been so close since they were children and she wondered if he was thinking that too.

'*Beni affet.*' A third time.

'*Baba.*' Emin clasped his father's hand. 'I do. I do.'

Meryem withdrew. She had heard correctly. Emin too. Emin, who never got to hold his mother's hand again after the age of seven, for whom she had become mother and sister. His everything... yes, she would have given him the sun if she could.

'Forgive me.' Her father's last dry words. In English.

Meryem looked down at her hands.

'Meryem,' Emin urged. 'He is asking for your forgiveness.'

She didn't move.

'*Tell him!* There won't be another chance.'

And it felt to Meryem as she looked back at her brother that time had finally done what she had once wished so hard for. Once prayed for, before she stopped praying. It had rewound. Spooled back. And there was her brother as a child, his eyes wild with grief and bewilderment looking back at her as if she, and only she, could put a stop to the torment his world had become. But even when they were children she had not been able to comfort him and it was the same now, and knowing that tore her heart anew. 'Emin,' she whispered, her throat tight, because if she allowed herself to cry, he might mistake the tears. He might think they were for the dying man in the bed between them, and *that* she would not allow.

'*Tell him.*'

Meryem took a breath in and it filled her lungs so violently, she shuddered. She pushed her shoulders back and lifted her chin and turned away from the bed and looked again at the open window to where she had seen the lone oleaster tree out on the plain. At first she couldn't see it, and suddenly she could, and although it was a moment away from being swallowed by shadow, the leaves glittered still. The day's last show of defiance. She turned, gently lifting her father's hand, her lips so close to his ear they left a trace of iridescent pink from her lips.

'*Ben degillim,*' she whispered, and then, '*ana la.*' And finally, in a voice that was strong as he himself had once been. 'I don't, Baba. I do not forgive you.' And she let his hand drop, stood, picked up her handbag and left the room without a backward glance.

How close she came. With one hand on the door handle and the housekeeper across the hall, another moment and she would have been gone.

But Emin was there, his hand covering hers, his grip so hard the emerald cut into her flesh.

'Meryem!'

She didn't turn to face him, even as her skin burned.

'Where are you going?'

'Home,' she hissed and wrenched her hand free.

He took a step back, watching her. 'Dubai?'

'Yes. Home.'

Emin's laugh was harsh. 'This is where you call home now?'

Meryem looked down at her hand, twisted the ring, loosening it free from the engorged skin.

'What is *home* there, Meryem, that makes you leave now? When our father is *dying*?' Emin stood, hands on hips. 'You have no family there. You have no friends there.'

Turning away, Meryem stared at the housekeeper.

She stared back.

'Of course!' Emin shook his head. 'What am I thinking? Of course, it's *home*. You have your money there! You must go back to your money, Meryem. Money is all you have left. You have no family. No friends.'

She didn't answer. She took her glasses out of her handbag and began rubbing them clean on a corner of her blouse. 'What do you want, Emin?' she said quietly.

'Our father is upstairs dying!' he said, eyes widening in disbelief. 'He is asking for forgiveness—'

'And he has had my answer.' She lifted the glasses, checking for smudges.

For a long moment Emin was silent. When he did speak, his voice was soft. 'What is wrong with you, Meryem?'

The corner of Meryem's mouth turned up. 'What's wrong with *me*?' she said and waited, allowing a moment to pass between them, a moment as wide as the plain she had just crossed, in which she watched him, watching her. When he didn't answer, she looked down, gave her glasses one last wipe and pushed them back on her head. '*You* are asking what's wrong with *me*?' Her voice was ice. 'You heard what he said, Emin.'

Emin tipped his head, as if he was confused, as if she wasn't making sense.

The gesture enraged her. 'You heard him, Emin!' And now her voice cracked with an anger that was electric, that bounced off the walls like a striking snake. '*She wrote to us!* All those years, when we were imprisoned here! She wrote us letters and he sent them back to London. All those years he made us think she didn't care!'

In the shadowed corner, the housekeeper stepped back.

'Meryem, we were never imprisoned—'

'Not you!' she cried and wheeled away from him. 'Not you! You weren't.'

'You weren't either, Meryem.' His hand reached her arm.

'*Don't* tell me how it was, Emin!' she hissed. 'You were a child, and you were a boy! *Don't ever try to tell me how it was!*'

'Meryem.'

'Don't you see what this means?'

How long it took for him to lift his head and meet her eye. 'It doesn't mean anything,' he managed, his voice like broken rock. 'She's dead. You heard Baba. When he collected her things, there was nothing. He doesn't have them. It's too late.'

Meryem turned, opening the heavy front door with one swift movement. Across the square she could see the driver leaning against the taxi. She didn't look back as she crossed to the gates that enclosed her father's house. 'Let's go,' she called to the driver.

He rubbed at his forehead, the stub of his cigarette an extra finger. He was looking beyond Meryem, back to Emin.

'Let's go!' she said again and opened the passenger door.

The driver nodded but he didn't move, and suddenly

there were footsteps very close behind, and then Emin's hand was on hers, squeezing hard, trying to push the door closed. 'You can't, Meryem. What you do, the way you live your life, it brings shame on all of us. I won't allow you to go back to it. I forbid you.'

'Emin.' Exhausted now, Meryem slumped her forehead to the door of the taxi, almost too weary to stand. *You can't... I forbid... You will...* These were her father's words, and then they had been her husband's words. Now Emin too? As the warmth from the taxi door spread across her forehead, Meryem felt herself consumed by a sadness as profound as any she had ever felt.

The driver took a step towards her, his hands raised in a conciliatory gesture.

'She is hysterical,' Emin said, nodding for the driver to step back again.

The word was a whip, yanking her upright. She turned and grabbed the handle. 'Get out of my way.'

Emin's face darkened. 'I won't let you go back to that... To...'

'Say it, Emin.'

He glared at her.

'*Say it.*'

But he didn't.

'You can't.'

His head dropped and he stared at the ground.

Meryem nodded. Her poor little brother, trying so hard to make his world right. When would he ever learn how unfixable it all was? For both of them? She tipped her head to the sky, pinched the bridge of her nose and closed her eyes. Once, long long ago, he had a toy car, a silver DeLorean that could travel back in time. He used to whoosh it across his pillow and whisper, *Take me back*, and no God had ever listened to him, and so he had learned to accept and build his world on the laws of men instead. Something she had vowed never to do.

The wound in her heart ripped open again. Such a deep and searing pain that she had to lean her weight against the taxi just to stay upright. Her mother had written. Letter after letter. And her father had sent every one of them back. Every one.

Flat 7. Sydney House. 5 Layton Rd, Enfield. London.

A place she hadn't been back to in thirty years. A place that if she ever allowed herself to think about it, felt as unachievable as the cities in snow-globes. Had she ever lived there? Had she really been that schoolgirl? The one who danced to pop music, who'd once kissed the most popular boy in class, who'd had a best friend with whom she had shared every secret and every dream. The girl who had had a mother, whom she had loved very much, but had let down in the worst possible way.

Because this last thought was always too difficult, Meryem did the only thing she could. She turned to the driver, opened her handbag and took out her Gucci purse from which she pulled another pile of clean notes. 'Back to Ankara,' she said, 'the airport.'

The driver opened his mouth, his eyes on the money.

'Ankara.'

Still he didn't answer.

Meryem counted more notes. 'It's enough?'

And, finally, the man nodded.

She had the passenger door wide open, but she didn't get in. Hand on the doorframe, she stood staring at a lone stork wheeling high above. Up the bird went, higher and higher, before turning to sweep down in wide arcs. Three perfect circles, she counted. For almost all of her life, she had been the girl without a mother, the girl who had had to learn to close her own circles, except the one for which she could find no beginning, and no end. Was it really so terrible, what she did? Was it really so bad? Was that why her mother never came?

'If you go back to Dubai, Meryem, I warn you, I will disown you.' Emin had stepped away, watching her intently.

And to her surprise Meryem laughed. His words were ants, tiny at the foot of what was already flowering. Hope. 'There's no need for that, Emin,' she said. 'I'm not going to Dubai.' She still had her hand on the door handle, her brow furrowed in thought, and for a long moment she didn't move.

Emin didn't either, and although Meryem could sense him watching her she wasn't thinking that he would try and stop her again. She was thinking through an idea that had blossomed in an instant. She wasn't going back to Dubai; that was as obvious to her now as the nose on her face. Her mother was long since dead, and she hadn't been back to Enfield in decades. But Alma might still be there. Alma, her best friend. And more than that, Alma's mother, who had been her mother's best friend. And maybe, just maybe she might find a different answer to the question that had haunted her life. She got into the taxi and pressed the window switch open, her hand shaking. 'He lied to us, Emin,' she said as she leaned out of the window.

'Where are you going?'

Meryem smiled. 'I'm going to England.'

The taxi driver started the engine.

'You won't find anything, Meryem.' Emin shook his head. 'They won't be there. The letters are gone.'

'I'm not looking for them,' she said, pressing one hand on top of the other. Hiding a nervous excitement she would not be able to deny. Thirty years. Emin was right. The letters would be gone. But what if they weren't? What if every word her mother had written was still there, waiting to be read. Pulling her sunglasses down, she took a deep breath and turned to him. 'You're wrong,' she said.

'Meryem. It's been too long––'

'You said I had no friends, Emin.'

Emin looked at her.

'But I do. And I'm going back to England to find her. I'm going to find my friend. Alma.'

I'm going to find the truth, she didn't say. *I'm going to find if my mother wanted me. If she missed me. If she loved me.*

SONJA

Flat 7, Sydney House
5 Layton Rd
Enfield, London

Saturday 10th May 1986

My darling Meryem,

You've been gone so many months already and I am thinking that you will have many questions when we see each other again. You will want to know why this happened. The only way I can think of to tell you, is to start at the beginning. To explain how things came to be the way they came to be. Emin too, he will have his own letters. This way, I may be able to answer your questions before you can ask them.

Your story started on December 13th 1971, on the fourth floor of North Middlesex hospital. I remember how the soap came from a bottle attached to the wall and the water ran from taps so clear you could see your face in them. But I was used to this now. Everything was pure white, and there were cupboards full of medicines to take away every pain. Still I cried for the Ebe.

Maybe you remember me sometimes telling you these things?

What you will not remember, for I never told you, is that if I had written this letter at the time of your birth, or even in the first years after, this is what I would have been able to write: X

For that is how I signed my name. That is how I gave my permission. That is how I trusted my future. So perhaps it is better that I have had to wait.

I wanted to tell you of the day you were born, because I do not know anything about the day I was born. I do not know if there was sun or wind, or even if it was night or day. I do not know the day, or the month, or the year. But you will. You will know.

Your afternoon was clear and sunny. And that is what the doctor said. This one has a sunny face. Very early, he said, for the eyes to open so wide.

I did not understand English then, so your father translated for me. I remember thinking it was because you did not want to miss a moment of living. And I was right. You were so inquisitive, you wanted to try everything life had to offer.

Your father carried you to the window and whispered the *ezan* into your ear, and then the name that we had chosen together, *Meryem*. He had never seen the city from such a great height and neither had I. We were so very happy and London was a strip of yellow-orange, and behind the sky was clear and cold and blue.

But it is only now, Meryem, that I understand how your father always saw something else in that strip of colour. And from this distance in time, I can see it more clearly than he could then.

Let me tell you about your birth. It wasn't easy! You came into this world with the cord tight around your neck, struggling to breathe, fighting to live! The doctor who saved you was called Dr Saunders. He told us something that I have always remembered. He said that even if the space of time between life and death can be less than a hair's breadth, it is still wide enough for human hands to intervene. What words, Meryem! Your father was crying when he explained them to me. Dr Saunders was a kind and good man and we were lucky to have him, but I could not let him touch me again. I cried. I wanted the *ebe* who tended the women of our village back home.

He understood. He sent for a nurse, and I could not believe it when I saw who came. Alma's mother, Kathy. I knew she lived very close to us, for I had seen her pushing her own baby in a pram. Alma, three months older than you. I'd wanted to stop and speak to her, but I never dared. Oh Meryem! Back then Kathy was the strangest woman I had ever seen. Her hair was jet black, cut short like a man's, and she was as wide as she was tall. Your father said she looked like Ahmet, the strongest man in our village. She did. But when she led me to the hospital bathroom that day, her hands were gentle as a child's. She did not let go of me. I was so weak, I would have fallen and she knew that. She tucked my hair behind my ear. She turned the shower dial and, together, we watched the blood wash away down my legs, until she had washed me clean.

She put me back into bed and spoke to your father and even though I did not understand the words, I knew that she was telling him she would be back. I knew she would look after me.

Later your father sat in a chair by my bed and held you in his arms and watched the yellow-orange of London fade to black. He thought that I was sleeping, and sometimes I was. He thought that everything would be alright now, and that everything seemed possible. It might have been.

The corridor outside was silent and I wondered if the nurses had forgotten that he was there. I know he did not want to move. I know that eventually he closed his eyes and joined us in a sleep so peaceful I have been searching for it ever since.

Love always, Mamma

2

HARD DAY

London, present day

Alma's lips moved as she folded knickers, one pair, two, three. All the same colour, same style. She placed them in a pile at the far end of the table, took two white t-shirts from the laundry basket, folded them and added them to the knicker pile and stood looking at it. She needed jeans, a jacket, a cardigan and something with a bit of glitter, or colour. And that would do. Would it? The pile looked small, what she needed so little. She pushed her glasses up her nose, tightened the band of her thin ponytail and turned to look out of her kitchen window. Did she even have anything with a bit of glitter, anything with colour? Not that she could think of.

From along the hallway, canned laughter floated through. She glanced up at the clock. Her soap would be starting soon. Another thing she did on a Thursday night –

along with a cup of tea, white, no sugar. She took the kettle to the sink and began filling it.

On the table, next to the laundry, lay a pile of photographs. Twelfth-century figurines that formed a part of her next restoration job. As the kettle boiled, she tapped the photographs into a neat pile and slipped them back into their protective cover. She'd save them for the weekend. Sammy and Gary would want time for themselves, and she would definitely want her own time. If it hadn't been for the support she knew Sammy was going to need, she wouldn't have accepted the invitation. An Eighties nostalgia weekend didn't sound like her idea of fun. But as she wasn't anyone's go-to person for fun, what did she know? And Sammy would need her. Was there anything harder for a daughter than saying a final goodbye to a dearly loved mother? As she looked up and caught sight of her reflection in the window, Alma's smile was rueful. She was definitely the go-to person for that.

As the TV laughter died away and the kettle stopped boiling, another sound began. Her phone. Familiar of course, but strange. No one rang in the evenings. Sammy sent texts and... no one else rang. Frowning, Alma walked out to the hallway and picked it up. *Caller unknown* flashed across the screen. She refused the call and put it back down; not answering unknown numbers was an established habit of, if not a whole lifetime, then certainly too many years to count.

She poured her tea and stood stirring in the milk.

Maybe she should try and pick up something with a bit of colour when she met with Sammy in Harrods tomorrow. It wasn't too late, was it? And when did that rule start? Alma frowned. The rule for not answering unknown numbers. She rinsed the teaspoon under the tap, flicked the excess water off and turned it upside down to sit in the drainer. It would have been another one of the precautions taken by her mother to make her feel safe, when she was still almost a child. Precautions that had grown into rules, that she had become equally good at nurturing, so her mother too had felt safe. Rules that settled into iron bars, multiplying until they had jailed her into this corner: days spent in the dimly lit back rooms of the British Museum, a week in the Lake District in July, laundry on a Thursday evening. And now this, dragged along like a middle-aged gooseberry, on an Eighties nostalgia weekend, with wardrobe needs smaller than a sparrow. How, if she even wanted to, was she ever going to escape? By dying, like her mother? And suddenly her hand was at her mouth, her head shaking. The pace of her thoughts had been too quick, ambushing her as they had with an intense sadness. She picked up her cup, and walked back to the window.

Across the park, bricks of amber sunlight shimmered on the lake. At some point of every day she found herself doing this, watching this view that never changed, and was never the same, thinking, always thinking, that if she just stood long enough, she might slip through those bars and out into the world of this view.

From the hallway came that familiar and strange sound. Her phone, ringing again, loud in her empty home. A home that was barely twenty minutes from where she had grown up, from her old primary school, and her old secondary school. Down the street, the bus-stop – seventeen minutes to the station, change at Hackney Downs, number 56 into the city. It was a small life. No one could disagree with that. She lived a small life that she could only imagine becoming smaller. Her throat hurt as she swallowed a mouthful of tea and turned away from the window.

In the hall, her phone was still ringing, growing, it felt to Alma, only louder. She put her cup down and looked along the passageway. There was one last gridline, that bordered the map of her world. The cemetery across the road, where her mother was buried. Where she too, would surely end up. The thought swept her along the hall. And then the phone was in her hands and she was swiping the screen and the line had opened. She held her breath, everything stilled; a voice tumbled into her world.

'Alma?'

Alma. The voice was the echo of a voice she knew. Her blood ran cold.

'Alma?'

'This...' She stalled. 'Yes,' she managed. 'This is Alma.'

'It's me. Meryem!'

Exactly what she'd been expecting. Still, the name hit her like a bullet. Stunned, she turned, walking blindly back to the kitchen, coming face to face with her reflection in the quickly darkening window.

'From school,' Meryem was saying. 'I left. In the second year. We lived above you, remember. Flat seven.'

'Meryem?' Alma's fingers reached for the hem of her cardigan, rolling it to a ball. *Meryem from school* didn't *leave. Meryem from school was taken.* Her brother too. 'Meryem,' she repeated. And Meryem wasn't *Meryem from school* either. Meryem had been her best friend.

The voice on the other end laughed. The voice that said it was Meryem.

Alma held her phone away and looked at it. From the living room she could hear the TV.

'Alma, are you there?'

She brought the phone back to her ear and as she did

the voice laughed again. 'Are you okay? I think I've given you a heart attack!'

'I'm okay.' Hand at her mouth, she nodded. In the window, she could see her shadow-self, nodding back.

'It's been a long time, Alma.'

'Yes... yes it has. How are you?' she managed, the words escaping before she could stop them. *How are you?* After half a life-time?

'I'm fine, Alma!'

But Meryem sounded so much more than fine. She sounded happy and light in a way that, here in the squat light of her kitchen, next to a pile of folded laundry, was incomprehensible to Alma. 'How are *you,* Alma?'

'I'm... I'm fine too,' she stuttered and fell into a chasm of silence. What to say? What could she say to someone she hadn't seen since she was fourteen years old? Someone to whom she was once closer than any other person on the planet. The walls wobbled, her eyes burned with tears and a heat swept up her throat.

'Take a guess where I'm calling from?'

Alma shook her head.

'I'm in London!'

'London?' She wrapped her arm across her stomach, a protective instinctive gesture. 'Oh... That's a surprise.'

'Isn't it? And I was thinking...' For the first time, a note of hesitation crept into Meryem's voice. 'I was hoping we could meet? Tomorrow, perhaps?'

Alma opened her mouth. Nothing came out. She wasn't sure she'd heard right. Tomorrow?

'If you have time, that is?'

'How did you find me?' she said and was shocked by both her question, and the directness of it.

'How did I find you?' Meryem repeated. She paused. 'It's

not so hard, Alma. You haven't gone far. You have the same name.'

No, she hadn't gone far at all, and yes she had the same name.

'Not me! I'm back to Saylan, from Saeed.' Meryem's laugh was deep and throaty. 'It doesn't sound much, but it is.'

Alma didn't speak, she was thinking of the names. Saylan, Saeed.

'You're not happy, Alma? That I found you?'

'Of course,' she stuttered. 'Yes, of course I am.' And once again she looked across at her reflection. The woman in the window did not look happy. The woman in the window looked as if a ghost from her past had just walked in, bringing with her all the other ghosts of her past.

'Alma.' Meryem's voice was soft now, as if she were coaxing a child. 'Do you think you can make tomorrow?'

'Tomorrow?' Alma's knees went soft. 'I have to be at Harrods. I—'

'You shop at Harrods? You've done well, Alma.'

'It's not... I'm not... I don't shop there—'

'Alma?'

Alma didn't speak. She clamped her mouth together and nodded.

'I'm teasing,' Meryem purred. 'Only teasing.'

'I know.' But she didn't. She hadn't.

'Anyway, my hotel is very close to Harrods, because I *do* shop there.' Meryem laughed. 'Do you think you can fit me in? Just a coffee? Half an hour?'

'Yes...'

'Wonderful!' The line went silent. 'Wonderful,' Meryem repeated.

'I have to meet someone there,' Alma said quietly. 'Sammy. Samantha Bowman, actually. From school.'

'From school.' Meryem's echo stretched the long vowel sound. 'You're still friends? That's so nice for you.'

'Yes,' Alma managed. 'Still friends.' And she fell silent and when Meryem didn't speak she added, 'I mean, we've always stayed in touch.' Because they had. Sammy had been a loyal and consistent friend, but... but what? But she wasn't, and never had been, her friend like Meryem had once been her friend.

'Good. That's good,' Meryem said, back on track. 'So tomorrow then? If I'm not interrupting anything?'

'No. It was just a shopping trip before—'

'So nice. Shopping.' Meryem's pace changed as she interrupted again. Quickened as she went through arrangements. 'Tomorrow then!' she finished. 'Oh, and give my regards to your mother, Alma. It will be such fun to see you again!' And the phone clicked off.

Give my regards to your mother.

The words were pins and Alma was nothing more than a bubble, and the pin-words burst her. If the table hadn't been right there for her to lean on, she might have fallen.

Give my regards to your mother.

Obviously Meryem wouldn't know that her mother was no longer able to receive regards, that her mother was dead. She sat down, her phone in her lap, her tea going cold, the laundry basket bearing its silent load. The clock ticked and from the living room came the closing credits for the soap she'd missed. The soap she never missed. She took her glasses off and rubbed her eyes and found her knuckles were wet with tears. Meryem was back. How strange those words were. Meryem was back and tomorrow they would meet and understanding this, Alma felt as if she were caught in a shoal of emotion, multi-coloured, fast-turning and immeasurable.

At at some point in her life, too long ago to remember, the idea that Meryem would come back had slipped away as unobtrusively as the sun slips below the horizon, never to resurface. But it had. She was back. And it was too late. The world that that sun had set upon was long gone, replaced by another world with a lower horizon and darker edges, a world that had been born in water and blood, from which her mother had spent all her remaining energy trying to protect her.

3

WHERE DID YOUR HEART GO?

London, present day

SAMMY'S LIST TO live for!

1. Be blonde!
2. Scatter mum's ashes
3. Buy Versace jeans and wear them
4. Renew passport
5. Ride in a Porsche 911
6. See George Michael

COMPLETELY BALD, wrapped in a fluffy white dressing gown the belt of which barely knotted across her stomach, Sammy sat at her kitchen table. A snowman, with a pink billiard ball of a head. Her fingers drummed the wood as she read through the pencilled list once again.

If it was funny when she'd written it, it was ridiculous now. Now that it wasn't just a list. Now that the Porsche was parked on the drive and the weekend booked. She'd been too surprised to protest when he'd turned up in it yesterday. Although she had no idea why she should be. It was on the list, therefore he would get it done. The irony was she'd only added it because she couldn't think of anything else. And she'd only added George Michael because that was impossible. It hadn't stopped him.

Is that it? Gary had said when he first read her list. After he'd left her alone for half an hour to *really* think about it. Umm, yeah, that was it. God knows she'd tried hard enough, but she really wasn't bothered about swimming with dolphins, or seeing the Northern Lights, or the Great Barrier Reef. And she felt guilty about that. About what? Lack of ambition was the answer that long afternoons on the sofa watching TV had brought her to. That, and a complete inability to see through the little ambition she did have. Because why for example hadn't she ever dyed her hair blonde? Or renewed her passport? When had her world grown so small? She picked up her mug and took another slurp of tea and it burned her throat. Renewing the passport now, like Gary had suggested, was plain ridiculous. Ten years? It could last longer than she would. And probably would.

She picked up her mug and in an attempt to taste the tea, took a long, determined slurp. Nothing. Only a warm wetness in her mouth. Chemo spoiled everything. When she put it down again, it left a splodge on the paper. *See George Michael* was already illegible. Sighing, Sammy picked the list up and folded it in half, and then half again. What did it matter anyway? Her bottom was too big for Primark jeans, let alone Versace. And blonde? Well she'd fancied trying that since she was sixteen. If she hadn't got around to it by now...

A loud bang made her jump, so much that she dropped the list. Scowling she turned to Gary. He was at the hob, frying bacon and generally knocking pans around as if he were on Masterchef. How long had she been cooking for the family? Twenty-five years! Twenty-six actually, without ever finding the need to handle a pan like that! Male chefs had a lot to answer for. Delia Smith never banged a pan in her life. At least she still found herself funny! And yes, twenty-six years she'd been cooking, but barely once since her diagnosis. He had taken over, wrapping her in cotton wool so thick it suffocated. Sheepishly she unfolded her list, and using the sleeve of her dressing gown, blotted it dry.

'You okay?' Gary turned; he had the spatula pointing to heaven.

'Fine,' she muttered. '*Fine*.' And she put her head to one side and feigned an interested expression, as she pretended to the study this list she knew so well. He was *always* asking her that. And what was she supposed to say? No, I'm not okay? I'm terrified. I'm mutilated. I wander the house at three am looking for shoes to polish! *Renew passport, renew passport, renew passport...* She was still reading the same words when Gary plonked a plate of bacon and eggs on the table.

Startled, Sammy looked from the plate to her husband. She couldn't even smell it. How the hell was she going to eat it? 'Thanks, darling,' she managed. 'It looks lovely.'

He grinned back, and she thought what she'd been thinking a lot recently. If she ever won the lottery, the first thing she'd do was get his teeth fixed. Picking up her knife and fork, she smiled. Get his teeth fixed? What would he fix about her? Twenty-six years this year they would have been married, and every time the anniversary was mentioned he made the same joke. *You get less for murder.* Every. Single. Time. She gave him a reassuring nod, took a mouthful of food and waited for him to turn back to the hob before she began the laborious process of chewing. From the first day of her diagnosis, the entire family had approached her illness with such a *Can Do!* positive attitude that Sammy had often felt that she had no other choice but to make merry and get on board, when sometimes, like right now, she craved a little space... To begin to come to terms with the fact that, although her prognosis was good and the cancer hadn't spread, she had lost the most womanly part of herself – her breasts. To grieve, to be miserable, to be left alone so she could get on and chew her tasteless food in peace.

And chew...

And chew...

God, it really was tasteless.

Gary started whistling, elbows wide, scrubbing the frying pan.

She put her hand across her mouth and forced a mouthful down. Sighed. Readied herself and scooped another forkful in. Desperate for distraction, she picked up her list again.

Scatter mum's ashes

This... This was a hard one. Why in five years hadn't she managed to fulfil the promise she'd made to her mother and scatter her ashes? Fleetwood wasn't the North bloody Pole for God's sake! Why had it taken cancer to move her? Because it had, and she was under no illusions about that. A cancer-free Sammy, she knew, would have shrugged and said, *I'll get round to it.* But Sammy-with-cancer? This

Sammy was different. A significant part of her body had been removed. If she felt less solid now, so did life itself. One more day gone and now she knew... Those left were countable. None of the old excuses worked anymore. So it was time. It was beyond time to say goodbye.

'Right.' Gary turned. He was wiping his hands on a tea towel. 'Are you going to be okay? I can still drive you there?'

'I'm fine,' she said. 'I'll take the train.'

'Okay.' He took his anorak from the peg and pulled it on.

(That was another thing... if she won the lottery, she'd throw that old thing away and buy a Calvin Klein. If Calvin Klein did anoraks.)

'I'm going to check the oil and the tyres. Alma knows what time we're leaving?'

Sammy nodded. Alma knew. Everyone knew. Gary had told them at least seven hundred and fifty-six times.

'I just want to be sure,' he said, and was gone.

She stared at the drainer. Funny. The boy she'd fallen in love with had been the rogue of the class. Her handsome Irish rover. Cheeky and rough around the edges. Now? Now he went through life with a permanent checklist. She blamed parenthood. He'd taken it all so seriously.

She waited until he was in the car, had backed out the drive and disappeared around the corner before she stood up, and fished out her cigarettes, hidden in a secret pocket of her handbag. This was another thing she craved – the space to pretend everything was normal. He'd hate it if he saw her smoking. But she'd never said she'd given up. Then again, she hadn't said she hadn't either, although the day was soon coming when she knew she would. When she'd join everyone else, and get positive! And get on with getting well! She scraped the bacon into the cat-bowl, lit the cigarette and opened the door. Then, leaning against the frame, inhaling deeply, she sank into the moment. A moment in which she was herself again, whole and unmutilated, just Sammy, quietly enjoying a quiet cigarette as she watched the street she knew so well go about its business.

They should sell. Now the kids had gone, the house was far too big for just the two of them. A century had passed over since they were the new kids on the block. She brought her thumb to her mouth and bit free a thread of loose skin, smoke stinging her eyes. What did Gary say when he came home yesterday in that car? It made him feel young again. He'd been saying lots of stuff recently. Just last week, she'd heard him on the phone to an old friend. *Yep. Same house, same job, same old, same old.* And the row they'd had when she'd gotten cold feet about visiting their son in Australia! If she hadn't fallen ill, that could have turned into something huge. He'd been so disappointed. She looked at the cigarette again, went into the kitchen, drowned it under the tap and buried it deep in the bin. Then she ran her hand over her smooth bald head and looked at the clock.

Ten-thirty already.

Thank God, Alma had put their meeting back an hour! Imagine if she hadn't. Alone in her kitchen, Sammy laughed. *You'll be late for your own funeral,* her mother used to say... which was a bit too close to the mark these days. Still, she was glad to have this little bit of extra time and because this was the new Sammy, she remembered to be thankful that she was glad. A fleeting victory.

SONJA

Flat 7, Sydney House
5 Layton Rd
Enfield, London

20th September 1986

My darling Meryem,

You have been gone exactly nine months. Almost enough time for me to have grown you inside me again.

Back then, when I was growing you, there was a programme on the television I used to watch. I could not understand what was being said, but I liked to watch the pictures. It was about a farm. I remember seeing the cows let out of the barn after winter, how they jumped and ran with happiness. I remember because I was jealous of their freedom. In my first year in England there were many days when I never left the living room, never mind the flat. I unrolled my prayer mat and made namaz there, I even carried potatoes in and peeled them there. I couldn't use the kitchen, because strangers, when they passed on the walkway, could look straight into the window and see me. So, in the beginning, I would stay in the living room, and stand at the big windows and look out at the trees of the park. No one could see, we were so high up. Then I would go to the other side of our apartment, to the bedroom, and watch people walking below and long to be able to do the same. Like the cows, I wanted to be free, but I did not know how.

Back in the village, Meryem, animals were my friends. In England we did not even have a cat, but back home the goats were so close they woke me. I knew how to talk to them, to make them give up their milk. This was why I liked the television programme. If I closed my eyes, and listened only to the sounds, it was possible for me to imagine I was back home.

Perhaps you will think how funny all this is, if you remember the afternoons in our kitchen? Alma and you played with dolls at the table while I cooked, with the windows open and the neighbours walking past waving and sometimes stopping to talk. But it is true; in the beginning I was too scared to use my own kitchen, too scared to leave the flat and too scared to take a bus, in case a stranger sat down next to me. For a long time, it felt as if every day in my new life only brought something new to be scared of. If I had known how hard it would be, I am not sure I would have come, even for three bedrooms and a kitchen with seventeen cupboards and a bathroom with taps and hot water.

Seventeen cupboards, but not one friend and no family.

I had a friend in the village. Her name was Afife. I think you must know her by now. When I came to try and bring you home last month, she told me that she had not seen you. I think she was lying. And I think I know why.

I did come for you, Meryem. I came to take you and

Emin back. Do you know this? The police here, said they didn't know where you are. They said your father is not British, and there is nothing they can do. I told them where you are, and still they said this.

So I came myself.

What a house your father has built! The biggest in the village. So easy to find. And so silent. He took you away again. I do not know how he knew I was coming. People talk. I should not have told anyone where I was going.

Go back to England, Afife told me when I stood outside the gates to your father's house. The men are talking to him, she said. Be patient, she said. You know how proud he is.

We grew as girls together, Afife and I. She was one year older than me and I thought she knew everything. But when I heard I was to marry your father, I asked her what England was and she did not know.

Then I asked the *muhtar.* He told me that England was a long way away. He said it is dark and there is always rain and that the city is covered in smoke clouds so nothing can grow there. I believed him, Meryem. We all believed the *muhtar.* I told your father I could not live there.

Your father laughed. He took out his wallet and showed me how it was full of strange money. This is what grows in England, Sonja, he said. And if it rains, I will keep you dry.

So I came to the land of rain with every pair of salvar I had and my favourite pieces from my ceyiz. They were on the table in the living room. You will know what I am talking about, the two long white runners embroidered over with yellow and red. They were the most colourful things in our flat, weren't they? I never told you this, but they reminded me of the rugs we weaved back home, in colours so bright and vivid that when we aired them out of windows or stretched them over rooftops it was like a rainbow had been cut into squares and dropped from the sky.

These runners are in so many old photographs. I look through sometimes. You and Emin, leaning over the table on Emin's fifth birthday, 1981. You, squeezed onto your father's lap, Bayram 1978. Alma and you, dancing to your records. You were eleven years old. Was it four years already?

The most beautiful thing from my ceyiz, I could not bring. It was a wool quilt. The cloth was black, printed with large red and blue flowers that were all connected by leaves an incredible deep green. I chose that cloth because I had seen that green colour in a picture book my father brought back from Ankara when I was very young. I never thought that one day I would live in a land where I would only have to look out of the window, to see it. Greens everywhere. I did not know such a colour, not until I came to England.

Can you still see the green of the park, where you played with Alma and Emin? If you close your eyes, can you see it? Sometimes, Meryem, I hope you will have forgotten, so that you will not be missing it. Because now you will know only the grey of the steppe, now you will be able to count the trees, there are so few.

Oh, Merym. What am I saying? We don't forget. It has been over fifteen years, but I remember everything of the day I left the village. Your father pointing to a cloud of brown dust that was the taxi coming for us. Fatma, my neighbour's daughter, scratching a stick in the soil. The sound was loud and the copper jug that she had just filled with water winked with sun. Your father asked her what she was drawing. 'England,' she said and then she asked us, 'Does it look like England?'

It was just swirls in the dirt, Meryem, but for all I knew it could have looked exactly like England.

We had a pact. Afife and I.

When we were girls, we promised each other that if we had daughters we would marry them to our sons. So Afife would be a mother to you, Meryem, and I would be a mother to her girl. I left my quilt with her. The centrepiece of my ceyiz. If I was willing to trust a daughter to Afife, it made sense that I would trust my quilt with her. It was too big to carry to England.

I will keep it perfect, for when you return. It will be soon, she said.

But fifteen years is not soon. And I did not keep my promise. I did not promise you to anyone. You were never mine, I learned, to make such a promise. And I think this is why she would not help.

Do you think it is possible to inherit loneliness, Meryem? Before you were born, back in those days when I listened to the sound of cows on the television and peeled potatoes at my feet and did not know what day it was, I grew loneliness like rain grows seed. And you too were growing inside me. So I ask again, is it possible to inherit loneliness?

For your sake, I hope that it is not.

Love always, Mamma

4

A DIFFERENT CORNER

London, present day

'ALMA! AAALMAA!' The woman stretching her name to distortion, grabbing her wrists, swinging their joined hands, like a skipping rope on a playground, was astonishingly glamorous. All hair, and glossy lips. Huge eyelashes. And loud laughter. 'Alma, Alma, Aaalmaa!'

'Meryem.' That was all Alma managed before the squeaking and the crackling started, and arms were by her ears and she was squashed up against something scratchy. As she managed to extract herself she saw that the scratchy thing was snakeskin. Snakeskin! She flinched, her glasses slipping sideways, as she stepped back.

'It's not real!' The woman laughed, looking down at her gilet. The woman who must be...

'Meryem?'

'No snakes died!'

'Oh...' Her eyes went back to the gilet. 'No... I didn't think they had. I—'

'*Aaalma!*' Meryem's eyes shone with amusement. 'I'm not that cruel!'

'No.' Alma stalled. She couldn't seem to get a coherent word out. 'I didn't think you... I...' Giving up, she put her hand to her mouth and pulled at what felt like hair. A strand of Meryem's hair? Sticky and sweet, it tickled her mouth as she eased it free.

'It is so good to see you! So good!'

'It is,' she managed just before perfume hit the back of her throat, making her cough, and cough again.

'Here.' Meryem reached across the table for a carafe of water. 'Take this,' she said as she poured a glass. As she handed it over, she smiled, revealing a wide crescent of polished white teeth. 'You look well, Alma.'

Alma took the glass. And as she stood sipping, feeling like a child with hiccups, she couldn't help it, she ran her tongue over her own chipped incisor.

'Shall we sit?' Meryem beamed.

It was Meryem. She was wider, and, seemingly, shorter. And yes, almost absurdly glamorous, dressed in skinny jeans, white sneakers and a fiercely scarlet blouse. Topped by that gilet. Lashes like spiders, thick pencilled brows. Skin, mirror-smoothed by a layer of foundation, and hair that had been curled and tonged. And jewellery! Jewellery dripped from Meryem like baubles from a Christmas tree. Alma glanced down at her own plain cream blouse. The last time they had seen each other had been sunset, on the darkest day of the year, thirty-six years ago. But she'd known the moment she'd first seen this woman, sitting alone at this table. Meryem was miraculously the same, and yet completely different.

'*Vanilla Mooseline*,' Meryem mumurmed. She was reading from the menu, lime-green reading glasses halfway down her nose.

'Mousseline,' Alma corrected before she could stop herself. Meryem spoke English with an accent? Of all the things she hadn't expected, she hadn't expected this. She blushed. 'Sorry.'

Meryem smiled. 'It's okay, Alma. You must correct me. I don't use English much. My ex-husband was Saudi, so I've been speaking Arabic for a long time.'

Feeling a chill along her arms, Alma nodded. She knew about a husband, about Meryem living in Saudi Arabia. The news had come decades ago, in the last letter Sonja had ever received. She remembered because of the sound Sonja had made when she read it. More animal than human, Alma hadn't heard anything like it before, or since. The wail had filled every room. Even the closed door of her bedroom had not been barrier enough, and sitting on her bed, staring at her old Wham! posters, she'd wondered how her mother could bear to stay next to Sonja, to be so close to that noise. Remembering this, her chin dropped. Barely a decade after Sonja's death, her mother was dead too and there was no doubt in Alma's mind that the stress and the worry had been to blame. 'You're not married anymore?' she managed, her voice wired tight with emotion as she watched Meryem remove her reading glasses.

'We divorced years ago.' Meryem shrugged. 'From Meryem Saeed, back to Meryem Saylan again!' She held up the menu card. 'Now, I can't decide between a profiterole, or a puff pastry. Which is better do you think?'

'They're both good...' Alma's voice trailed off. She was

looking at Meryem's hand as it held the menu. The carefully sculpted nails and the two huge rings, one an emerald, neither on her wedding finger. Despite the adornment, it was not the hand of a young person and what she saw among the creases and lines of three decades was the expanse of life that separated them. And then she found herself glancing down at her own hands. Plain, dry, with creases and lines of their own. They said Nivea cream and resin from work. Sometimes she could still smell it.

'I think I'll just have coffee,' Meryem said and turned to wave at a waiter. 'For you, also?' she asked, as a waiter arrived.

'Yes,' Alma managed. 'Yes, coffee is good.'

Meryem ordered, turned back to the table and smiled again. 'It really is good to see you, Alma!'

'It is... It is.' Alma smiled back, her face already stiff with the effort, with the pressing down of the melee of questions she knew she couldn't ask.'So you're bi-lingual?' she said, and it sounded ridiculous, but she didn't know what else to say. 'That's impressive, Meryem.'

'Alma!' Meryem laughed. 'Call me, Mery! Like before!'

The smile faltered. It was strange enough to hear her own name on Meryem's tongue after all this time, but Mery? Mery was another lifetime ago. Even the sound of it jarred. It was too much, too soon – an old and precious intimacy that couldn't be yanked up and thrown back on. Uncomfortable, she picked up the water carafe and poured herself another glass, busying herself with anything to hand. 'I mean I can't speak anything other than English. Mind...' She coloured. 'I haven't really been anywhere to...Well, I mean I haven't travelled much... at all.' And feeling the warmth in her cheeks, she put her glass down and looked at it.

'Travelling,' Meryem said, as she lifted her hair off her shoulders, 'can become dull, Alma. I never thought I'd say this. When I was married, I wasn't allowed to travel.'

'In Saudia Arabia?'

Meryem shrugged. 'I couldn't go anywhere without my husband, and he never wanted to go anywhere. But it's true!' She laughed. 'When you travel a lot, it can become dull.'

'Oh.' Alma nodded. Here she was, forty-four, with money in the bank and no commitments, unable to get further than the Lake District.

The waiter arrived with a tray, and Alma watched as Meryem took the coffee pot and began pouring, her gold nails flashing like little shields. Meryem, she thought, must sail through airports and customs all the time, switching languages like shoes. 'Do you travel a lot?' she said. And this didn't sound so ridiculous.

'Enough.' Meryem murmured, sliding a cup across the table.

'Thank you. With your work? Do you travel for work?'

'Sometimes.'

Alma picked up her cup. 'What do you do?'

Meryem didn't answer immediately, and in the silent moment that followed, Alma experienced a rush of familiar but long-forgotten excitement. The feeling that, for her, had almost defined their old friendship. Whatever Meryem did would be exciting, would, of course, have her travelling all over the world. This was Meryem. The smartest girl in the class. A hot-house flower, amongst all the weedy seedlings of North London.

'Hospitality.' Meryem smiled. 'I work in hospitality.'

'Oh.' Her face finally relaxing, the smile real now, Alma leaned forward. 'Where do you get to visit?'

Meryem waved a hand. 'Lots of places.'

And there was another silence. This time too long. In a final strained attempt to keep the conversation going, she pushed on. 'Where was the last trip?'

'I really can't remember,' Meryem murmurmed. 'Gold Coast? South Africa?'

Alma shrunk. The cup rattled in the saucer as she put it back down. She felt chastised, as if she'd overstepped a mark. Pushed too far into Meryem's life, which wasn't after all, hers. Those days when everything from hair clips, to socks, to classroom crushes had been shared, were long gone. 'Well,' she said, swallowing her words. 'It all sounds very glamorous to me.'

And again Meryem dismissed the moment with a wave of her hand. 'Oh, it's not really. And nowhere near as interesting as what you do.'

'Me?'

Meryem nodded. 'I read about you online,' she said. 'Head of Portable Antiquities! I'm impressed, Alma, but not surprised. You were always smart.'

'Really?' Her mind was scrabbling now, trying to picture the photograph, the dry biography Meryem might have read. Her Facebook profile was private. Not that she did social media. And Meryem obviously didn't either, because although she'd spent an hour or more last night trying, there had been no trace. Nothing.

'Anyway!' Meryem leaned across the table. 'I'm sure you don't want to talk about work either! Not after all these years! I want to catch up! I have a couple of days free, and I thought that now is a good time to see you. I want to hear *all* about you, Alma.'

'There's honestly not much to tell,' she said.

'There *must* be!' Meryem laughed. 'It's been so long! Are you still dancing? You loved to dance.'

'Umm, no.' She flushed. She hadn't danced in... Well, she couldn't remember, that was how long.

'Children?'

'No.'

Meryem nodded.

'But it's okay,' she started, as she always did when this question came up. It was as much about appeasing the discomfiture of the questioner than her own. Children, for her, had never been on the agenda. Watching Sonja had been example enough. The world was too dangerous, the decision never to make herself that vulnerable had been easy. 'I never wanted them. How about you?'

'One boy and one girl.' Meryem's smile was small. 'But they are twenty-six and twenty-four now. I don't see them much. My daughter is in Singapore, and my son lives in Riyadh.'

Twenty-six? Twenty-four? The numbers wheeled in Alma's head. That made Meryem a mother by eighteen. The same year Alma had started university. The same year Sonja had died... *that Meryem's mother had died.* She reached for her cup and her hand was a jumble of tingling nerve-ends. Those years immediately after Sonja's death, her student years, had been an oasis of much needed calm. Her mother had insisted that she study far from home, and with hind-sight she had been right. Three years, with the quiet friend-ship of two other students and the freedom to immerse herself in a subject she loved, had been the respite she needed. A healing time. And although happy might be too much of a stretch after everything that had happened, content wasn't. Yes, she had been content. And Meryem had been a mother. Had she also been content then? A warmth rushed Alma, pricking tears. How could she have been, considering the plans they had made together as teenagers, the university they would attend together... the way her mother had died... 'You were...' She paused. 'You had your children very young. Was it... was that tradition?'

Meryem looked at her.

'I mean, in Turkey. Where you... went.'

'Yes.' Meryem smiled as she glanced down at her phone and swiped the screen. 'And no.'

'What was it like?' The question that had burned away in her for years, slipped out. She couldn't have stopped it, even if she had known it was coming.

'In Turkey?' Meryem mumurmed. 'Like anywhere else, I suppose. Lots of family. Lots of sheep. Not much school, so that was fun!' She looked up. 'Yes, it was good.'

'And—'

'Are you still in Enfield?'

Alma held her eye. 'Yes,' she said and when Meryem smiled and said nothing, she reached for the sugar. She didn't speak as she stirred it in, and neither did Meryem. As much as she wanted to believe that Meryem hadn't cut her question off, it was clear that she had. She tapped the spoon on the edge of her cup and resting it on her saucer, tried again. 'I often thought of you when I was at university, Meryem. I remember you wanted to go.' Looking up, their eyes met. 'I hope,' she said, 'I hope you were happy.'

And although Meryem smiled, her eyes were empty as moons.

Alma nodded. There were fences around Meryem's life that she wasn't going to be allowed to see over, that was clear. A part of her felt resentful, another part confused. Maybe it was too long ago. Too far away. They were grown women. It wasn't as if she was spilling forth all the details of her own life. Then again, if she did, she'd be finished in five minutes. Not even that. Three cats, been and gone. One flat in London. Decades, nearly a whole life, in the back room of a museum. That was it. The smallness of it, spelled out like this, overwhelmed her. She glanced again at her pale blouse and her pale hands, and then across at Meryem's scarlet blouse and glossy lips and what she thought was *Why? Why don't I ever wear red, let alone scarlet?* She was burning hot with embarrassment, and overwhelmed with sadness. In a sudden decisive movement, she pushed her chair back, and stood up. It had been a mistake to come. Probably, a mistake to have answered the call in the first place. The woman opposite her was Meryem only in name. There was no friendship to be found here, that safe place she had remembered all her life, the two of them, schoolgirl backs against the wall, planning life, was long gone. 'I'm sorry,' she whispered. 'I think I should go. This... this is difficult.'

'Alma!'

The quiet resolve in Meryem's voice made her turn.

'My father died.'

Alma stared. A long moment passed. 'I'm sorry—'

'Don't be.' Meryem interrupted. 'I wasn't.'

Holding Meryem's eye, Alma didn't speak. She wouldn't have known Meryem's father if he passed her in the street, and after all that had happened she wasn't sorry. She was polite, that's all. But it was clear from the way Meryem was looking at her now that there was no need for politeness, that the time had passed for customary responses, for niceties, for small talk.

'Please, Alma.' Meryem indicated the chair. 'Please sit down.'

Hands cold, legs weak, Alma sat down. Talk of children and missed opportunities was one thing. Talk of death was something else altogether.

'I want to be honest with you,' Meryem whispered. 'I'm

not just passing through. I came because I wanted to ask you something.'

Blood pounding her ears, Alma nodded.

'He said something before he died. Something that has brought me back here.' Tracing the edge of the tablecloth with a golden nail, Meryem paused. 'Do you remember my mother, Alma?'

'Of course.' The words were rocks, scraping their way through. Of course she remembered. Was Meryem going to ask? Here, amongst the starched tablecloths and polished cutlery, was she going to have to tell it here?

'I wanted to ask...' As she twisted her emerald, Meryem's eyes glassed over.

A pang of intense sympathy almost felled Alma, and her own words, just a few minutes ago, echoed... *I hope you were happy*. Whatever Meryem had been, it hadn't, Alma knew, been happy. And now she understood she wouldn't leave. And it was so like a feeling she had once known, a memory of Meryem bound up with friendship and loyalty. She would stay. And yes, tell Meryem whatever she needed to know, however difficult.

'I wanted to ask,' Meryem began again, 'if you remember my mother talking about me after I left.'

Left. Alma stared. Meryem hadn't *left.* Meryem, and her brother Emin, had been taken. *Abducted,* the newspaper had said. The question was so different from the one she had been expecting, it left her dumb. *Left.* She couldn't get beyond the word.

'Anything at all?' Meryem smiled.

Alma nodded, watching as, opposite, with every moment that passed, Meryem's smile became weaker, her eyes softer with a surging disappointment. But Alma had nothing to say. Nothing to offer. She couldn't remember Sonja talking about Meryem. Grieving and crying, she remembered, not conversations. What had been said between her mother and Sonja, she didn't know. They talked all the time, but never in front of her. Ever. Shaking her head, she said, 'I'm sorry, Meryem. Your mother didn't talk to me. They tried to keep me out of it. To protect me I suppose.'

Meryem nodded, but her eyes were almost liquid now.

'She talked to my mother,' Alma added. 'They spent a lot of time together.' She felt as if she was juggling. One ball on that strange word, *left,* another keeping Meryem afloat. 'I know it helped,' she continued, encouraged as Meryem reached for the coffee pot, her face a shade lighter.

'I understand.' Meryem topped up her coffee. 'Of course.' She lifted her cup. 'And how is your mother, Alma? Maybe then it would be better if I could talk with her? If that is okay with you?'

Goosebumps raced along Alma's arms. She frowned, her mouth twitching as it struggled to voice the words she hated. 'My mother is dead, I'm afraid. A long time ago now.' And she watched as the blood drained from Meryem's face.

Meryem's cup went down. She stared at it. 'Ah,' she whispered, blotting her eyes with her thumbs. She smiled, picked the cup up again, and then just as quickly put it back down. 'Excuse me,' she gasped.

And before Alma was on her feet, Meryem was gone.

5

ONE MORE TRY

London, present day

HEAD DROOPED OVER THE BASIN, hair dangling, Meryem took breath, after breath. Emin had been right. It *was* too late. The realisation was so bright it hurt, and every time she understood anew, needles stabbed and she had to concentrate just to get the air into her lungs.

She reached behind her neck and, scooping her hair back, lifted her chin to the mirror. Every one of her forty-four years looked back. Every hurt, clearly etched. Turning away, turning the tap, she patted cooling water onto the back of her neck. It was over then. The idea born outside her father's house was already dead. Her mother had written, but the words in those letters were as lost now as her mother herself. Alma couldn't tell her anything, and the one person who might have known, the woman in whom her mother might have confided, was also dead. So now she would never know. She looked up, and the face that looked back at her was brutal with misery.

Locked in Saudia Arabia, about to give birth to her first child, when the news of her mother's death had reached her, understanding that she would never know why she hadn't come, was something Meryem had survived. It was the shadow she'd learned to live under, a weight that had so nearly crushed her. And it had taken years for the shell to grow. For composite layers of hurt to harden into a protective mantle. So why had she weakened herself by allowing hope in? Why had she made herself as vulnerable as that girl who'd sat on the hill, scanning a horizon for a dust cloud that never appeared? She looked up, and her hollowed eyes looked back.

Because there were letters, Meryem.

The voice in her head was that child. Stubborn, naively persistent. Ignoring it, Meryem took a brush from her bag and began pulling it through her hair.

It changes everything.

And if there were letters, there were planes. Her mother could, and should, have come for them. Jamming her hands against her ears, Meryem closed her eyes. The voice scared her. If she continued to listen to it, it would lead nowhere but bitter disappointment. And she'd already lived enough bitter disappointment to last a thousand lifetimes.

She wrote to you. She wrote...

The hairbrush clattered to the floor. 'STOP IT!' she cried. And her voice bounced across the cold tiled walls.

There was a moment's echoing silence and then, as if in answer, a violent retch behind the furthest cubicle door.

Meryem turned to the sound.

Another retch tore through, raw and ugly, followed by a gasp and a tiny voice. 'I'm sorry. If I could, I would stop. I really would—' And a third, equally violent retch cut the voice off.

Meryem bent and picked up her hairbrush, slipping it into her bag. She didn't know if she should answer, or leave, or wait. Someone was ill. And that someone had thought that she had demanded they stop being ill. And Alma was waiting back in the tea room and... She turned to her reflection, and did what she always did when there was nothing else left to do. She pinched her cheeks for colour, and blinked a brightness back into her eyes. And just as she was about to leave, the cubicle door opened and a woman wearing a blue headscarf came out. Her face was pale and shiny as white satin. Through the mirror, they looked at each other.

'Are you okay?' Meryem said, when it became clear that she should speak first.

The woman's chest rose as she gasped air, held it, let it out again. She gave a terse nod and moved to the sink.

Stepping aside Meryem watched as the woman began washing her hands. 'I didn't mean *you* should stop,' she said. 'I... I'm sorry if you thought that.'

'I'm not thinking much at all right now,' the woman muttered. 'Except that I'll probably skip Versace.'

'No. You shouldn't do that.'

'I'm sorry?'

'You should never skip Versace.'

The woman's mouth twitched. 'So I've heard,' she said and reached for a paper towel, but it seemed to be taking all her strength to pull one free.

Stretching past her, Meryem handed one over. 'Is there someone with you?' The woman was so frail.

'I'm meeting someone.' The woman nodded and looked at the mirror. 'God, I need to clean my teeth.'

'I can help with that.' And from the depths of her handbag, Meryem wrestled out a neat wrapped package – new toothbrush and mini-paste, holding it up triumphantly.

'You're very prepared.'

'I travel a lot.' Meryem shrugged. 'I'm always prepared.'

'Well... thank you.' The woman took the package. 'I'm Sammy,' she said, then, 'and I'm glad you weren't telling me to stop. I did think it was odd.'

'Sammy?'

AND BEFORE SAMMY COULD RESPOND, the door swung open and Alma came in, her face etched with worry.

Alma looked from Meryem to Sammy, and then back to Meryem. 'Sammy,' she said. 'I didn't know you were here.'

Sammy grimaced. 'I was going to have a little browse first. Came over a bit funny. I think it was the bacon Gary made me eat.'

'Have you...?'Alma swung to Meryem. 'I didn't know if I should wait. If...' She paused. 'I didn't know if you were coming back.'

'Of course!' Meryem smiled. 'It was rude of me. If you've paid, I will reimburse you.'

'No. That's not what I meant.' Alma paled. She didn't care about the bill. She cared that she wouldn't see Meryem again. That Meryem had disappeared as swiftly and permanently as before. With every minute she had waited, her panic had multiplied. There was so much to say. They hadn't even begun. And although she had no idea how they would begin, she was sure that they must. That this was something she hadn't understood she needed to face. Something she'd never expected to face. 'I was worried,' she said. 'That's all.' She turned to Sammy. 'This is Meryem, Sammy.'

'Meryem?'

'Meryem Saylan.'

'Meryem Saylan?'

And for a long moment, standing with her back to the door, Alma watched as Sammy and Meryem looked at each other.

Stretching out her hand, gold nails flashing, Meryem smiled. 'Sammy. It's been a long time.'

Sammy stared at the hand as it were a fish. Helplessly she turned to Alma, then back to Meryem. 'I didn't even recognise you!'

And as Meryem shook her head and laughed, her tonged curls bounced back to life. 'Why would you?' she smiled. 'It's been so long.'

'I'm sorry. Alma did say... Last night... I... you... Wow, well you look great!' As Sammy stopped talking, she gave a short, embarrassed laugh and her hand fluttered up to her headscarf. 'As you can see, I'm not looking my best.'

'I think you look great too!' Meryem said, emphasising the *great*.

There was a long, uncomfortable moment.

Still hovering by the door, Alma said, 'Are you okay, Meryem?'

'I'm fine!' Meryem turned to the mirror, put her hand inside her blouse and straightened her bra strap. She flashed Alma a wide smile. 'No need to worry.'

'I'm sorry. I don't know why, I thought you would have known.' Turning to Sammy, Alma added, 'Meryem didn't realise my mum had died. She was—'

'It was just a shock, that's all,' Meryem said, her palm held high in a stop sign. 'I'm fine. And you,' she smiled at Sammy. 'You *really* shouldn't skip Versace, Sammy. Their jeans are fabulous. Nothing fits my bottom so well.'

'Really?' Sammy's laugh was easy now. She glanced at Meryem's bottom and looking up caught Alma's eye. They exchanged a smile. 'It is on my bucket list.'

'Bucket list?'

'Your List to Live For,' Alma corrected.

'Yes, well.' Turning to Meryem, Sammy said, 'I'm a bit under the weather.'

Meryem nodded. 'I understand.'

No one spoke.

The door swung open and a young girl wearing white headphones came in. They waited for her to pass, Meryem leaning against the sink. Alma by the door.

The girl closed her cubicle door and as she did, Sammy said, her voice determinedly bright. 'So, anyway! This one here,' she nodded at Alma, 'along with my husband, made me make a list. I mean, Versace jeans! Can you believe it? What a thing to put on a bucket list!'

'What else did you put on the list?' Meryem closed her handbag and swung it over her shoulder.

'Oh...' Sammy shrugged. 'Silly stuff. The jeans of course. Renewing my passport, and then actually using it.'

'That's what they're for.' Meryem smiled.

Sammy smiled back. 'Yes. Oh, and seeing George Michael of course.' She turned to the mirror. 'Not like this though. God, I look dreadful!'

Over the top of Sammy's headscarfed head Meryem mouthed to Alma. '*George Michael is dead.*'

'*I know.*' Alma mouthed back.

'*You wanted to marry him, remember?*'

Alma's lips twitched. She wanted to laugh. What a thing for Meryem to remember! She had. She really had wanted to marry George Michael.

'Sammy.' Meryem put her hand on Sammy's small

shoulder, her emerald ring winking in the overhead lights. 'You do know that George Michael is dead?'

A whole head shorter, Sammy looked up. 'I'm not that far gone, Meryem! Of course I do. Cried buckets, I did! Absolute buckets.'

'Oh, so did I!' In a genuine gasp of empathy, Meryem's hands flew to her chest. 'They played 'Careless Whisper' on Radio Dubai every day for a whole week. I cried and cried and cried.'

'Me too,' Alma whispered.

'And I thought of you, Alma!' Meryem turned to her. 'I thought of you so much!'

'Did you?' Alma said, dumbfounded. She had no idea how to respond. Should she say, *And I thought of you too*? Which wasn't nearly enough. Because she'd never really stopped thinking of Meryem. Not, as the years had passed, in the acute, overwhelming state that had plagued those first weeks and months. Rather as an underlying layer of sadness, an absence in her life that was unresolvable and that she had learned to accommodate. Listening carefully if a news item came on about Turkey, answering polite enquiries if she bumped into an old school teacher: *Did you ever hear? No, nothing.* The view of Sydney House, their old flats, from the top deck of the number 56. And then of course with the arrival of the internet, the novelty and hope of *Friends Reunited* and *Facebook. Twitter, Instagram.* But not once had she found so much as a trace, and the absence had settled again, like sediment in a riverbed. So this *And I thought of you* was like a sonic wave from the bottom of the ocean. It reached her, and it displaced her. Meryem had thought of her too.

'Yes!' Meryem's face lit up. 'I did, Alma! You used to write

Mrs Alma Michael all over your schoolbag in that white liquid thing... what was it called?'

'Tipp-Ex?' Sammy offered.

'Tipp-Ex! Yes!'

'Well, let's face it,' Alma smiled, feeling inexplicably lighter, 'we all wanted to marry George Michael.'

'Not true,' Sammy said. 'I was into Simon Le Bon. Duran Duran. And you...' She turned to Meryem. 'I remember now. You always said you were never going to get married, Meryem! I remember that. You were going to be a scientist. You wanted to work in space.'

Meryem smiled. She turned back to the mirror, smoothing her eyebrow with the tip of her finger.

'Well not *in* space,' Sammy blustered. 'I mean *with* space. Rockets, I think...'

Alma watched. Meryem's life, the life she had lived between then and now, was as unknowable as the far side of the moon, but it didn't, she was very sure, contain science.

'Did you?' Sammy asked, but her eyes were on Meryem's blouse, her jeans, the snakeskin gilet, the shiny white Chanel sneakers. 'Did you carry on with that?'

In the mirror, Alma's eyes met Meryem's. She looked away.

'No.' Meryem smiled, twisting the length of her hair into a rope and pushing it over her shoulder. 'I didn't become a scientist, Sammy.'

And a long wide moment passed.

'Well,' Sammy said. 'It's obviously not the real thing we're going to. It's a tribute act. George Mightbe, would you believe?' She turned to Alma, the indents where her eyebrows had been arching with unspoken questions.

In response, Alma gave a tiny shrug.

'It's all part of an Eighties weekend,' Sammy said. 'And,

as I'll never see the real thing now, my husband went and booked it. I persuaded Alma to come. Well... I asked Alma to come. I have to... There's something I'm doing...' Sammy's hand went to her headscarf.

'An Eighties weekend?' Meryem's mouth turned up at the corners. 'That sounds fun.'

'Doesn't it? My husband arranged it all.' Sammy laughed, her voice lighter now. 'Actually you might remember him? He was in our year as well. Gary Collins?'

'Gary Collins.' Meryem brought her palms together, holding them under her chin as she narrowed her eyes and shook her head.

Alma watched. There was something forced about the reaction, as if Meryem was trying too hard to remember someone she clearly didn't remember. Or someone she clearly did but was pretending not to.

Meryem smiled. Smoothing down her blouse, she turned to Alma. 'So, Alma. Did you ever see him?'

'Who?' Alma startled. The question had been swift as an arrow.

'George Michael? You really wanted to. Remember?'

'No.' She blinked. 'I didn't.'

Meryem nodded. 'What a shame,' she murmured. 'What a shame.'

What a shame. Yes, it was. Like her life draining away with Thursday night laundry and TV soap operas. What a shame.

'But really Sammy? Don't skip Versace! You're here now and you must grab the opportunity while you can!' Meryem looked at Alma, her face brightening. 'Do you know what? There is nothing I like more than shopping. What do you think, Alma? If we both help, we can get Sammy her jeans.' She didn't wait for an answer. 'Every woman *needs* a pair of

Versace jeans. Remember Topshop on Enfield High Street? We used to spend every Saturday there, didn't we Alma? Such fun times we used to have, trying on everything in the shop!'

Alma smiled, not because she was remembering fun times but because it was what the situation required. In truth she was as dazed by this sudden remembrance of something else forgotten, as surely as if she had been slapped. Fun times? Was there, had there been, a time in her life when an afternoon trying on clothes in Topshop was such easily accessible fun? And if so, where had that Alma gone? The Alma who did things like that? The Alma who had fun?

'You're right, Meryem!' Sammy grinned. 'You're absolutely bloody right! Carps a gem! Or whatever the expression is. Let's get it done!'

'*Carpe diem*,' Alma murmured, but it was too late. Like a battleship in full sail Meryem, and Sammy, had already swept through the door.

6

CREDIT CARD BABY

London, present day

'I'M NOT SURE. I'm just not sure at all.' Sammy stood in front of the full-length mirror in a pair of jeans, the back pockets of which were covered in bright diamante studs. 'It's like having headlamps on my arse,' she muttered.

Standing next to her, Meryem winked. 'All the better for attracting attention.'

'I don't know.' Sammy did a little half turn to look at her rear view. 'They're not too blingy are they, Alma? I mean, I could see myself wearing them in Dubai, but Enfield?'

Sitting a few feet away, on a plush red couch, Alma wrinkled her nose, her face caught between the encouragement she thought it should display and the emphatic *No* it strained to express. 'Well...' she started and was cut off by Meryem leaning across to smack Sammy's bottom.

'Buy them!' Meryem declared. 'Why not? They look great!'

Half a second passed as Sammy's face froze and then broke apart in a wide laugh. 'Bugger it! I will. Why not indeed!' She turned to Meryem. 'What about you? Are you going to buy that?'

'Maybe. What do you think?' Turning away from the mirror, Meryem looked at Alma. 'Is it too tight?'

'No,' Alma said and tried to smile, but it was more of a grimace, and she knew it. While Sammy was busy with jeans, Meryem had tried on dresses. The one she had on now reminded Alma of a bandage, a full-length, maximum-strength compression bandage that she wasn't sure how Meryem had gotten over her shoulders. Nut-brown skin poured over every seam. From the gentle rolls at Meryem's underarms, to the scoop of the back and the huge, suspended tsunami of bosom at the front. Too tight? Not, if Meryem intended to stand all day... and not breathe... or eat.

'I need heels!' Meryem cried and nodded at her discarded sneakers. 'I never wear those things! Only in London when I have to walk.' Rising up onto the balls of her feet, she turned sideways. 'And I *never* walk in Dubai.'

'I guess it gets hot out there?' Sammy said, still admiring her sparkling bottom.

'Sammy, you have no idea! I refuse to go anywhere unless there's air-con!'

'I can't do heels anymore,' Alma murmured.

'Me neither,' Sammy said.

Meryem twisted around. 'Alma!' She pointed. 'Do you remember those white ankle boots you had? You had to change into your plimsolls at lunchtime, because you couldn't walk in them.'

Alma frowned.

'They were all funny and bunched up.'

'Periwinkle heels?' Sammy laughed. 'That was Eighties fashion for you! I had a perm. Mind everyone had a perm back then.'

'I don't remember that,' Alma said, smiling herself now. She didn't and it seemed funny how Meryem did. How, by comparison to her own, Meryem's memories were clear, as if they had stayed all these years in a bright and sunny place.

Sammy turned to the mirror. 'Do you remember we used to change on the bus, on the way to school? We'd take off our ties and roll the waistband of our skirts up?'

Meryem's face opened with delight. 'We did, didn't we?'

'We did everything on the bus!' Sammy laughed. 'The back three rows. Six stops, I could eat breakfast – one packet of salt and vinegar, smoke a fag and still get a full face of make-up on. Even eyebrows.' And suddenly she dropped her head and folded over, her shoulders heaving up and down.

Alma froze. She looked at Meryem, and they both looked at Sammy.

'Sammy?' Alma whispered, standing.

Sammy shot upright, tears streaming down her face, fist at her mouth as great silent roars of laughter rampaged through. She was shaking her head and trying to speak, wheezing and gasping and holding her chest. 'Wait a minute,' she managed, putting her hand up. 'Wait a cotton-blinking minute.'

Watching Sammy trying to control her laughter, Alma's mouth twitched. And when she looked across, she saw that Meryem too was smiling, on the edge of laughing.

'I shaved them all off!' Sammy gasped. 'I shaved my eyebrows off, just so I could pencil them back in! I mean, what the hell was all that about?'

And now Alma did laugh. Sammy's eyes were alive, her cheeks had flushed and she looked to Alma like she hadn't looked in months. It was impossible not to smile back at such a face.

'Mind,' Sammy continued. 'I wouldn't really need to do it now, would I?' And those bare dents where her eyebrows had been jumped once, then twice and then a third time.

'Stop it!' Alma slapped her hand over her mouth.

'Stop what?' Sammy winked, making her eyebrow dents dance again.

Meryem too folded over, shaking with laughter, her bosom spilling over the dress as the zip burst open under the strain.

'Stop it!' But Alma was helpless with giggles now. Loose as string. Crossing her legs and un-crossing them, just like a kid. Her sides hurt. 'Stop it,' she moaned holding her stomach.

Meryem stumbled back to lean against the mirror, one arm across her mouth, the other holding the dress up, tears of laughter streaming down her face.

'We were such idiots,' Sammy managed, long minutes later, as one by one they regained their composure. 'Or I was.'

'We were kids.' Alma smiled.

'We were, weren't we?' Meryem said. 'Just kids.' She turned to face the mirror and beside her, Sammy did the same and together they stood looking at themselves, and Alma sat, watching them.

'It is a lovely dress, Meryem,' Sammy said finally.

Alma nodded. 'It is. It's just...' She paused. 'Would you ever wear it?'

Meryem turned, her eyes wide. 'Of course! If I buy it, I'll wear it, Alma. And...' She took one last glance at her reflection and said, 'Yes! Yes, I think I will.' And she disappeared into the changing room.

Neither Alma nor Sammy spoke. With Meryem gone, Alma could now see herself clearly in the mirror and it made her uneasy. Why had she asked such a question, when Meryem had so resolutely shut down every other enquiry into her life. She tipped her head at the ceiling, at the rows and rows of white spotlights. She'd asked, because that wide-open moment of easy laughter had had her feeling as if a portal had been opened, a gateway into the past, where questions had flowed between them easy as water. *Which boy do you like? What do you want to be? Where shall we live when we're older?* She lowered her head and looked back at her refection, her eyes narrowing. There she was, forty-four, the spotlights concealing nothing. And there was Sammy. And the portal hadn't been anything more than a fleeting mirage. And there was another reason she had asked that question. She was envious. She could, and probably would, get through an entire lifetime without ever finding an occasion to wear such a dress.

'Alma?' Sammy padded across. 'Did you see the price?' she said, keeping her voice low. Three thousand two hundred pounds!'

'What!'

'She's obviously loaded.'

'I guess.' Alma fell silent. She looked across at the changing room: £3,200 was vast amount of money. Three hundred pounds was more than she'd ever spent on a piece of clothing. More than she'd ever spent on a piece of furniture. In fact the only thing she'd spent more on was her mother's coffin.

'She's fun though. Sort of exactly how I remembered,' Sammy said.

Alma turned to her.

'Don't you think? I mean you were her friend.'

'It's been a long time.' It was all she could say. Hidden behind the make-up and the jewellery, it was true, there were parts of Meryem that she recognised. But the very fact that they were hidden made it clear that, unlike Sammy, this was not how she remembered Meryem. The Meryem she remembered, her friend, her confidant and constant companion, had had nothing to hide. Had seemed to her younger self to be as free as the wind, leaning into life with a courage and confidence that had inspired and scared her.

'How long is she over?' Sammy whispered, sitting down.

'I don't know.'

Sammy nodded. Her shoulders drooped and she seemed to sag.

'Are you tired?'

'I am.' Sammy sighed. 'But I'm also really looking forward to this weekend. All of it. I know that might sound strange, but I'm so ready to let go of Mum now. If you know what I mean.'

'I do.' Alma smiled. Having had far too early a head start on this journey, she understood exactly what Sammy was talking about. It had taken years, and there had been times when she never thought she would, but one day, without noticing, she had woken to find that she too felt differently about her mother. It wasn't so much being ready to let go, that wouldn't have been how she described it. It was more a case of being ready to accommodate the memory of her in a different way, to find a lighter space for it in her head. A space with softer edges, that didn't re-open the wound every time.

'Speaking of letting go, I still have your box in the attic.'

'What box?' Alma frowned.

'Your mother's.' Sammy smiled. 'You left it with me years ago.'

'Oh.' Alma's mouth made a small round shape. She'd forgotten. Her own flat had no attic, and in the immediate aftermath of her mother's death, it had been too destabilising to open a wardrobe door and see it sitting there. 'You know,' she said, 'I actually forgot you had it.'

'That's good,' Sammy said. 'In a way.'

'Yes, I suppose it is.'

'It's not very big. We could bring it. I'm not sure when we'll next see each other.'

'Then bring it, yes.'

'Okay.' Sammy stretched her legs out, and looked at them. 'I don't know about these. Maybe I should go for the first pair. Without the bling.'

'No!' Twisting on her seat, the force of Alma's response surprised her. Alma shook her head, a little too hard, but Meryem, she was thinking now, was right. Why the hell not? Sammy should buy, and then wear, diamante-studded jeans. While she still could. 'No,' she insisted, as much for herself as for Sammy, because she was thinking about that dress, and all the other dresses she might have worn. 'You should buy these.'

'Okay, okay.' Sammy held her hands up in mock surrender. 'I promise, okay? I definitely will.' Lines ploughed across Sammy's brow as, deep in thought, she looked up at the dressing-room curtain. 'Has she said anything about what happened?'

Alma shook her head.

'Her father just took her, didn't he? It was in the papers and everything. I remember that much.'

Alma didn't speak. *Left.* That was the word Meryem had

used. 'I haven't asked,' she said. 'There hasn't really been an opportunity.'

'No.' Sammy was still staring at the curtain. Suddenly she sat up and turned to Alma. 'We should ask her to come, Alma. Is that silly?' And before Alma could respond, she added, 'I mean, why not?'

Why not? Those words again.

'It just feels...' Sammy paused. 'You know... It feels like we should at least ask. Don't you think?'

Slowly, Alma peeled her hands from the couch. They were inexplicably clammy again. She too looked across at the changing room. There wasn't a reason in the world for her not to ask Meryem to join them, which didn't stop her feeling... uncomfortable? The way Meryem had fled the tearoom remained like a warning siren in her head, a wail in the background of what otherwise had been an enjoyable hour.

'It's an Eighties weekend!' Sammy was saying. 'I think Meryem would enjoy it! I mean, I don't know about you, but I haven't laughed like that in ages. Plus, we're really going to need a laugh this weekend, aren't we?'

And how could she disagree with that? The weekend, despite what she said about being ready, was going to be hard for Sammy. She'd held onto her mother for five long years, but it was time. Sammy could be facing her own mortality. It was beyond time. She nodded again. Everything Sammy was saying made sense. They should ask Meryem – who would, of course, say no. Who would have something more important to do. Who travelled to the Gold Coast and spent three thousand on a dress without blinking. Meryem wouldn't be interested in an Eighties weekend in Blackpool, with a George Michael lookalike. 'She's just passing through,' Alma said quietly. 'I doubt she'll be able to make it.'

'We'll ask anyway,' Sammy decided. 'It would give you two a proper chance to catch up. I'm sure there's a lot to catch up on.'

Catch up? Alma smiled. Ever since they were children, running through the park, she hadn't been able to catch up with Meryem. It was funny how she remembered that. How it used to upset her. They couldn't have been more than five or six. But, Sammy was right. She too hadn't laughed like that in ages because Meryem was fun. She went to stand and as she did, Meryem swept out of the changing room, the dress slung over her arm like a sequinned carcass.

Sammy stood. 'Alma and I were talking.'

'About me?' Meryem said, her smile as generous as it was fixed.

'No!' Sammy turned to Alma, then back Meryem. 'No. We were talking about the weekend. We wondered, actually, it's a bit of a long shot, but we wondered if you'd like to join us? It's going to be fun. I mean I don't know how long you're here for and you're probably tied up—'

And to Alma's astonishment, Meryem's eyes brimmed with tears. Feeling her own fill up, she watched as Meryem put her fist to her mouth and shook her head and said, 'An Eighties weekend? Why not?'

SONJA

Flat 7, Sydney House
5 Layton Rd
Enfield, London

20th April 1987

My darling Meryem,

You have been gone one year and four months exactly.

Spring is coming. We have longer days. Yesterday when I wrote Emin's letter it was warm. I told him about the tulips I planted with you both and how he tried to eat the bulbs. This time of year always reminds me. It also reminds me of my first English lessons which I will tell you about now. Perhaps you read each other's letters? You will both laugh I know, and then maybe one day we will all laugh together about it.

It was Kathy who taught me. We had seen each other many times, on the street and on the stairs. But we could never talk. Then one day she invited me in and asked me if I would like to learn English. 'Learn English' – I understood that much. And I wanted to, Meryem, but I was not confident I could. I had come to know some Turkish women, and although like me, they couldn't understand what the midwife was telling them, they didn't seem to care. Maybe they already knew how to care for their child. Maybe they had learned by watching their own mothers. But my mother had died when I was a baby. I had no one.

We started on a warm day, just like today. I remember because Kathy wore a short dress that showed her arms and her legs. It was pale green with large white flowers and I was shocked when she opened her kitchen window and stretched her legs out on a chair to smoke a cigarette. She wasn't very tall. Later, when I tried my first cigarette, I had to push the chair much further away to stretch my legs.

The first word was sugar. And the next, icing sugar. Back home we had one word, and one sugar, seker. I was pulling packets out of Kathy's kitchen cupboards because I could not understand what to fill my own cupboards with. Kathy poured little piles onto her table to show me how icing sugar was different to sugar, and how there was flour, and raising flour and baking powder. And I began to understand why there were seventeen cupboards. This was when she told me about birthday cakes.

She was training then to become a fully qualified nurse. She told me the name of her village in Ireland, and I told her the name of my village. It made us laugh, all the things we couldn't pronounce, all the things we couldn't say to each other. She had less furniture than we had. A table in the kitchen, a cot for Alma, and a television she was paying for every week.

I found out that she was three years older than me, and Alma was three months older than you. I also found out that Alma had come to her from a man she was not married to.

This was why she left Ireland and came to England. I found it so hard to understand, Meryem. Children have sometimes come to women who are not married, this I knew. But to travel to another country and raise the child alone? That was something beyond my comprehension. From the beginning I understood how different she was to any other woman I had known. I couldn't imagine living the life she lived, wearing the clothes she did. And at the same time, with every new thing I learned about her, how close in age our babies were, how alone she also was, I believed more and more that God had sent her to me to be my friend. Why else would it be that the woman who had washed me clean after you were born, lived so close? Only one floor lower. If I called from my kitchen window, she would be able to hear. Just like the village.

It was the opposite for your father. He would never enter her home. He did not call her any bad words but he would not enter her home.

Yes, my first English lesson. I can see that day so clearly. It was the beginning of happiness.

'Flour is for cakes,' she said. 'Like birthday cakes?'

I did not know what a birthday cake was.

'No birthday cakes?' When she stubbed her cigarette out, it was stained pink with her lipstick. She went to the sink and filled the bowl with water, the backs of her knees patterned with the lines of the chair. 'When is your birthday?' she said. ´I'll make a cake for your birthday.'

'My birthday?'

'The day you were born.' In the beginning, Kathy spoke very slowly because my English was so bad.

Somehow, I managed to get her to understand that I didn't know the day I was born and I remember that when she turned, her hands were dripping soap bubbles.

'What do you mean, you don't know?' She sounded angry.

I was afraid, Meryem. Afraid of losing someone I hoped would become a friend. She dried her hands and left and I didn't know what to do. If I should leave too? But she came back to the kitchen, and she had her passport and she pointed to her birth date and told me that my birthday was also in my passport.

I understood immediately. But she was wrong and I couldn't explain that. I didn't have enough words. She asked me if your father was home. He was, but he was sleeping. He worked nights now.

'Your birthday will be in your passport.' This is what she kept saying. She was pointing all the time at her own passport and her pointing was an angry point and I was so ashamed, because she was thinking I was stupid. Already, she knew I couldn't read. But how could I explain, Meryem, that what was in my passport was not the day I was born? That was when I stopped being afraid. I wanted to be able to talk to Kathy. I wanted to explain myself. I did not want anyone to think I was stupid and I decided I would learn English as quickly as possible.

And as you know, I did. But it was many months afterwards, Meryem, that I was able to tell Kathy what I will tell you now.

Your father returned from England when the fields were being prepared for the autumn seeding. Two days later, my brother's wife, Nur, sent the little ones out to buy sweets and had me sweeping all through the house. She called me 'el kizi': stranger girl. It was not her fault she wanted me married. I was grown and there were too many mouths to feed. My mother and my father were in the cemetery. Even though I had never known my mother, I missed her. But when everyone says it is God's will, you cannot dwell on things. We did not talk about her.

And then your father's mother came to visit and I knew it was happening. Nur sprinkled lemon cologne on her hands and sent me out to make the coffee. It was an exciting time. I wanted them to know I was pleased with the match, so I used twice as much sugar in the coffee. I remembered your father before he went to England. Everyone did. He was handsome and strong. He ran up mountains.

After it was agreed, we went to Ankara for my passport and when the public recorder asked the date of my birth, my brother could only say it was after the lambs were born.

How old was she then? they asked.

My brother said I was sixteen. But we didn't count birthdays. He wanted me to be sixteen because it was old enough to marry.

I was counted as sixteen, and given a birthday of 21st June 1952. I left Ankara with a birth certificate, and a civil wedding certificate, and a passport, none of which made any sense. I remember the women in the city rushing past with nothing covering their heads, and in one day I saw more cars than I had ever seen in my life. Wires dangled between buildings, so that everyone was connected to everyone else. How strange it all was to me.

So you see? What was in my passport was not the day that I was born.

That birthday cake day, our first English lesson, was interrupted because Lenny banged on the kitchen window and I ran away. I was not accustomed to seeing men I didn't know and I could not understand how Kathy could lean out of the window and talk to him. Her arms were bare! She was like the women in Ankara. I remember moving back against the cupboards. Kathy tried to get me to come forward and say hello. I wouldn't. And then I saw him lean through and put his nose an inch from hers. She pushed him back and they laughed and she stuck her tongue out like a child and waggled it at him.

I knew that I could never behave the way that she did, and Meryem, whatever else you have been told – I never did.

When Lenny left, Kathy called after me. I would not come. I was angry and embarrassed and confused but I could not tell her these things. She found me and saw my face and hugged me for a long time. Then she went to the kitchen and came back with a book and showed me a picture of a cake and said 'birthday cake' three times, pointing at me. She was telling me that she would make a birthday cake for me. I understood.

Much later, when I carried you back up the stairs to our flat, I whispered in your ear and promised you that you too would have a cake on your birthday. I would always make you one, Meryem. I whispered it again and again in your ear because I was determined my daughter would always know the day on which she had come into this world. But you will not remember this. You were six months old and fast asleep, and this was the beginning of my second summer in England.

And I kept my promise, Meryem. I have made you a cake every year. Every year.

Love always, Mamma

PART TWO

7

CARELESS WHISPER

London, 1985

'You are coming, aren't you?' Across the classroom, Gary stood in the doorway, looking back at Meryem from under his floppy brown hair.

As Meryem nodded, Alma's stomach clenched.

There were five of them in this maths group. Sammy Bowman, Ed Cutter, Gary, Meryem and herself. Collaboration was something their teacher encouraged, and Meryem, until now, had always resisted. She said she gave more than she got, something Alma couldn't argue with. No one was better at maths than Meryem, but this time they had been grouped with Gary Collins. And Gary's best friend, Ed, had suggested an after-school homework session. At his house. With music. And all week, as Meryem had become more excited, Alma had only become more worried.

She didn't want to go. Gary Collins was the most popular

boy in the class and Ed lived in the most expensive part of Enfield. 'We were going to practise the dance,' she pleaded as the door swung closed behind Gary.

'Aaalma. Don't you want to see what his house looks like?'

Alma turned away. She hated it when Meryem stretched her name like this. Like she was talking to a baby. She wasn't a baby. Out of the two of them, she was the oldest and Meryem had promised that they would practise the dance routine they were performing for the end of term show. 'You know you won't be allowed to,' she fired back, using the best ammunition she had. Meryem's parents.

But Meryem only smiled and fired back her own best ammunition. 'I will, if you go.'

Stumped, Alma kept her chin down, stuffing her schoolbag with books. It was true. They had been friends since they were babies, and that, Alma understood, afforded Meryem a degree of freedom that wouldn't otherwise have been possible. They lived in and out of each other's homes. Dolls and hair clips, magazines and tape cassettes, moving between the flats in a continuously circular motion. They had explored Trent Park together, had the same Snoopy t-shirts, slept top-to-toe in Meryem's single bed, when Alma's mother worked nights. Once, Alma had even moved into Meryem's home for a week when her own mother was recovering from what she'd said was flu, but Alma had always suspected was more to do with her boyfriend, Lenny, moving out. Apart from the one time Meryem went to Turkey, Alma couldn't actually remember any days when they hadn't seen each other. School fêtes, birthday parties, pantomime trips. If she was going, Meryem could go. But this felt different. This felt like new territory. And it was to do with the way Gary and Meryem looked at each other.

It wasn't for herself that she was worried. The succession of boyfriends her mother had had, was enough for Alma to feel that a boyfriend of her own would not have caused problems. Not that that was likely to happen soon, boys simply didn't look at her the way they looked at Meryem. No, it was for Meryem, she was anxious. And that was because of her father.

He frightened Alma. When he was home, the atmosphere changed in Meryem's house. Her mother would tell them to play more quietly as she closed the bedroom door, and Meryem's face would harden and it was, for a moment, as if a shadow had fallen. The one thing Alma was grateful for was that he *never* came into her home. It wasn't that he was rude to her mother, but if he came to collect Meryem he would stand at the doorway and wait, no matter how many times her mother had invited him in. She'd given up now, shaking her head and walking away to leave him on the doorstep, no matter how cold, no matter how long Meryem was taking to get her things together. Those were the times Alma was secretly grateful that it was just her and her mother. No boys and certainly no men.

'Anyway.' Meryem said brightly, linking her arm through Alma's. 'I've already asked my mum and she said it was okay. Please? I promise we'll practise at the weekend.'

And as always, she just couldn't find a loud enough way of saying, *No.*

'*Hide me!*'

Halfway along the road up to Ed's house, head low, shoulders hunched against the freezing wind, Alma had her collar up and her eyes down. She didn't see Meryem stop, jump aside from their group and duck, so the urgency of

Meryem's repeated whispered *Hide me!* took her by surprise. Startled she looked to where the voice had come from.

Meryem had scuttled from the pavement to crouch behind the gatepost of the nearest house. She was all bare knees and green socks and giggles. 'Stand in front and hide me.' She was still whispering, as she nodded across to the other side of the road.

Alma turned. On the opposite pavement, a dark-haired, middle-aged man was walking down the hill, towards them. But he too had his head low against the wind.

'Hide me, Alma!'

From behind, she felt hands on her back, manoeuvring her into place, holding her like a dummy as the man passed by.

When enough distance had opened, Meryem stood up. 'My dad's friend,' she whispered, tugging her socks up. 'Tariq. Mister know-it-all.'

At the bottom of the rise, the man turned the corner and disappeared.

Meryem watched. 'Did he see?' she said.

'I don't know.'

'Do you think he did?'

'I don't know!' Alma frowned. Hadn't Meryem said that she'd asked her mother about this homework group? 'Why are you hiding?' she said. 'Your mum knows.'

But Meryem only laughed. 'Come on then!' she called, hurrying ahead, keen it seemed to Alma to catch up with the rest of the group, who had disappeared into the paved driveway of a large expensive-looking semi at the top of the rise.

Hands deep in pockets, Alma followed. Meryem hiding like that had unsettled her, which didn't help because she was already nervous enough for both of them. She'd never been to this part of Enfield before. Never been in a house the size of the one they were heading for. She looked up, caught a glimpse across the rooftops ahead and gasped.

And at the same time, standing in the driveway, waiting for her, Meryem gasped too. 'Look, Alma!' she exclaimed, pointing. 'Just look at that!'

Alma couldn't speak. They were right at the top of the rise, both of them looking across to the expanse of Forty Hill Park and its lake, which had partly frozen. The view was astonishing and beautiful, and the more Alma looked, the more it seemed to change. Low sun splaying rays across the ice of the lake, patches of water rippling grey in between. A living patchwork of light and movement. Eyes smarting with cold, she blinked. 'Imagine,' she said, 'living up here and seeing this every day.' She was thinking of her bedroom at home, where the only variation of view came from the orange-striped curtains of the window in the tower block opposite. They were either open or closed. And then all the other windows repeated as far as she could see, left and right. And the layers of windows divided by white balconies and below, the cars, litter bins, lamp posts, entry doors. This was her view, had been her view for all of her life. 'Imagine,' she whispered again.

Meryem had walked the few steps back and was now standing beside her. 'We will,' she whispered. 'One day, we will.'

'What are you two looking at?' The voice came from behind. Gary, bounding out of the house like an excited labrador.

'We're looking at the water,' Meryem said calmly.

'Oh.' Gary waited, but Meryem didn't move.

Alma shuffled her feet.

'You can still see it from inside,' he said, looking up through the flop of his fringe.

'Of course you can,' Meryem whispered as she grabbed Alma's arm. 'You can probably see it from the toilet!'

And despite herself, Alma laughed, one step behind as she followed Meryem into a hallway scattered with the debris of discarded bags and shoes. Placing her shoes carefully on the shelf, Alma went to close the front door. She'd never have admitted as much to Meryem, and despite her nervousness, she had really wanted to see what a house on this road looked like. Because boys and Meryem's father aside, Ed, along with most of the kids in their class, moved in a world that left Alma as envious as she was uncomfortable. A world of grandparents and family half an hour away. A world without drama, and sudden sleepovers because a mother wasn't well, or worked all through the night. A world with houses like this, which of course she'd been curious to see, and of course, never would have, without Gary conjuring this invitation to Meryem, which would, by default, include her.

Closing the door, she stood awkwardly now as Meryem kicked off her shoes, walked into the living room and threw herself down on the large leather settee, as if she had been here a thousand times before.

'ONE THOUSAND TICKETS WERE SOLD. *Adult tickets cost eight pounds fifty, children's four pounds fifty, and seven thousand three hundred pounds was collected.*' Meryem read from the paper in her hand.

'So what's the question?' Ed yawned.

'I haven't got that far.'

'Idiot.' Gary threw a cushion at him. He lunged to catch it, before flinging it back, just missing Meryem.

'The question,' Meryem said, 'if you're interested, is how many tickets of each kind were sold?'

'I hate these.' Sitting at the end of the settee, Sammy fell back, a cushion over her face.

'How many of each kind *of what*?' Ed drawled.

'It's sooo boooring.' Sammy's voice was muffled by the cushion.

'And it's sooo easy,' Meryem replied.

'What's the answer then, *M-e-e-r-r-y*?' Ed said, and leaned across the coffee table, his chin on his folded knuckles as he looked at her.

Perched on the edge of her chair, Alma pushed her glasses up her nose. Ed had made Meryem's nickname, Mery, sound longer than her name.

No one spoke.

Meryem gave Ed a withering stare. She put the paper on the coffee table and, using her pencil, made a series of swift marks in the bottom right-hand corner. As she did, Alma sipped at the horrible watery tea Ed had made, a slurping sound escaping that had her blushing crimson-red.

Meryem glanced up and winked at her.

Another minute of silence passed, then Meryem put her pencil down and pushed the paper towards Ed. 'My name, *Edwa-a-a-rd*,' she said, 'is Meryem.'

Ed didn't answer; he picked up the paper, lips moving as he went through the calculations.

'You know she'll be right,' Gary said. He was sitting at the far end of the settee, an empty cushion between him and Sammy. He leaned back now, hands clasped behind his neck. 'She always is.'

And watching, Alma saw how Meryem now blushed.

Not the livid red she herself always turned, but a dusky pink across her cheeks.

'Enough maths!' Sammy stood up, threw her cushion aside and looking at Gary said, 'Let's put some music on?'

No one answered.

Ed slid the paper back to Meryem. 'I'll pay you to do my homework,' he said.

Meryem's answer was instant. 'Two pounds,' she said.

'That's cheating!' Alma gasped.

Meryem turned to her. 'I'm not going to help him in the tests.' Looking back at Ed, she said, 'I won't do the tests for you.'

He shrugged.

'But you can't. You can't do his homework.' Alma could feel the next blush creeping up her neck. Stronger and more insistent than the last. Everyone was looking at her.

'Why not?' Meryem said.

'Yeah, why not?' Ed yawned.

'You'll get into trouble.'

Meryem didn't speak; she looked down at the paper on the table.

'Oooh,' Ed whispered nastily. 'Better not then, you'll get into *trouble,* Meryem.'

'Shut it, Ed!' Sammy said swinging a cushion at him.

Alma pinched her knuckle, tears of embarrassment threatening.

'I'll be careful,' Meryem said quietly. She lifted her chin to look at Alma. 'I'll be really careful.'

'Okay.' Alma shrugged and her voice was tiny.

'It wouldn't work anyway! He'll go from dunce to genius in one lesson, and Mrs Knights will definitely suspect.' Sammy laughed.

'That's true!' Gary said and he too, laughed.

'Dickhead' Ed hurled a pencil at Gary.

And leaning out of the way, clutching her mug, Alma briefly closed her eyes, weak with relief that the moment was over.

'So! Music? Sammy tried again.

'What do you want?' Ed hauled himself to his feet.

'Anything, as long as it's not maths!'

Shrugging, he left the room, coming back moments later carrying a boom box that he placed in the middle of the coffee table. Looking at Alma, he pressed the play button and the heavy metal sound of Metallica's thrashing guitars burst into the room.

Alma shrank. Now she just wanted to go home, back to the view of those orange striped curtains... open or shut.

'Not this, Ed!' Sammy shouted. Her hands were over her ears. 'What else have you got?'

'What?' Ed mouthed. 'Can't hear you.'

Meryem stretched forward and turned the cassette off.

'I said,' Sammy shouted, 'not this!' But she was laughing as she pushed a reluctant Ed out of the room and into the kitchen. 'Find us something else.'

The moment they disappeared, an electrical charge surged through the room. Alma felt the static at her fingertips, the buzz in her ears. She didn't look up to see what had caused the change, she didn't need do. It was all there in front of her. Gary edging off the settee, next to Meryem now. They had their backs to her, but she could see. The waves of Meryem's black hair, her green sock sliding across the floor to touch Gary's green sock. Gary turning and leaning in.

Feeling foolish, feeling conspicuous, feeling that she wanted the world to swallow her up, Alma dipped her head to her cup. On the opposite wall, a huge glass cabinet soaked up the sun's rays. And as she focused on the rectangles of rippling light, all she could think was how Meryem was right, the view was everywhere.

LATER, as they walked back down the hill in a deep, prolonged silence, Meryem nudged her. 'What are you thinking, Alma?'

'Nothing,' she murmured. But she was thinking a thousand things. She was thinking that she was jealous, that kissing a boy seemed as impossible to her as climbing Mount Everest, yet Meryem had done it. She was thinking she was stupid for not being able to drink tea without slurping and stupid for telling Meryem she couldn't do Ed's homework, that Ed was mean, but his house was probably the nicest house she'd ever been in. And most of all, she was thinking that Meryem's father must never, ever find out.

'Tell me.' Meryem linked her arm through.

'It's nothing.'

'Alma.' Meryem stopped and made her turn. 'If you're that worried, I won't do it. I won't do his homework.'

'I'm not worried.' But she was. She was worried in a way that she didn't understand.

'You can tell me.'

Could she? She looked back at Meryem without speaking. For as long as she could remember, Meryem had worried her. Jumping into the deep end of the swimming pool without armbands, jumping off the swing at full height. Worry, and Meryem, were almost one thing, but the feeling she had today was new. It went beyond the swimming pools and swings, of their childhood. This feeling had a vein of malevolence that stretched away from kitchens and park playgrounds. That flowed instead towards the unknowable world of boys and men. One man in particular, Meryem's father. She pulled away. 'If you must know,' she said, trying to shake off the feeling. 'I'm thinking that one day I want to live where I can always see water.'

Meryem laughed. 'Me too! I was thinking exactly that too! We think the same! Isn't it exciting?' And she threw her arms around Alma and hugged her.

'I'M TELLING YOU, England is run by a one-woman dictatorship!' Under the flare of harsh fluorescent lights, against a backdrop of fogged windows, Tariq was holding court at the Turkish club.

On a long bench opposite, a row of old men, cardigan-clad tortoises, shook their heads in agreement, their rheumy eyes narrowed with mirth. Seated on upright chairs, working men tapped cigarette boxes, played with car keys and chuckled into their cups. Even the youngest men in leather jackets who leaned against the wall with hands stuck deep into pockets smirked. And the boys, cross-legged on the floor, rocked backwards with glee, although they were not at all sure what they were laughing at.

Arslan sat next to Tariq. The room was busier than normal, and it was obvious why. With the closure of the printworks there were so many more who had nothing to fill their afternoons with. Stifling a yawn, he leaned back in his chair. He should, he supposed, feel thankful that he still had a job. The same position he'd had for a decade, packing heavy-duty machinery for export. And, it was looking like, the next decade. Just last week he'd received the news that he hadn't got the promotion he had applied for. It hadn't surprised him. What surprised him now was that he'd bothered applying in the first place. That after all the previous rejections, he'd allowed himself to hope that this time it would be different. It hadn't. A younger, more inexperienced, whiter colleague had been given the job and the only thing Arslan felt at this moment was relief that he hadn't told Sonja. He couldn't face her disappointment. Not when she was doing so well. She was earning more than him now.

'That means you are working for a woman, Tariq!' one of the young men called.

Tariq drew his hand across his mouth, brushing away beads of tea that clung to his moustache. 'My friend.' He shook his head. 'We are all working for a woman.'

'You'll be sleeping in the kitchen next!´ came a second voice.

'Like Nabil!' called the first man.

'You mean Nabila!' The second man shot back.

Everyone laughed. And seizing the moment, one of the smallest boys reached a hand up to a nearby table to grab a fistful of dried peas. He was slapped back by his father.

Nabila. The whisper reached across the room like the hiss of a snake, and Arslan watched the old men suck air through yellowed teeth, and shake their heads.

Everyone knew the story. A couple of years ago, Nabil was made redundant. With his wife working, he had taken over the household duties, doing all the cleaning and all the cooking. And now, in a fit of insanity that no one had been able to shake him from, he slept in front of the oven at night, the last thing, Arslan supposed, the man had any control over.

'It won't be the kitchen for me!' Tariq answered loudly. 'I'll be gone.'

Arslan frowned. He leaned forward, elbows on knees. 'You're leaving us?'

'One day.' Tariq nodded. 'One day.'

'We're all leaving *one day*!' a man in a baseball cap called.

Tariq raised his hand. 'Be careful. You sound like Ali Tekin.' At the sound of his words, the room fell quiet.

Arslan spread his hands on his knees and looked at them. Everyone knew who Ali Tekin was. He'd worked harder and longer than any of them, and the house he had built himself back home wasn't even complete before he'd died of a heart attack. His wife had found him in the armchair, glasses on the floor, Radio Ankara on.

Tariq lifted his eyes to the ceiling. 'Who knows when it is their last day?' He shrugged. 'I have made my plans. I've bought the land already.'

The silence changed. If it was flatly respectful before, now it rose, expectant.

Arslan turned. 'Is this true?' he said. 'You've bought the land?'

'Yes.' Tariq nodded. 'Next summer I begin. After that, one more year.'

'And there is something else,' Tariq said, his voice hushed. 'I was waiting to speak to you about all this, but...' He shrugged. 'I think after today that it is better to tell you now.'

'Tell me what?' Arslan frowned.

'The Pamuk house is falling down, Arslan. I know his children would be glad to see the back of it.'

Arslan nodded. From the day they had arrived together as young men, Tariq and he had talked of returning. Everyone did. But talk was all they did. A way of passing time at work.

'It's a good position,' Tariq said. 'Pamuk was too lazy to do anything, but there is enough water for a garden.' He leaned closer in. 'I can see you there, Arslan. Sitting on your fat arse, watching the others sweat into old age. I'll be sitting next to you!'

At this, Arslan laughed.

'I'm serious,' Tariq said, and the tone of his voice echoed his words. 'It's been many years now. London is no place to raise a family. The riots? The people are animals.'

'The riots weren't close,' Arslan said, but there was no conviction in his response. Tariq was right. Across the river, just a few months ago, a policeman had been surrounded by a mob and hacked to death, on the streets. He had sat with Sonja and watched the news and yes, he had thought the same. What had happened on the streets of London was unimaginable back home. This was no place to raise children. Still, moving back had remained an idea. Something to consider for another time.

'Perhaps,' Tariq said, 'it is time for you as well?'

Arslan shook his head. 'The children must finish school first.'

'There are schools back home for Emin.'

'Meryem too.'

At the sound of Meryem's name, Tariq let out a snort of air. He shook his head and sat up straight. 'It would be better for you,' he said, 'if Meryem finishes and marries as soon as possible, Arslan.'

Surprised, Arslan laughed. 'She is only just fourteen.' He turned to look at Tariq and as he did, his face changed.

Tariq wasn't smiling, or laughing. On the contrary, his mouth had bunched to a tight ball, as if there were a bad taste in his mouth. 'She is nearly a woman. And it would be better,' he said.

Arslan looked at him. The truth of what Tariq was saying was undeniable. His daughter was on the cusp of womanhood. But girls here did not marry so young. As long as they behaved themselves... His thoughts ran adry. Tariq was looking at him with an expression he hadn't seen before. An expression that infuriated him. Concern, mixed with pity. Out of the two of them, he had been the first to buy a ticket for England. He had led the way. Tariq had always followed. *Pity?* 'Do you have something to tell me,' he said, his voice black.

Tariq took his cap off and pulled his hand through his grey-streaked hair. 'We have known each other a long time?' he said.

Arslan didn't speak. The knuckles of his fingers were white as he balled his fists. Tariq, of all people, had no business *pitying* him.

'And you trust that I would not be telling you lies?'

He nodded, short and terse. This was true. He could feel a heat at the back of his neck. Glancing around at all the other men, he leaned in, lowered his head and said, 'Tell me.'

Tariq also lowered his head, and his voice. 'For your honour, Arslan I will. For your honour, I saw Meryem yesterday walking along the road by the park. She was with two boys.'

Exhaling, Arslan leaned back. Slowly, he turned his hands over and looked at them. Across his left palm ran the thin white scar he'd received on his first job in England. Washing dishes in a windowless kitchen, while London slept. Pans went straight from the hob to the sink so quickly that one night he'd forgotten to use a glove. The ridged line was a reminder, as if a reminder was needed, of that time. Of those five long years he had waited for an answer from the government. Sixteen-hour shifts, washing his hands raw, falling into bed fully clothed, slapping his face awake in the mirror each afternoon. Eating macaroni cheese, and bread and onions, sharing a room with five other men and watching them go out for steak, paid for by their English girlfriends. Not him. Never him. He had stayed true to the promise of Sonja. And for what? He looked around the room. At the old men, condemned to finish their days in a high-rise flat, at the young men full of an energy England would stamp out of them, as it had him. At the boys, his own son soon old enough to join them. A son obsessed with an American TV show where men wore jewellery and ran around shooting people.

He had his residency now, but he was no better off. Would his son be? Dishwashing had been replaced by a production line, where he stood for twelve hours and would do so until the day he retired. His mother had died holding his photograph, and his children were growing towards something he didn't understand. And Sonja? She was a different woman to the woman he had married. A woman he barely saw. She worked days, he worked nights. It wasn't that he wanted to go back to the beginning, when she wouldn't leave the flat, but... Linking his fingers together, Arslan flexed his wrists. He couldn't decide. The ways in which Sonja had changed confused him. He was glad that she wasn't like so many of the other Turkish wives, who stayed home and grew fat on their husband's wages, baklava and gossip. But after her company's Christmas party she had come home smelling of alcohol, she had told him about bosses kissing younger colleagues under mistletoe. What he was more certain of was that they were only going through the motions of being married. Neither of them was happy. It wasn't unusual, it happened in marriages, and Sonja always behaved respectfully... But Meryem? He closed his eyes, and just as quickly opened them. Meryem, with two boys? How could Sonja have allowed it? In the far corner some younger men were laughing, and he was almost sure he heard it again, that whisper, *Nabila*. It would be him next. Again his hands balled to fists. They would be laughing at him next, at a man who has no control over his family. A daughter who is behaving like this.

'I only tell you for your honour. You understand?' Tariq's voice was close.

For his honour. Arslan nodded tightly. 'Perhaps you are right,' he said. 'Perhaps it is time to go back.' And the words made more sense out loud than they ever had in his head.

JOY BURSTING EVERY PORE, Meryem lowered the *Sky & Telescope* magazine she was reading, to stare out of the window. Daylight had narrowed to an inky twilight, the sky veiled by curtains of spiralling snowflakes. She was lying shoulder to shoulder, hip to hip with Alma, on a blue bean bag in Alma's bedroom. The walls were covered in posters of George Michael. Clothes spilled from the partially open wardrobe and, tucked into the mirror of Alma's dressing table, strips of black-and-white photo-booth pictures peeked out. Meryem and Alma grinning from every tiny square.

A scatter of school books lay on the floor. There was a Walkman on Alma's lap, and they both had their head-phones plugged into it. They were listening to Wham! Alma's lips moved as she sang along.

Smiling, Meryem watched the snow falling. She could, if she concentrated, still feel the imprint of Gary Collins' lips on hers, and it sent a tingling between her legs. He'd asked her to go and see *Back To The Future,* with him. Her first date. And as if that wasn't exciting enough, next year – she'd just read it! – Halley's Comet was coming. What a day! What a perfect day it had been. The excitement that had been building all afternoon was uncontainable. She wanted to shout it from the window! She had kissed a boy, and he had kissed her back and she didn't know how she was going to keep all the feelings that gave her to herself. 'Alma!' she pulled her headphones off. 'Look!' And she spread the open magazine across Alma's knees. 'Halley's Comet is coming! We should go to the Observatory and see it. You won't get a second chance. Not for something like this.'

Alma took her own set of headphones off and looked down at the magazine. 'I thought you didn't believe in astrology?'

'This isn't astrology! It's science, not superstition.'

'I don't know. I'm not as interested in all that stuff as you are.'

'What stuff?'

'Astronomy stuff.'

Meryem stretched her arms and clasped her hands together as she looked up at the ceiling. 'I just think it's interesting. Space. Stars. I mean, if Halley's Comet comes by every seventy-five years, where does it go in between?'

'In between what?'

'There could be a whole parallel universe going on.'

'I suppose so.' Alma yawned. 'Do you think that's possible though?'

'Maybe.'

'And is that what you want to be? A space scientist?'

'Maybe... Yes, then. Yes, a space scientist. What about you?'

Alma giggled. 'I want to be Mrs George Michael.'

'I know that!'

Alma turned to her. 'Is that why you want to see *Back To The Future* so much?'

'Actually,' and Meryem looked down at her hands. 'Gary asked if I would go with him.'

Alma gasped. 'He asked you out?'

'At Ed's house. When you were in the toilet.' She turned to Alma. 'But I won't. I'll tell him no, if you still want to go.'

'I don't mind,' Alma said. 'If you come and see *A Chorus Line* with me.'

'Ugh.' Meryem pulled a face, but she wasn't serious. 'Deal,' she said, then, 'Are you sure you don't mind?' She wasn't convinced by Alma's response. If she went with Gary, it would be the first time she would have gone anywhere, with anyone, except for Alma or her family, and it felt as odd to her as she was sure it felt to Alma.

Looking up, Alma pressed the stop button on her Walkman. 'I don't mind,' she said and her face was serious. 'But your dad will, Meryem.'

Meryem shrugged. 'Then I'll have to make sure he doesn't find out.' She turned to look back out of the window, her chin set. Alma was right, of course. Keeping Gary secret would be a problem. But if there was one thing she knew she was good at, it was solving problems. And anyway, her father worked all night and slept all day.

'If you say so.' Alma settled back down on the beanbag.

Meryem turned to look at her. Kissing Gary Collins had been the most exciting thing that had happened in her life, so far. But it was just a start. She had toes on the edge of a brink, above a plain so vast she could feel the upward draught of a life beginning. And although she couldn't wait to start living it, she wanted her best friend along for the ride. As she always had been. As she always would. Because what a life they were going to have! They'd already begun to plan what university they would attend. Up and away from these flats, away from Enfield! To make up for her insensitivity she said, 'Let's practise the routine,' because she wanted Alma to know that they were friends, and they always would be.

Surprised, Alma turned to her. 'You mean it? I thought you didn't even want to do it.'

Meryem shrugged. 'I don't mind.'

'Okay! In the kitchen then!' Alma was already halfway out the door. She stopped. 'In costume this time?'

'It's December, Alma! I don't even know where my shorts are.'

But Alma was opening a drawer, pulling stuff out. 'I can't find mine either,' she said and straightened up. 'PE knickers then? I still have mine on!'

'Me too!'

And giggling they slipped off their school skirts, and tied knots in their blouses.

'Make-up!' Meryem cried. She grabbed an eyeliner from Alma's dressing table.'I'll do yours.'

'It tickles!' Alma giggled as Meryem drew the pencil across her lids. 'And why can't I be Pepsi for once?'

'You haven't got the hair. Keep your eyes closed.'

But Alma didn't. 'What was it like?' she whispered as she opened her eyes and looked straight at Meryem.

'The kiss?' Meryem's eyes danced with light.

'That good?'

She nodded and together they leaned forward, arms clutching as they burst into a fit of prolonged giggles.

'SEE YOU TOMORROW.' Standing at the bottom of the steps, Sonja watched as Kathy bent her head, lit a cigarette, and walked to the gangway that led to her flat. Her friend was, she knew, desperately tired. And she had another night shift tonight. She wanted so much to be able to invite her up and sit her down. To look after her, just as Kathy had looked after her all those years ago when she was new to the country, to the climate, to the culture. When she was new to everything. Arslan had never been in Kathy's home, but he'd been welcoming enough, if reserved, when she came to theirs. Not now. Recently he'd made it clear she wasn't welcome, and that, Sonja thought, was because of Lenny. Or the boyfriend Kathy had had after Lenny. Or because she smoked, or because of the way she went to the pub with her work colleagues. Sonja didn't know. She couldn't keep up with the complaints her husband had begun to find, not just with Kathy, but with life in general. *Their* life in general. He wasn't the same easy-going man she had married, and she could not invite Kathy up. With heavy legs, she started up the concrete stairs to her own home, Emin at her side.

She'd only just dumped the shopping on the table, she hadn't got the front door closed, when she heard Kathy call up the stairs.

'Sonja? Get yourself back down here and look at these two eejits of ours will you!'

Emin on her heels, Sonja hurried down the stairs. Kathy was standing on the balcony outside her kitchen. She'd positioned herself to one side, so she couldn't be seen. She was pointing at the partially open window, through which pop music seeped out. Her hand was at her mouth, she was laughing so much.

Coming up alongside, Sonja peered in, saw Meryem first, then Alma. Their foreheads were shiny with sweat as they bounced and bumped into each other, as they danced and laughed, and laughed and danced. They were like the baby goats, that, as a young girl back in the village, Sonja had had to round up. Kicking and running and jumping around her as if life was just one long game. The memory made her smile and the sight of her daughter, so loose limbed, so joyous, made her smile again.

Kathy pointed at her front door, and ducking low, they scuttled past the window.

Inside they waited by the kitchen doorway, Emin's small head bumping against her thigh, as he too bopped along. The music was irresistible. When it finished, Emin burst into the room, grabbing Meryem's bare legs and Kathy and Sonja cheered and clapped. They didn't see the shadow that crossed the walkway outside. No one did. And by the time Sonja had gathered up Emin, and left Meryem to follow, and made her way back up the stairs to her own home, the shadow had already slipped back into the gloom..

'HELLO.' Arslan spoke his quiet threat from the corner of the kitchen. His bare forearms, folded across the blue of his overalls, bright in the gloom.

Startled, Sonja turned. She hadn't even switched the hall lights on. As she closed the door behind her, a gust of wind swept up the stairs and along the walkway, a whooshing ghostly sound. 'Go,' she said and put a hand on Emin's small back, steering him towards the living room. 'Go and put the TV on.' Slowly, she took her coat off and hung it on the hook, brushed her skirt down and went to the kitchen table, where the shopping bags sat bunched and bulky, just as she'd left them. He shouldn't be here. She looked at the clock. His shift started in twenty minutes.

'I've just seen Tariq.'

Sonja didn't speak. She took a cereal box and turned to put it away. When she closed the cupboard door, her hand stayed on the handle. Tariq, oracle of the Turkish club. She didn't like the man, and neither did Arslan. Not since Tariq had moved to day shifts, and been promoted. She was surprised Arslan would even listen to him, so bitter he'd been when he found out. Tariq didn't have the A levels Arslan had studied for at night school. Tariq had nothing. 'At the club?' she said, her voice light. Of course it was the club. Arslan never went anywhere apart from home, and the club. He didn't even go to the mosque anymore. She moved to her handbag, took her cigarettes and went to the window. And she no longer prayed either.

'You don't want to hear what he said?'

'No,' she said quietly, bending her head to light the cigarette. 'I don't want to hear.'

'About your daughter, Sonja?'

'*Our* daughter, Arslan. And no. If it's coming from Tariq I don't want to hear. I'm surprised you did.'

Arslan's eyes narrowed to deep black slashes, as he studied her face. 'He saw Meryem walking with two boys. After school. By the park.'

Sonja nodded. Reaching for an ashtray, she flicked a layer of ash from the cigarette, and ran her fingers through her hair, buying as many extra moments as she dared. 'I know,' she said finally, as she looked at him. 'Except it wasn't *just* Meryem and two boys. It would have been Meryem and Alma, and another girl and yes, I think two boys.'

'You knew about this?'

'They have a study group, Arslan. One of the boys lives there. She asked me if they could go to his house for the study group, and I said it was okay.' And when he didn't answer, Sonja balanced her cigarette on the ashtray, and began taking yogurt pots out of the shopping bag, lining them up on the table, allowing time for the lie to settle. Meryem hadn't asked. She'd said it *might* happen. She'd tiptoed around the subject for a week, and Sonja had avoided giving her an answer. The children were her domain. Arslan had never interfered with the decisions she had made, and although she had always known this could change, she had come to think less and less about it. He wasn't a traditionalist. On the contrary, he was the one who had encouraged her to become more independent. This was the man who had pinned her first wage slip to the kitchen noticeboard, to show how proud he was. He had been the one to suggest she stop wearing her headscarf. Her hand rested on the last yogurt pot. All this was because, as his wife, her propriety had never been in question. But, Meryem? Meryem was not her, and she had stalled in giving her daughter an answer because she had been trying to intuit his response. But they had grown too distant for anything as intimate as intuition, and she didn't know. She just didn't know. How far, was far enough? How much was he even interested? He slept through the days, and worked through the night. They barely saw him. And now with Tariq's whispered gossip, she was beginning to understand something else. Something that scared her. Meryem wasn't going to wait. For either of them.

'You,' Arslan whispered. 'When is it that you decide this, Sonja?' And in the dark, his eyes glittered, black quartz.

Sonja picked up her cigarette, her fingers clumsy. 'Do you even know what they are studying?'

He didn't answer.

'It's maths.'

He looked away, out of the window, and what she felt was such a welcome relief to the darkness of a moment ago, it could only be hope. Her husband was a clever man, he had been ambitious. And Meryem, it had always been clear, was the apple that had fallen closest to his tree. 'Meryem is top of the class,' she began. 'She has been for the last year, Arslan. She doesn't even like these study groups because she's the one who always does the work while—'

Whipping away from the window, he slammed his fist on the table. A yogurt pot jumped, the plastic cracking as it hit the floor.

Cigarette mid-air, Sonja stared at it.

He pulled his hand back, nursing it to his chest. 'Have you also decided that it is okay for her to be dancing in her underwear?' he said. 'Like a slut! Is this okay as well?'

Still looking at the spilt yogurt, Sonja felt the extraordinary lightness of terrible fear. Had he seen? Had he seen Meryem dancing? If he had, she knew that he would have experienced the same cold shock that she had. Dressed in so little, the curve of Meryem's hips and the shape of her breasts had been undeniable. It had been many months since she'd seen her daughter so exposed. For Arslan it would be longer. But it was clear their daughter's body was making a woman of her, long before she was ready. She glanced to the hallway, the living room where Emin was watching TV. 'It was just a bit of fun,' she managed, her cigarette held low so he wouldn't see her hand shaking. It *was* just a bit of fun. An end of term thing. No outsiders. Nothing to worry about. Nothing to tell Arslan about.

'Fun?'

'It's for the class. That's all. Alma was too shy to do it on her own, so Meryem said she'd do it with her. You know how close they are.' And resting her cigarette again, she bent to pick up the yogurt, cleaning silently and swiftly. She didn't look at him as she stood and rinsed her hands at the sink, but she heard him move towards her, closer, until they were shoulder to shoulder, her facing the sink, him facing away. Never had she seen him so angry. She looked sideways to him. His face was drawn and tired, and he had twelve hours on a production line ahead. 'This is not you, Arslan,' she whispered. A moment passed, a moment in which the physical space they shared was closer and more intimate than it had been for as long as she could remember. She looked down at her hand on the sink and wondered if he would lift it to his cheek and kiss it, as he once so often had.

He didn't. He walked to the ashtray, picked up her cigarette and stubbed it out. 'I don't want to see you smoking,' he said. 'You are becoming like an English woman.'

Sonja stared. She wasn't surprised that he hadn't taken her hand. They moved around this flat, and their marriage, as companionable strangers, and she was happy enough with that. She knew so many other women who did not enjoy the freedoms she had. But this? Telling her what she could and couldn't do? Thumping the table? This was not a man she had seen before.

'Where is she now?'

And because suddenly it felt as if she was pushing her daughter into a lion's den, she could not speak Meryem's name.

'*Where is Meryem now!*'

The anger in his voice confused her. 'With Alma,' she whispered. 'Only Alma.'

'*It stops, Sonja!*'

'What?' Sonja pressed her hands together. 'What stops?'

'From now on, she comes straight home.'

'She has her friends, Arslan. The library––'

'*No* friends! *No* library! *No* study groups. It stops. I will not be a man who cannot control his daughter. I will not be pitied for being the father of such a daughter! Do you understand?'

'Arslan.' Sonja shook her head. 'No one thinks this. No one is saying––'

'If you cannot control her, Sonja, I will.' And moving across, he pressed his palm to her cheek, too hard for affection. 'She is becoming a woman, Sonja. You can see that as well as I can.'

'She's still a child––'

'Shhh!' He put his finger to her lips. 'What will she need study groups for anyway? When she leaves school, she will marry.'

Sonja's hands found the edge of the sink and leaning away from him, she gripped it hard. *Marry?* 'This is not something we have discussed,' she managed, her voice hoarse with shock. 'Meryem wants to go to sixth form. She wants to go to university.'

He didn't speak.

'She is like you, Arslan. It was what you wanted too. Your night school courses––'

'*Got me nowhere!*' he hissed. He took a step back, and, crossing his arms, looked out of the window. 'There is something else. Something we should be thinking about.'

'Something else?'

'Going home.'

Home? Sonja stared at him, at the curve of his shoulder, a silhouette against the pale dusk of the kitchen window. Home was an idea that over the years had become as nebulous as the clouds above. In the beginning it was, or had been, a balm they would lovingly anoint each other with. She him, after a disappointing time at work for him, he her after a lonely week at home for her. Both of them, one to the other, in the midst of a grey February. A balm they had found they no longer needed, no longer wished to apply. Or was it just her? Had the need diminished only for her? Home? Once it was all she thought about.

'Let me speak,' he said, and as he turned his face had softened and his voice was gentle. 'There is the chance of a good house, Sonja. It has enough water for a garden.'

'No.' The strength of her response, surprised them both.

From under heavy brows, his deep-set eyes looked at her. 'You could have your garden. It's what you've always wanted.'

'No,' she said again, and emphasised it by shaking her head. As a girl she had wanted a garden. As a newly wed, illiterate bride, watching farming programmes on TV, hundreds of feet from the ground, she had dreamed of gardens. But on their one and only visit back home, she had seen the calloused fingers and dust-etched lines of the villagers' faces. And she did not want what they had: she had felt it in her bones and it had shocked and shamed her. But breaking her back on a square of dry Anatolian dust was not what she wanted.

Arslan nodded. 'We don't have to decide anything now. We have enough money saved to buy it anyway. When Meryem finishes school, we can go then.' And his hand was on her shoulder. 'Two years?' he said. 'Maybe less? We can find her a good husband there.'

And as he tried to pull her towards him, Sonja's hands went back to the sink, holding fast.

'Come now, Sonja?' He looked at her. 'We've both done our time here, haven't we?'

ONLY AFTER SHE heard the front door close and his footsteps echo down the stairs did Sonja unpeel her fingers. Her hands grooved now with angry pink lines.

We've done our time.

It sounded like prison. He had made their life in England sound like a prison sentence, when for her it had been a freedom beyond imagination. She earned more money than even the schoolteacher in the village. She left the flat in the mornings, slipping into the pattern of London commuters as seamlessly as the stitches she had once embroidered for her *ceyiz.* She bought pretty blouses and wore them for her job as a receptionist on the front desk of a company that had offices in New York and Singapore. And in Kathy, she had the best friend she could have wished for. But as much as she had tried to engage him, as her world had expanded, his had only shrunk. She knew why. His A levels hadn't been needed for the managers' positions he'd applied for. What had been needed, it turned out, were qualities she'd come to accept he did not possess. Patience, not pride. Flexibility, not stubbornness. Compromise. Sometimes his increasing apathy towards life had worried her. But she got lost behind work and children and home, and if she'd ever stopped to give the problem any serious thought, the conclusion she had always reached was that it was a problem for tomorrow.

Slowly she turned to the kitchen window. There she was, and reflected behind her were her seventeen kitchen cupboards that she'd learned to fill so well. And beyond them, the door that led to the hallway, that led to the living room where Emin would be lying on his soft stomach, watching *The A-Team.* The same room, where she used to sit and peel potatoes and wait all day for Arslan to come home. Had she really been that woman? It felt as unreal to Sonja as the idea that tomorrow had finally arrived.

MERYEM COULDN'T SLEEP. Alma, it seemed, could. It had been forty minutes since she'd responded to her floor-bangs, and knowing how uneasy Alma felt when her mother worked nights, she was glad. She was also restless, and bored.

The room was light, a combination of moonlight and snow that filtered through the curtains. On the opposite wall she could see her homework schedule, the row of small neat ticks showing work done. Sighing, she rolled onto her back and put her palms on her breasts, moving them up together, so her fingertips touched, then letting them slip apart, feeling the weight. They had come so quickly. By day she wore a bra that ironed her chest flat, but by night she'd begun to touch and hold them, exploring the novelty, circling a finger across to feel again and again the tingling sensation. To Alma, she had complained that they were a nuisance, that already she hated them, but secretly Meryem already knew that if sex had anything to do with her breasts, she was going to enjoy it very much. And then she was thinking about Gary Collins, and the way they had sat next to each other, how his foot had felt as it rubbed hers. And the kiss... Her first... Smiling, she rolled onto her side, one hand still cupping her breast. She would never forget that first kiss. Ever.

From the living room she could hear a woman's voice singing. '*Sezen Aksu*', her mother's favourite. When she was younger, if she couldn't sleep, she knew to find her mother in the living room, sewing, or nowadays reading. Serçe singing, and the album cover, with its flowered green background and Sezen's beautiful face, on the coffee table. She'd never liked the music much, it always sounded to Meryem as if something horrible was going to happen, but folded in her mother's lap, she could have stared at Serçe's face forever.

Another voice started up. Meryem stretched her arms to the ceiling. Her mother had begun to sing along, which meant that her mood had improved. All through dinner, she'd been distracted and quiet, packing Emin off to bed early, sending Meryem to her room. Sitting up, Meryem threw her quilt back. The room was too light to sleep. And she was too excited anyway. She tiptoed over the pale wood of her bedroom floor, and out into the hallway. She was too big now for her mother's lap, but never mind.

The door to the living room opened as silently as the falling snow outside. Meryem gasped. Her mother was sitting by the window, chin raised, little finger poised, cigarette smoke twisting and fading, a glass of wine in her hands. Too beautiful to be disturbed, far too beautifuL. Like a movie star, in the blue moonlight. She shrunk back, and as she did, Sonja turned to her and said, 'Come in, Mery. It's okay.'

Suddenly shy, knowing how closely her mother watched, Meryem inched across the room, tugging her nightie over her knees as she sat opposite, and tried to look at her mother without looking at her.

'Couldn't sleep?'

'No.'

Sonja wiped at her eye.

'Mamma? Are you okay?'

In response, Sonja leaned forward and tucked a lock of Meryem's hair behind her ear. 'Don't lie to me, Mery,' she whispered, 'I know where you went today. And so does your father.'

Meryem's eyes widened. 'It was just homework,' she blurted. 'That's all we did. Alma was there, you can ask her. She—'

Sonja brought her finger to her lips. 'I understand,' she said. 'But your father doesn't.'

Meryem nodded. 'Is he angry?'

'Yes,' she said. 'He wants you to come straight home from school now.'

'Every day?'

'Every day.'

'But that's not fair, Mamma!' Meryem's voice was loud as she thrust her chin forward. 'I have rehearsals.'

'I know.'

'He's not even here! He wouldn't even know!'

For a long moment Sonja studied her daughter's face, but, closely as she looked, she could not see fear, only defiance. How like her father she was.

'I want to do the show. It's not fair, at least let me do the show.'

Sonja didn't speak. She turned away and smoked her cigarette. She was thinking of the way Meryem and Alma had danced. The innocence and joy of it.

'*Mamma.*'

And Meryem was right. Arslan was never here in the afternoons. She doubted he even knew what time school finished. Today had been an exception, fuelled, she understood now, by Tariq's gossip. And this sudden talk of going home? Of marriage? It could fall away as swiftly as it had arrived. If she kept calm, they could get through the next weeks. After Christmas there would be time to take a closer look at what this tomorrow looked like. If indeed it was really here. Turning to Meryem, she said, 'Alright. But you must be truthful with me.'

Meryem nodded. 'I will. I promise.'

'Do you understand, Meryem?'

'Yes.'

Suddenly, Sonja leaned across and grabbed her daughter's arm. '*Do you understand?*'

'Yes, Mamma,' Meryem whispered. 'Please let go, it hurts.'

And there it was at last. An unmistakeable shadow of

fear that passed across her daughter's face and squeezed her heart so she had to turn away. Meryem wasn't a toddler, leaning too far out of the window. She was a girl, on the brink of becoming a woman. Scaring her back into the cave was wrong, and Sonja felt it with every fibre of her being. She didn't speak and neither did Meryem, and they sat for a long time, Sezen Asku's voice, as rich as velvet, filling the silence, outside, the lights of London beckoning. Her smile, as she watched, was small. Once, this view had scared her. But she had learned to read and write, to navigate her way through one of the greatest cities in the world. How much further could her daughter go? Closing her eyes, she tried again to make sense of what had happened earlier. Arslan's behaviour had been so out of character, it was hard to believe he was serious. Tomorrow, she would make his favourite, honey chicken. On Sunday she would suggest they go for a walk on Hampstead Heath. He always liked the view from the hill. He'd carry first Meryem, then Emin on his shoulders. There were many things she could do to make things better between them. Turning, she stretched a hand forward to stroke Meryem's hair. 'It will be okay,' she said. 'It will be okay.'

And together they sat, the celestial light of an unknowable moon shaping mother and daughter alike.

8

PATIENCE

Blackpool, present day

'AND YOU'RE NOT JOKING?'

The young man from reception blushed again. He'd been blushing on and off, since Alma had completed her check-in leaving Meryem alone with him.

'Umm, no,' he stuttered.

They were standing in the doorway of a small single room, the man having volunteered to show Meryem what was left in the way of last-minute accommodation.

'Mmm.' The room was tiny. One laminate wardrobe, the width of a coat-hanger. One laminate table, the size of a laptop. One bright red chair. One fridge, one kettle, one narrow single bed, dressed in a grey-striped duvet. At the window, a grey-striped curtain. She took a step in, turned and looked at him. There was an orange grease stain on his shirt, nearly as orange as his cheeks were. 'I'll pay double,' she said.

'Double?'

Irritation rose. Smiling she said, 'Triple then.'

'I… I'm not sure I understand,' he stammered. 'Triple what?'

Meryem watched him. He was far more of a boy than a man. In a cheap suit, with a razor nick on his fresh-faced cheek. Of course he didn't understand. Speaking slowly, she said, 'I'm saying that I'm happy to pay above the asking price for a bigger room.' Her eyes flicked down to the stain on his shirt.

The man looked down himself now, saw the stain and made what he obviously hoped was a discreet attempt to scratch it off. The noise of his nails loud against the starched cotton.

Meryem winced.

He flicked away whatever he'd scratched off, looked up and coloured an even deeper shade of orange. 'We don't have anything else,' he said. 'Eighties weekends are always popular.' And he too, looked over the tiny room. 'I don't know why,' he added miserably.

Meryem turned away. Poor boy. He was obviously bitterly regretting his decision to accompany her. What was he thinking might happen? He was younger than her son. Tapping the arms of her sunglasses against her lips, she walked towards the window. She hadn't seen Hassan in four years. What she had said to Alma this morning wasn't true. It wasn't that she didn't see her children infrequently, it was that she didn't see them at all. Four years now for Hassan and three for Saarah. And if she had thought that Saarah, who after all had grown up in Saudi, would be more understanding, she had been wrong. Her calls and texts went unanswered. The last email she had sent was a year ago, on Saarah's birthday, when she had received one line back,

Thank you, followed by her position and title.

And now Hassan, she had heard, was engaged to be married. The news had left her quietly happy. The girl was a medical researcher. So along with Saarah there would be another educated woman in the family. And although it hadn't escaped her, the towering irony of her husband's encouragement of Saarah's education and subsequent career, it did not detract from her pride either. Her children remained her proudest achievement. Nothing could diminish that, neither centuries of silence, or deserts of distance. They were hers, and they always would be.

A muffled cough from behind broke her thoughts. Without turning, Meryem nodded. He wanted out now, this boy-man standing in the doorway. Out of whatever he thought he was getting into. He coughed again, and her irritation flared. How was she supposed to spend two nights in a room no bigger than a prison cell? And now she was thinking of her apartment in Dubai, the floor-to-ceiling windows and sleek marble bathroom. It wasn't even big, not by Dubai standards and certainly not compared to the villa in Saudi Arabia, with servants' quarters and swimming pool. Folding her sunglasses away, she leaned up to the window. The view here consisted of three disabled parking spaces and a row of wheelie bins. From her apartment in Dubai, she could see the turquoise of the marina. What on earth was she doing here? She'd been in some strange and uncomfortable situations before, but this? The boy-man coughed again. Meryem squeezed her eyes shut in irritation. This wasn't her world, she didn't belong here. From deep in her handbag she felt the vibration of her phone thrumming. She reached in and pulled it out and Alma's message flashed up. *I'm going to take a shower and freshen up. Gary and Sammy are about an hour away. I suggest we meet at the bar at 6?*

As she slipped her phone back into her bag, Meryem stared out at the wheelie bins. It had been fun, the time spent with Sammy and Alma in Harrods. Really fun. She'd laughed in a way that she couldn't remember doing for a long time. Like a shutter on a window, her mind went dark and she stared and stared at the wheelie bins. She couldn't remember. She could not remember when she had last laughed out loud like that. Once, a few years ago, with a client, they had stood on La Mer beach and laughed at children, who had been laughing at themselves. Their joy had been contagious, impossible to resist. But other than that, she couldn't remember. It might not have been since her own children were young. Those precious few years, she had been able to live through them. When, as if her life had depended upon it, she had thrown herself into every childish activity they demanded of her. Building tents from blankets, castles from Lego. Long afternoons of Disney movies, which could be relied upon for a happy ending. Remembering all this, Meryem closed her eyes. Her life had depended upon it. All the years of her marriage she had been unable to leave the house unless accompanied by her husband. Lego bricks and Disney movies had been the only escape. And now she was thinking of Hassan. Would he have his own children soon? Would she ever be allowed to meet them?

A third cough came. Distinctly louder now.

Smiling, Meryem turned and once again looked over the single bed, and the single wardrobe, and the single chair. The Dubai marina was beautiful to look at, but nothing about it had ever made her laugh. And the huge villa she had spent years roaming in Saudi Arabia was far more of a prison than this little room could ever be.

And there was something else.

Something that made her smile easy now. Emin had been wrong. She did have friends. For the next two days, she had friends and she was meeting them at the bar at six.

'I'll take it,' she said. 'I'm a fan of Eighties weekends too.'

9

OLDER

Blackpool, present day

'Gary.' Meryem held out her hand. The man Sammy had just introduced her to was almost bald, the mop of dark hair falling shy across his eyes that she remembered so well, gone. He was dressed in a cheap, short-sleeved polo shirt and pressed jeans, the kind of mass-produced outfit all western businessmen sported on their days off in Dubai. Were she to pass him on the street, she would not have recognised him. But his face? A warmth spread through her chest, reaching her smile. Gary's face, the boy with whom she had shared the only consensual kiss of her life, was as recognisable to her as if it had been last week, not last century. There were changes of course. He had a broader jaw, flesh under the chin, hollows under the eyes. But those eyes were the same light blue, and she was struck for a moment by the realisation that, with his hair gone, she could see them more clearly than she ever had before, which seemed somehow ironic, and it also disturbed her because she could see how they had clouded with embarrassment. She laughed, because she was strangely nervous too, and this was the best way to hide it. 'Hello, Gary. How are you?'

'You remember Meryem, don't you?' Sammy said.

'Of course I do.' A crimson tide swept up his neck as he reached out his hand to shake Meryem's. 'I'm great,' he said. 'Yes, um... great.'

'Lovely sweater,' Alma said.

Sammy looked down at her chest. 'Gary bought it for me. No reason. He just came home with it. Said I needed some sparkle in my life. To make me smile.'

'Very pretty.' Meryem smiled. The sweater was awful, cheap, and shapeless. She wouldn't have been buried in it.

'So how was the journey?' Alma said.

'Oh it was lovely,' Sammy beamed.

'Did you drive?' Alma asked.

'No... no, I didn't dare.'

'What's this?' Meryem looked from Alma to Sammy.

'Gary rented a Porsche 911, for the weekend,' Alma said.

'I see.' Meryem smiled. 'That's nice.'

'It's my dream car,' Sammy said. 'Probably the only time we'll get to ride in one, don't you think?' And she turned to Gary.

But before he could answer, Meryem leaned forward and tapped Sammy's hand. 'Then you must drive it, Sammy!'

'Thank you, Meryem!' Gary said. 'That's what I kept telling her.'

Sammy turned to him, her voice tight. '*And* as I kept telling you, I will. In my own time.'

'You just need a little confidence,' he said.

Sammy pressed her lips together. She didn't speak.

'It's easy enough. Once you get used to where everything is.'

'Leave it,' she muttered through lips that didn't move.

'It's a great car,' Meryem said, 'but I can understand why it's intimidating. It's also a powerful one.'

Gary looked at her.

'I had one,' she shrugged. 'But it was too small for me. I changed it for a Range Rover.'

There was a moment of silence. Then, giving Gary a look so pointed it could have speared fish, Sammy muttered, 'I didn't say I was intimidated.'

Alma shifted her weight. 'Talking of cars,' she said a little too brightly, 'have you seen the DeLorean out there? I wonder who that belongs to.'

And with palpable relief, everyone turned to look across the car park.

'I can't see that getting up to eighty-eight miles per hour,' Gary said.

Sammy frowned. 'Why eighty-eight?'

'That's the speed you have to reach to go back in time.' As she spoke, Meryem turned and looked at Gary.

He laughed, then blushed, looked away from her and immediately looked back, and to ease his discomfiture, she added, 'My little brother had a toy DeLorean, so I remember this.'

'It's very low.' Sammy peered.

'It's a sports car, Sammy,' Gary muttered. 'That's the design.'

Staring straight ahead, Sammy released a long and tightly controlled breath.

'You know,' Meryem said, still looking out of the window, 'I've always wanted to ride in a DeLorean.'

'Perhaps you should,' Gary mumbled. And he pushed his hands deep into his pockets and looked past Meryem, as if he were talking to someone behind her.

'Anyway!' Sammy said. 'Here we all are! I hope it's going to be fun,' and as she got to the end of her sentence, her voice crumpled.

'It's going to great,' Alma said reassuringly.

'It's going to be really fun, Sammy.' Gary put his arm across her shoulders and pulled her close. 'I promise.'

Allowing herself to be held, Sammy was quiet a moment. 'Well,' she said as she straightened up, 'maybe you could find whoever owns it and persuade them to take you for a ride too.' She was looking at Gary as she spoke. Turning back to Meryem, she said, '*Back To The Future* is his favourite film.'

Meryem nodded, and, although her smile stayed in place, inside everything slipped. How funny. How ironic. How sad. From the corner of her eye, she saw how Gary's head had dropped, how he kept his eyes on the floor.

And she too looked down, at the emerald on her hand, twisting it hard.

'Every time it's on the telly, he makes me sit through it,' Sammy babbled on.

Meryem looked at her. Her face was as featureless as a desert. No eyebrows, no lashes. Bloodless lips, bloated white cheeks. And jealousy of other women was something she had never felt, so the feeling she was experiencing now was inexplicable. What was there to be jealous about? Gary? A middle-aged man, with very little hair. A middle-aged man, who still put his arms around his wife, who bought her glittery sweaters to make her smile. She didn't know what hurt most. The fact that she had been so easily forgotten. Or the fact that no man had ever bought her something just to make her smile.

'Honestly, I think I must have seen it at least twenty times!' Sammy laughed. 'I said to Gary, I'll be as grey as the Doctor if he keeps insisting we watch it. He will be too! Mind,' she turned to him, 'that's if either of us have any hair by the time we watch it again. We're not doing so well in that department, are we?'

Gary looked up. 'What?'

'I'm saying, we'll be as grey as the Doctor.'

He looked at her blankly.

'By the time you stop making me watch that film.'

'No one makes you.'

'Oh, come on!' Sammy laughed.

But Gary had already turned away. 'I'm going to get us checked in. We're late enough as it is.'

For a long moment, Sammy stood, watching as Gary walked away. Then, turning, she said quietly, 'I don't know what's wrong with him. He's turning into a grumpy old man.'

'Women grow old, men grow grumpy,' Meryem murmured. She too was looking at Gary. At what was left of his hair – the thin tuft of black, peppered grey. How long, she wondered, had he waited for her to come back? To take her to the cinema, as he had promised. How many years, watching and re-watching, his beautiful thick hair thinning, had he remembered and thought of her? And then she had to blink, rapid as gunfire, and turn her head and bring her finger to her eye and press hard. She took a deep breath. What *was* she doing here? 'Excuse me,' she managed, her smile tight as a tripwire. She moved across to the window, put her handbag on a side table and busied herself with opening it. Then, arms folded tight across her chest, she stood very still, breathing in and looking across the car park at the DeLorean, so conspicuous amongst all the Fords and Volkswagens. It was parked in such a way that the rear window caught the evening sun, winking at her. Twice. And in her mind she was back, in the long deep nights of her grandmother's house in the village. Lying next to Emin. That tiny car glinting silver off the huge Anatolian moon as he wheeled it across his pillow. *Take me back,* he'd whisper, over and over. And there she was. Fourteen. Rigid as a steel rod. If she breathed, she'd cry, and if she cried, Emin would cry and what was the point of that, when she couldn't take them back? Not then and not now. Because it wasn't and never had been a time machine. Hand trembling, she took her lip gloss out and drew it across her lips. Behind she could hear Sammy's voice and it was like hearing a radio in another room.

'Meryem!' Sammy waved her over. 'We were talking about the film and I was just saying to Alma, my first job was as an usherette at the Odeon. I was there for all the sequels, *Back To The Future II* and *III.* I loved that job. Loads of free ice cream.'

'I hated mine,' Alma said. 'I had a Saturday job at the laundrette on the high street.' She laughed. 'I remember I had to collect all the stray socks and pants. Sometimes I even knew who they belonged to.' She made an exaggerated expression of disgust. 'I wouldn't want to go back to that.'

'My second job was sweeping hair!' Sammy laughed. 'Me neither.'

Meryem smiled. When Sammy was sweeping hair, she was being beaten for not keeping hers under her headscarf. When Alma was sorting socks and underpants, so was she, having washed them in the ice-cold water of the village fountain. Only she didn't get paid, and she could never leave. She looked first at Sammy and then Alma. 'I wouldn't want to go back either,' she said, her voice cold as metal, her eyes glittering black. 'We didn't even have washing machines. We washed clothes at the fountain.'

No one spoke, which is exactly what she knew would happen. As she held her chin up, she felt, rather than saw, Alma's stare.

'Was this––' Sammy started.

But Meryem cut her off with a short harsh laugh, the reverse of a starting gun. She put her hands behind her head and scooped her hair into a loose knot. 'Yes. Turkey,' she said. 'My grandmother's house. But don't worry, Sammy. Everyone has washing machines there now. And actually, it was a lot of fun.'

'Fun?' Alma said.

'Yes, Alma.' Meryem turned. 'I didn't wash clothes on my own. I had loads of friends there. We all did it together. We did everything together.'

Before Alma could respond, a door swung open on the far side of the reception desk, and a burst of music flooded through. Two men and two women walked past, the men jowly, the women with waists as thick as their shoulders.

'Can you hear that?' Sammy said, the undercurrent of relief in her voice unmistakeable. 'That's the karaoke guy warming up.' She reached back and re-tied the knot of her headscarf. 'This is going to be great.'

10

ENJOY WHAT YOU DO

Blackpool, present day

EVENING SUN POURED through the windows, illuminating *Ales & Stouts* etched in gold on the bar mirror, making nectar of half-drunk wine and gilded globes of the beer taps. A fruit machine flashed ladders of neon-blue signs, and tucked away in a corner table, Alma leaned against the fat leather padding of her seat. Behind the bar, a young man with greasy hair and yellow teeth was opening another bottle of champagne. Paid for, again, by Meryem, who in leather trousers and metallic-silver blouse had strode up to the bar, dropping her platinum Amex card on it, as if she were dropping a post-it note. Was it platinum? Alma didn't know. She'd never seen one before and, judging by the look on the barman's face, neither had he. Either way, he had been instantly mesmerised, both by Meryem and by the card. He hadn't stopped looking across at her all evening.

Taking the corners of her wrap, Alma pulled it tighter around her shoulders.

At the end of the bar, three steps led down to the large function room, where, at the far end of an empty dance floor, a man had bent low, flesh hanging over his belt, as he plugged in a speaker. Background covers of 1980s hits played, and all around voices hummed, and for this camouflage Alma was grateful. She took her glasses off and rubbed the bridge of her nose, a snippet of that morning's unfinished conversation replaying over and over.

He said something before he died. Something that has brought me back here.

And it was unfinished, because although Meryem had said she wanted to be honest, she had, Alma knew, been anything but. It didn't matter what she wore, it didn't matter how glossy her hair and her smiles were, how shiny her earrings, they didn't hide whatever it was she didn't want seen.

'You alright, Al?'

The words had her jumping. She looked up to see Sammy, watching her carefully. Sammy, when it could just as easily have been her mother. Same knotted headscarf, same language. *You alright, love? Just checking. Alma, you alright?*

'Lost in thought you were.' Sammy smiled.

Her eyes smarted with the poignancy of déjà vu. *Lost in thought you were, Alma. Don't dwell, love.* Chemotherapy had transformed Sammy, just as it had her mother. The pale bloated skin, the blankness of missing eyebrows. And in the end, what had it all been for? A few more months in her mother's case. Overwhelmed, she made a quick nod of the head, picked up her glass and looked away. She needed a moment in which to compose herself. To separate reality from memory. She missed her mother every moment of every day. *Too soon.* That's what people had written. Or said. And it was, it had been far too soon. But Sammy wasn't her mother. The prognosis wasn't the same. She had to keep reminding herself of that. It wasn't the same. There was a hand on her arm, and she jumped again.

Sammy's eyes were soft with concern. 'Alma?'

Alma blinked. 'I'm fine.'

'You sure?'

'Yes.'

'Okay.' Squeezing Alma's arm, Sammy turned back to the table. 'Who's doing karaoke later?' she said. Her cheeks were flushed with champagne. She looked happy, and watching her, Alma smiled. It was good to see Sammy happy.

'Alma and me!' Meryem declared. 'We'll do Jitterbug!'

'What?' Alma looked at her.

'From Wham! Remember? *Wake me up, before you go-go!* You used to make me do that dance, all the time. You were Shirlie, and I was Pepsi.'

'No...' Alma said, her voice cracking with panic. 'I couldn't.' She felt weak with fear, helpless to prevent it happening. 'I don't think I'd remember,' she managed, swallowing down the bile in her throat. She wasn't fourteen. This wasn't school.

Meryem put her head to one side as she smiled. 'I'm teasing, Alma. Look at me? Do you think I could do the Jitterbug now?' And before Alma could answer, Meryem laughed, picked up the largest chip from her plate and held it up. 'These are the problem! I love English chips! We have a Harry Ramsden's in Dubai you know. It's very popular. I order from there a lot. Too much, far too much! But I always wash them down with champagne, so that's alright!' She was chewing and talking at the same time. Wiping her hands on a napkin, picking up her glass, she was indeed washing the chips down with the champagne that she'd ordered. Her cheeks too were flushed with wine, her lips were full, and her hair fell in black waves across her shoulders.

She was, Alma thought, as she watched, exceptionally beautiful. Of course the barman was entranced. So were Sammy and Gary. And so, she had to admit, was she. Meryem hadn't lost her magic. Just like it used to be, she was still capable of enchanting everyone who crossed her path, and, sitting in the shadow of the setting sun, Alma felt the stirrings of an emotion that was so far in her past, so small, she couldn't take it seriously. Envy. It belonged to another person, a person she hadn't been in decades. Because if there was one thing she remembered, one thing she was sure was true, it was that even before Meryem had vanished, she had been out-growing the dynamic that had characterised their friendship. Had begun to imagine a life in which Meryem wasn't the central character. Top of her class in every subject apart from maths, for Alma a life beyond school and home had beckoned. A life in which she might sometimes take centre-stage, in which she might shine. Then Meryem had disappeared and, for so long, her absence had shone brighter than she had. And just as the glare was fading, just as she was beginning to step forward, Sonja's death had sent her hurtling back so far she'd never ventured forth again. So much so that from this distance that brief period of time, when she had been on the verge of becoming someone other than the person she became, held for Alma the quality of a mirage. In her heart she knew it was real, but, exposed to the world, it glittered with so much never-to-be realised promise that it couldn't be true. And now Meryem was back. Seamlessly slipping into her allotted role. And if it wasn't happening in front of her, she wouldn't have believed it. She was forty-four, facing nascent feelings of childish jealousy?

'Harry Ramsden's?' Sammy was saying. 'In Dubai?'

Meryem nodded. 'It reminds me of home.'

Home? Alma looked at her glass. Meryem had lived more of her life away from the UK than in it. 'Surely Dubai feels more like home now? she ventured, surprised at the level of resentment that had arisen within her.

Meryem shrugged. 'What can I say, Alma? Nowhere is really home anymore, and yet everywhere is home. I consider myself a gypsy of the world.'

Tight-lipped, Alma nodded.

The barman came over and she watched as he set up fresh glasses and poured, the tip of his tongue pushed out in concentration. He didn't spill a drop and when he was done, it was Meryem he looked to for approval. But Meryem picked up her glass without so much as acknowledging him. Alma watched as, deflated, he left

'So...' Drawing the sound out, Meryem looked first to Sammy and then Gary. 'You're still in London?'

'Not quite,' Sammy said. 'We moved out to Essex. Been there twenty years, haven't we love?'

'We have,' Gary nodded.

'We needed the space, and now with the kids gone, we don't.'

'How many children do you have?' Meryem asked.

'Three. Two boys and a girl. Sean, Aiden and Sarah. All grown and left now. It's funny I still wake in the middle of the night thinking I can hear them kicking the walls.'

'My daughter is called Saarah,' Meryem said.

'Oh, how funny. How old--'

'They kicked the walls?' Meryem laughed as she cut Sammy off.

'Yes...' Pausing, Sammy glanced across at Alma. 'Just in their sleep,' she said, hesitant now. 'You know, when they turned over.'

Meryem nodded, a smile playing at her lips. 'Alma,' she said, turning. 'Do you remember our knocking code? I'd knock on the floor, you'd knock on the ceiling? Three times. To see if the other was awake?'

Alma frowned.

'My bedroom was right over the top of yours. Two knocks meant I'm going to sleep now. Three knocks meant, I'm awake—'

'Yes,' she said, because she did remember now. She hadn't, but now she did. And something else. It was always Meryem doing the knocking. As a nurse, her mother had often worked night shifts, and Meryem had known how it helped her get to sleep – that it was a comfort, knowing Meryem was only a ceiling away. Was, almost, in the same house.

Sammy smiled. 'You were such good pals, you two.'

'We were,' Meryem said, reaching across to squeeze Alma's hand. The warmth was tremendous.

Alma smiled, and – for the first time since Meryem had come back, since they had embraced, just a few hours ago, in the tea room of Harrods – they held each other's eye, both of them blinking back tears. 'We were good friends.'

'We were.' Taking a napkin, Meryem wiped her eye. 'Best friends, right up until I left.'

Left. There it was again. As she felt Meryem's hand slip away, she looked up to find Sammy staring at her.

'*Left?*' Sammy mouthed.

'Do you remember, Alma?' It was Meryem again, forging

on, lifting her glass, asking Alma, but addressing the table. 'Your mother used to get so angry, because you always waited for me in the mornings with the front door wide open? She'd be trying to get to sleep after work, and you'd be standing there letting all the cold air in? We saw each other every day, didn't we?'

Alma nodded. 'Yes, we did,' she said quietly. This was true. From the day they were born, until the day Meryem disappeared, they must have seen each other every single day of their lives. She pushed against the padding of her seat and flexed her toes. The only time she could not remember seeing Meryem every day was the summer Meryem's family went back to Turkey for a holiday. That was the only time she could remember walking to school alone, until... She looked up at Meryem drinking her champagne, and a flush of pink spread across her cheeks. *Until you were taken, Meryem*, she said silently. *Taken,* not *left*. After that, of course, she was always alone.

'And there was an old man who lived across the way,' Meryem waved her hand, smiling again. 'Alma's mother would be shouting at her to close the door, and he'd be shouting at her to stop shouting, and...'

Listening, but not hearing, Alma closed her eyes. A few feet away, outside the open doors, a man and woman stood smoking. This was another thing that brought her mother back. Just a passing draught of cigarette smoke, and there was her mother, feet up on a chair, blowing smoke out of the kitchen window. Opening her eyes again, she reached for her glass and took a mouthful of wine. It was numbing, a cold blanket on what was an increasing smoulder of unease. Then suddenly, once again, she felt the warm plumpness of a hand on hers.

'Well, here's to my favourite things!' Meryem beamed.

'Fat English chips and... champagne!' She raised her glass. 'And to friends. Thank you for inviting me. I'm so glad you did!'

Opposite, Sammy raised her glass and so, too, did Gary.

'Chips and champagne!' Meryem sang.

'Chips and champagne!' they chanted back, and sitting across from Meryem, Alma felt the reflected glow.

Meryem turned to Sammy. 'So, tell me all about your children.'

'Oh,' Sammy laughed. 'Where to start...'

But start she did, allowing Alma to once again lean back, nurse her glass at her chest and listen as Sammy talked and Meryem asked questions... and laughed... and waggled her fingers... and moved her hair off her shoulders, and deftly steered the conversation the way she wanted it to go. An image came to her. Meryem sat on a desk, swinging her legs with long green socks, moving her hair off her shoulders, just as she did now, waving her hand to describe something to the group that surrounded her. This *was* Meryem. And always had been. The nucleus of any situation. At school her hair had been jet black, like now, while everyone else had variations of dirty blonde, or mousey brown. And Meryem had had breasts, whilst the rest of them nursed bumps. If something was funny, it was Meryem who laughed first and loudest. She never needed to wait and check with the cool kids. Meryem *was* the cool kid. Her ambition, her plans... She'd been ahead of them all, running a sprint, while the rest of them meandered along in a marathon. Alma looked at her glass, biting hard on her lip. Something else was remembered. Something so deep it was undeniable. She had loved being Meryem's friend. Despite the hairline fractures of that last year, being Meryem's friend had been exciting. Had opened doors which never would have opened for her alone. Every day had been an adventure that she'd never been scared of joining, because Meryem had been there. Her eyes smarted with a sudden sadness. When was the last time she'd started her day without knowing what it would contain? And how it would end?

Sammy was tightening the knot of her headscarf. 'Well thank you, Meryem,' she said nodding at the second bottle of champagne. 'It's very generous of you.'

'No need for thanks!' Meryem beamed. 'I love bubbles.'

She seemed happy, Alma thought as she watched. As if being happy was the easiest thing in the world. And then she didn't know what to think. On the one hand, it was good that Meryem was happy. Nothing was ever going to erase the past, nothing could ever bring back those that were gone.

'So.' Sammy said. 'Now you know all about us, what do you do?'

'Always time for bubbles!' Meryem laughed, pretending that she hadn't heard what everyone else so clearly had.

Alma stared at her glass. On the other hand, appearances could be so very deceptive.

And then Meryem laughed. 'I work in hospitality, Sammy. It's my job to make sure the clients are happy. I take care of everything they need and, because they are usually very rich, they can need a lot!'

Over the top of his glass, Gary nodded. 'Sounds interesting.'

'Tell us more!' Sammy leaned forward.

Meryem smiled. 'Well, as I said to Alma, it's not so interesting.'

Opposite, Alma looked down at her hands. If it wasn't interesting, whatever Meryem did paid well. The champagne, that dress, the Amex card.

'I'm sure it's more interesting than anything we do.'

Sammy leaned forward, her chin resting on her folded knuckles. 'Do you get to travel much? You said you were like a gypsy earlier.'

'It depends on the time of year.' Meryem put her head to one side, and ran her fingers through her hair. 'But yes, sometimes we have to travel with the clients.'

'Oh! Where to get to visit?' Sammy's face was wide open with interest.

Alma turned away. Just a few hours ago, she'd asked almost these same questions of Meryem. And Meryem had skipped over them as if they were hot coals. But that was over coffee. Now there had been champagne.

'Everywhere, Sammy!' Meryem waved her hand and the silver of her blouse, on fire with sunlight, was like a giant sparkler. 'When it gets too hot in Dubai, I am often working in Europe. In January I'm in South Africa. It really depends.'

'Lots of air miles then,' Gary nodded. 'Hope you have a loyalty card.'

Meryem threw her head back and laughed. 'Not on private jets. Honestly? It's the only way to travel!'

'Wow!' Sammy shook her head. 'I've never been on a private jet in my life and you talk about it as if it was like catching the bus!'

'You've never been on a plane,' Gary said.

Sammy stared at him. 'That's not true. We went to Portugal once. Remember?' And holding his eye, she waited until he'd shrugged a response and looked away.

'I don't know what hospitality really means, but lucky you, Meryem.' Sammy picked up her glass. 'My job takes me to the walk-in fridges in Tesco. Gary's takes him to Felixstowe.'

'Felixstowe can be fun too,' Gary muttered.

'Yeah,' Sammy said. 'Rocking. Like that tomato juice.'

And Gary went the exact same shade as his drink.

Meryem reached for the bottle. 'Mostly, I enjoy my work,' she said, topping up her glass. 'But it's nothing compared to what Alma does.'

Slowly Alma raised her eyes. In the car, on the way up, there had been a brief conversation between Meryem and her about her work. It had ended with Meryem warning about the solvents she used causing premature skin damage.

'Senior Objects Conservator!' Meryem said. 'Isn't that what you said, Alma? That's what you are?'

She nodded.

'And not just in London!' Sammy was looking at Alma. She turned to Meryem. 'Museums all over the world use her. And they send her the work because she doesn't like to travel. That's how good she is.'

'You didn't tell me this, Alma?' Meryem put the bottle down, and again, reached across the table and took Alma's hand. 'I'm so proud of you,' she said, her voice splintering like wood. 'So proud.'

Alma flushed, her arm conspicuously stretched across the table, her hand imprisoned. The display felt over the top. Pulling her hand back, she picked up her glass and shrugged. 'It's just my job.' Close as they once had been, this wasn't a Meryem she recognised. This Meryem was a hall of mirrors, deflecting and magnifying, revealing nothing.

'Well,' said Sammy as the silence stretched on.

'What a gift!' Meryem clasped her hands together. 'To be able to make things beautiful again! You bring things back to life, Alma!'

'It's just restoration,' she said quietly.

. . .

A WAITRESS CAME and took their plates. As she did, a crackle of sound came over the PA. Alma looked up. In the time they had been sitting, all the tables around the dance floor had filled and across at the bar a crowd had formed.

Sammy pushed her chair back and stood up. '*Just going to put in a little request,*' she mouthed at Alma. '*For karaoke.*'

The lights dimmed and Alma saw that the young barman with the greasy hair had been joined by two other staff. She watched them as they moved back and forth, behind the bar, their white shirts bright squares of colour in the newly darkened room.

And suddenly, as if the dimming of the lights had given him courage, Gary leaned across the table. Raising his voice against the backdrop of sound, he said, 'Do you miss England, Meryem?' His head was lowered and he was looking at Meryem from under his brows, like a shy schoolboy, and it was so uncharacteristically the Gary that she knew, it sent a raft of goosebumps along Alma's arm.

Meryem put her head to one side. 'I miss the grass.'

'Grass?'

'Where I live, there is only sand. But English gardens with real grass and trees, and all the birds... In Dubai everyone keeps birds in cages.' Meryem smiled. 'I have a friend,' she said, 'who bought her bird cheap from the Chinese market. No one wanted it. Do you want to know why?'

'Why?' Gary smiled too.

'Because it could only say one thing. *Pulimak kay*!'

There was a beat of silence, then Gary said, 'Which is?'

'Fuck you. In Malaysian.'

He put his head back and laughed.

'The bird,' Meryem continued, 'came to the market from a Dubai lady. She had a new maid, you see, and this new maid had told her what the old maid had taught the bird to say. And –' Meryem paused. 'Do you know how long this bird had been saying, *Fuck you*?'

Again, Gary shook his head. So did Alma, watching as Meryem spun the threads of her story, unravelling the tension of a moment ago as easily as if it were silk and not the strange lumpen material of human hearts.

'Four years! Can you imagine? For four years the woman goes to the bird and says, *Good morning little bird.* And the bird says, *Fuck you!* And the woman says, *Hello little bird, here I am back from shopping.* And the bird says, *Fuck you!*'

Gary had dropped forward, his head shaking with mirth, and Alma too was smiling. Because it was funny. Meryem was funny. She put her glass on the table. She'd been here before. Watching from the sidelines before, as Meryem stole the show. Of course she had. She felt light-headed and almost completely submerged with memory. And then a fat warm hand on her back slapped her back to the surface. So hard she almost gasped. It was Sammy.

'Are you going to sing, Gary?' Sammy said.

'You sing?' Meryem laughed.

'Sometimes.' He shrugged.

'It's actually been one of the surprising side effects of that.' Sammy nodded at Gary's tomato juice.

Meryem frowned. 'Tomato juice makes him sing?'

'No,' Gary laughed.

'Sobriety makes him sing,' Sammy said. 'Since he stopped drinking, for health reasons, he's been known to do a bit of karaoke.' She picked up her own glass and winked. 'Who knew?'

'You have health reasons?' Meryem looked at Gary.

'*My* health, reasons,' Sammy said, and her voice softened. 'He stopped drinking, because I stopped drinking, because chemo and alcohol don't go well together. He did it to support me, and then just continued. How long has it been now, darling?' she said and standing behind him, she placed her hand on his shoulder.

'It doesn't matter,' Gary murmured, reaching back to clasp her hand.

'Drink can cause many problems.' Meryem's face was serious. A line of sweat had broken out around her hairline and underneath her eyes, mascara smudged a hard purplish line. 'I enjoy it at a party time like this, but in my family it was a problem.'

Alma turned to her. *My family.* Was Meryem going to start talking now? Answering questions no one had yet asked? What had it been like with her father? What had happened?

Against the backdrop of music and chatter, the little pocket of silence that opened up around their table was ocean deep, and consequently Meryem's voice resonated. 'My mother,' she said seriously. 'What I was told, was that for her, alcohol became the most important thing in her life. In the end it killed her. That's what they said. She just drank herself to death.'

Gary looked down at his glass. 'It's hard,' he murmured.

Sammy didn't say a word.

And completely still, glass in hand, frozen halfway to her mouth, Alma sat, her face utterly bloodless.

SONJA

Flat 7, Sydney House
Layton Rd
Enfield, London

18th Oct 1988

My darling Meryem,

You have been gone two years and ten months and I have learned, perspective is everything.

Now that I have it, I can see clearly the moments of my life in which I made choices that hurt us both. But they only became clear afterwards, like raindrops that have dried upon a window. And, like the raindrops, they always lead somewhere if you join them up.

Here is one.

Kathy had a boyfriend, Lenny. Do you remember him? I know that Alma does. Alma remembers everything. She is trying to forget, but I can see in her eyes how much she remembers. Kathy is so worried for her, and for me. It is not right for one person to carry so much worry. I am a burden. I know this.

Kathy allowed Lenny to move in with her. They were not married. Your father did not approve. For a while he would not let you visit Alma at her home, then he seemed to forget, or if I am more honest, lose interest. Things were not going well for him at work.

Then Lenny lost his job and started drinking. Every day he was happy to sit in the park with his friends and every week collect his benefit. He said he was sick because he couldn't stop drinking. Kathy said he was lazy. So did your father. This was the only thing Kathy and your father agreed upon. Kathy told Lenny he had to leave and Lenny hit her. He was drunk. She called the police and although he didn't have anywhere to live, he left her flat.

This happened a week before we were to make our first trip back to Turkey, for a family wedding. I know you will remember that. You were ten. Emin was five. You had never been before and you were so excited.

I was also happy to be returning. Neither your father nor I had been home in ten years. I was looking forward to seeing my family and especially my friend, Afife. But Kathy was then the closest person in my life and I was worried about leaving her alone, so soon after. Now that Lenny had gone, she was working even longer hours to pay all her bills and I often looked after Alma. And Kathy had loved Lenny. I knew that she missed him. I told your father this in the first hours of our journey home.

'She shouldn't have called the police then,' he said.

'But he hit her,' I said. I remember that your father wouldn't look at me, so I asked him, 'Do you think she should have let him stay?'

He kept his hands on the wheel. And because he did not

answer, I began to talk. I told him again how Lenny had bruised Kathy's cheek, had pushed her back into the kitchen cupboard so the handle pressed hard into her spine and left a bruise there also. It was then he raised his palm to me and said, 'Enough, Sonja! Sometimes these things happen between a man and a woman. It is not for outsiders to decide.' And he would not turn, even for a moment, to look at me.

So I looked at him. His skin was grey, and his jaw-line soft. But Meryem, if you came to me all those years before, from a husband I didn't know, your brother came to me from a husband I loved. We had been happy. We had worked hard, we had learned English and learned to look forward, not backward. His words shocked me, but who could blame me for thinking that I knew him? Who could blame me for not seeing that raindrop? He looked so tired. I reached across and put my hand on his and he turned and smiled and pressed his fingers through mine.

Let me tell you then about the trip. Do you remember the car journey? Three days. We were all exhausted, your father especially. His hair was streaked grey at the temple, the skin under his eyes, shadowed purple. But this was not just the journey. This was how he always looked.

It was late afternoon, on the third day, when we finally saw the village. You were both asleep in the back seat. I remember watching the shadow of the car as we drove across the steppe, my hair streaming, I leaned out of the open window to let it blow, because I knew that very soon I would need to cover myself.

You woke up. The sun was low. Most of the houses had already fallen into the long shadow of the mountain and the village was dark. I could see you did not like what you saw. And I can tell you this now. It was a shock for me also. The houses seemed so small, I hadn't expected the journey to take so long. This was when I understood just how isolated the village was. I know I was thinking of the view from our flat, the London skyline. But I was also thinking how, with the morning sun, everything would be different. I pointed out the lines of the mud-brick walls and the flat roofs, clear against the scrappy vegetation. The road was bumpy, unpaved. A boulder could bend it like a crooked elbow. In England we were used to smooth roads and horizons of green. Here, trees grew as randomly as the boulders, stubbornly single, or in small groves, because as I explained to you, the water came from the mountain, channelled into wells. You were so looking forward to collecting it every morning, as I had promised we would. And I was looking forward to showing you.

Sheep bunched on the hills and oleaster shimmered silver-grey, against the burned earth. I leaned out of the window again and breathed in. You asked me what I was doing. I told you that I wanted to smell the trees, so you wound your window down and did the same.

Your father said, 'They smell of nothing. It's the wrong time.'

I told him to try. That there is always a smell. And he did. He opened his window and filled his lungs and the breeze blew his thick hair back in a sleek line and we both laughed at him.

Then, as we got closer, behind the first lines of the village we saw the tower of the minaret, its shape and height so unlike anything else. You asked what it was, and your father's face darkened and I knew what he would be thinking. As if he had heard me, he said, 'Cover yourself, Sonja.' It was understood. The way we lived in England, was not the way we would live in the village.

Your grandmother had never met you, nor Emin. But when we arrived it was her son she cried out for. She threw out her arms and began a wail which scared you. I saw the confusion in her eyes at the greying stranger in front of her, the soft-stomached, heavy-lidded man who was too broad across the shoulders, too soft to be the boy who had left – her boy, who ran up mountains. And what is worse, what haunts me to this day, is that your father also saw. I will always wonder if this was when he began to make his choice.

I stepped back, you reached for my hand and I thought then of how very little your grandmother understood of the life your father lived. Of a working day that started not with prayer, or a shared meal, or the long white fingers of the morning sun. What did she know of working days, that were not days at all? That began with a card punched in at 17:00 and continued long into the night, when wives were home, sleeping alone. Of a job where everything he needed to know he had learned on his first day, so many years ago? Where he must have known he had gone as far as he was ever going to.

Then too, what would she have known of the life I lived with him? How we celebrated *bayram* alone, me cleaning windows and washing skirting boards, while you and Emin lay on your stomachs and watched The A-Team and we bought pre-packed lamb from Tesco.

And Ramazan? The many times I broke fast alone, in a kitchen of shadows, looking out at the stark outline of the high-rise opposite, while your father watched a conveyor belt. Both of us, in our separate ways, thinking of home. Purple shadows on the fields, tarhana soup, chicken and *dolma biba* spread upon a cloth on the roof top. The way the whole village turned their heads and opened their ears to hear the first notes of the ezan. And the way that sometimes, in late summer, a whole sunflower, torn open, would scatter its seeds like sweets.

Her son, my husband, your father – went to work, came home, drank tea at the Turkish club. There was nothing else. He would do nothing else.

I peeled Emin's hand from my waist. I can still feel how small it was. When I moved forward to kiss her, I pretended not to see the accusation in her eyes, but I wanted to whisper in her ear, it is not my fault, it is not my fault.

We all woke early the next morning. You complained of the divan, saying it was hard and lumpy. It was, for a child accustomed to a mattress of foam. We left your father sleeping, and I pulled two chunks from the loaf left out and gave them to you, whispering for you to follow. Outside the narrow paths were cool and hard, the soil not yet breaking to dust. A scraping sound startled Emin. It was a cock, two rooftops away. From much further the softer sound of lambs floated into the village. You dawdled behind me, chewing each mouthful of hard bread as if it were baklava. I understood. Everything tasted better there. Behind a half-open shutter someone coughed and you both twisted your heads to stare and I laughed when Emin stumbled over his feet in fright as a woman opened her door and, with a broom, chased the stones from her step. Life was so close up! It startled and fascinated you.

The sun had barely broken the horizon. We reached the last house before the lane opened into the square with the water fountain. The same spot from which I had left, so many years before. I told you to wait behind me and I stepped up to the house and knocked quietly. Moments passed, we heard footsteps and then the door opened a crack, enough for me to see a heavy woman with black spaces between her teeth, peering through the dark interior. I was shocked, Meryem. So shocked, so I did the only thing I could. I cried out, *Afife!* and I threw my arms around her, so that she would not see any confusion in my eyes. But there was no hiding the difference between us and of course, Afife saw immediately. She took a step back from the doorway and stretched my arms out.

'Let me look at you.'

'Afife.'

'England! Sonja. England is making you beautiful.'

I tried. I shook my head. 'Afife, you—`

But she would not hear, and she turned to you. 'And who is this? Who do we have here?' She tickled you under your chin, and she grabbed at Emin pulling him into her skirts. 'Who is this? Who is this?' But Emin turned his shoulder from the embrace, and you Meryem, you smiled, a reserved response. It was strange for both of you. Everyone was a stranger and you were not accustomed to being touched. Already I had seen the silent resentment in your face when, the evening before, you were passed like a package between the women of the family. They lifted your hair and ran their hands over your body as if it were theirs, talking in a language you understood, but didn't like to speak. That morning, when I awoke, I remember you were staring at me across the room, silent, wide-eyed. I see it still, and it haunts me.

I introduced you both to my friend, but Afife's eyes stayed on you. I told her she looked well, but she only said, 'No Sonja. I have eyes to see myself.'

She woke her younger children and we walked up to the rocks above the village. This is where Afife and I played as girls. This is where we talked about whom we would marry. But on this day I talked of my job in England. Now I could speak English and I could read and write. I was working in the post room of a big company, sorting letters into pigeonholes. And I sent faxes. I tried to explain it to Afife. 'Imagine,' I said, 'a piece of paper goes into a machine one end, and comes out from another machine in another place, another country. If you had a fax machine,' I said, 'I could send you a letter in the morning and you would get it immediately.'

And then it was Afifie's turn to surprise me because she said, 'I know these machines. We have one. In the muhtar's office. Pina, the school teacher, persuaded him it was a good thing, so if there is something urgent it can be sent straight away.' She picked up a stone and scratched a line in the dust. 'But so far there has not been anything urgent.' Then she looked at me sideways, like she used to when something funny had happened and we were not supposed to laugh. 'And,' she said, 'it would have to be urgent only in the evening, because there is no electric current in the day.'

Oh, Meryem, how we laughed! On the brow of the hill you were playing with Afife's daughter, Fatma, and you heard the laughter and turned to watch. I like to think now, Meryem, that as you watched your mother laughing, your heart lifted the same way mine always did when I watched you and Alma laughing over something silly, something private. Two girls with their heads together.

'Anyway,' Afife said, 'if you sent me a fax the muhtar would read it first. Even before Fatma.'

'Afife,' I said. 'You know it is me writing the letters myself now?' I said this because in the beginning, your father would write very short letters for me. I remember clearly what Afife replied.

'And you know it is still not me reading? It is still Fatma?'

'Of course.' I was ashamed. "It is me writing myself." It

sounded boastful. I changed the subject. 'Do you know what Arslan has bought the newlyweds?'

Afife shook her head.

I made her guess and she said, 'Salt?'

'Salt?'

'Hazan's daughter married a boy from the next village. He is also in England. They sent her off with five kilos of salt.'

'We have salt in England, Afife!'

'I know you do, Sonja. I was just trying to make you laugh.'

I felt ashamed again. 'Shall I tell you?'

'Is it gold?' She nodded at the bangles on my wrist.

'No. Much more useful than gold. Or salt.' I could not look at her. It was your father who had insisted that while we were in the village, I should always wear the bracelets. I would not have chosen to do so.

Afife did not guess again and we sat in silence. Back then I remember thinking that I had shamed her with my talk of reading and writing, with the bracelets, just with myself. Now I think it was not so simple.

From the moment her daughter had read to her from my letter, that we would be visiting, she too had been overjoyed at the thought of meeting again. Every letter I had ever written her, she'd kept. She told me that sometimes she would take them out just to look at them because even without understanding the words she could trace my progress. She would look at the short lines, the careful, neat squiggles from the beginning, like her own children's schoolbooks, and she could see how as time passed the marks on the paper became longer and smoother, joining together like notes. As if I were learning to sing. My letters from England, she said, were the thing that she looked forward to more than anything in the world. But they were getting less and less frequent. Because, Meryem, the more I could write, the less I did. Sitting next to me that morning, with my bracelets and my boasts, it must have taken a great effort for Afife to forgive me that. And, as I write this, Meryem, I remember how years later, she lied when I came to find you, and I wonder now if she ever really did. Forgive me.

'Something from England? Something to cook with?' she guessed again.

'Nearly.'

'Tell me then.'

'An electric knife.'

'What is that?'

'It is a knife that you plug into the electric current and it cuts.'

'You plug it into the current?'

'Yes.'

'What do you do when there is no current? '

'Then, I suppose you must use another knife.'

And we looked at each other as if we were both children again. As if we had run up here to escape another water fetching chore, as if we had nothing behind us but water fetching and nothing before us but spaces like this in which to lie back on the rocks and watch the storks circle.

'Well let's hope they won't need to do any cutting during the day,' Afife said before we burst out laughing for so long, and so hard, we had to hold our stomachs and wipe our eyes, and all you children turned and stared.

The sky was a clear white. Afife asked me if I liked England. I said that I did.

'Will you come back?'

'Maybe.'

Then she said, 'Meryem will marry soon enough.'

I can see you that day as clearly as if you are standing before me now. You are ten years old. I see too, the stork that circled over the poplar trees. I see it now, because I stared at it then. Stared and stared, until it disappeared into the shade of the foliage. Stared because I did not want to look at Afife.

'Remember,' Afife was saying, 'I will keep Mehmet for her. I have promised. Just like your quilt, I still have it, Sonja.'

Oh, Meryem. The quilt was a thing. A thing made of wool and cloth, folded away. Afife spoke of it in the same sentence as she spoke of you. As if you too were to be folded away, looked after, until someone else decided.

I remember exactly what I said. 'Meryem will not marry so young. She will stay at school. It is quite normal in England.'

We did not speak, nor look at each other. Finally, Afife picked a stone and juggled it between her hands and said, 'What does Arslan think?'

'We think the same,' I said, because I thought we did.

Afife narrowed her eyes and studied me carefully. I looked away.

Another raindrop that I did not see.

Love always, Mamma

11

NOTHING LOOKS THE SAME IN THE LIGHT

Blackpool, present day

HER BACK PRESSED to the door of her room, hands clasping the handle, Alma stood, heart pounding, blood ringing in her ears.

Feel very sick.

That's how she'd excused herself, leaving with the urgency sudden nausea allows. And she did feel sick, as Meryem's words echoed in her head.

In the end she just drank herself to death.

Sonja did not drink herself to death.

From the corridor outside came the sound of a door opening. She held her breath. The soft tread of anonymous footsteps came closer, passed and faded away. Her grip relaxed.

Something wasn't right. Something was very wrong. Meryem's mother did not drink herself to death and there was no one who knew that better than Alma. And her own mother of course, who was no longer here to share the knowledge. But Meryem? Didn't Meryem know?

The fear that had gripped her heart since those words were spoken relaxed, and in its place a landslide rushed in. She slumped against the door. On shaky legs, she went into the bathroom and stood looking at her ghostly reflection. *I was there,* she whispered. *I was there.*

The room didn't answer.

She took the kettle and filled it, staring out of the window as it bubbled itself to an angry climax. On a distant road, the yellow headlights of a car moved like fireflies in an otherwise black night.

As the shock subsided, exhaustion crept in. She made tea, sat down on the bed, and leaned against the head board. Did Meryem not know how her mother had died? It seemed inconceivable to Alma, but how else to explain what she had just heard? *Do you remember my mother talking about me?* That had been the question Meryem had asked, and she hadn't been able to give the answer she had sensed was needed. It hadn't occured to her that there were other answers she had, answers that Meryem wouldn't need, wouldn't want to hear, but must surely have.

Across the room, pushed against the wall, sat the box Gary had brought in from the car. The box Sammy had kept in her attic for the past fifteen years. Alma looked at it, and as she did, she forgot to count. Once upon a time, whatever was in there, had been too much for her to face. Not now. Now she was putting her cup down, and edging off the bed. Now it almost felt to her as if it had been placed there on purpose, ready for this exact moment. Because a box full of her mother's personal possessions was the next best thing to having her mother. And right now, she really needed her mother. She got up, dragged the box to the bed, and opened the cardboard flaps.

The first thing she found was a small cosmetic bag, containing her mother's glasses, and nursing watch. A rush of memory flooded. *Be a good girl now. I'll ring before bedtime.* This was the watch her mother wore over her uniform, and it was so easy to see her, standing in the doorway ready for work. Tears in her eyes, she pressed the watch to her heart, holding it there for a long and quiet moment. A fold of thick blue material covered the next layer. As Alma reached in and unfolded it, she realised it was her mother's old dressing gown. Carefully she held it to her nose, but the only scent now was that of musty abandonment. She placed it to one side and, one by one, began lifting out the pile of framed photos that had been packed underneath. They were harmless, and as she looked through them she wondered why she had packed them away like this. The family back in Ireland, a few of her and her mother when she was very young. One of her mother as a teenager, sitting astride a scooter, full of spark and hope. It would have to have been taken before she fell pregnant. Before she escaped the stigma of being an unmarried mother and fled to England to start anew. Tracing her mother's unlined face with her fingertip, Alma smiled. The last photograph was that of her mother and Sonja, holding their babies – herself and Meryem. It had been taken in the kitchen of their old flat and on the table was a cake that Sonja pointed to proudly. Alma studied it for a long time before placing it with the others and turning back to the box. A plastic storage box, stuffed full of the paperwork that details a life: death certificate, vaccination reports, insurance policies, expired passports. Taking everything out, she felt very peaceful. When she had asked Sammy to take this box, she hadn't even been able to open it and yet here she was, calmly sorting through the paperwork for her mother's long-ago funeral. And if it wasn't that time made grief easier, what did it do? She looked up, seeing herself in the wall mirror. Time, she thought, made grief lighter. That was all. The pressure lessened, it would have had to. Those first few months, even the first year, she had barely been able to breathe.

Underneath the folder lay another folder, with a small neat label: *Professional Qualifications.* She opened it, ready to take out yellowed certificates and diplomas, but what her hands found was much thicker – a bundle of envelopes, tied together with blue ribbon that had faded and frayed. Carefully, she untied the ribbon and as she did, a familiar feeling of detachment took over. It came from her hands. The way they were handling the letters with such slow and deliberate care made it possible for her to think of them as someone else's hands. And it was so familiar because this was her work. This was what she did.

All our efforts, Alma, are first dependent upon the object's safekeeping in antiquity, and favourable burial conditions thereafter.

Alma looked down at the ribbon. The words she remembered now, had always remembered, were those of the lead curator on her very first job. She'd been allocated a Roman lamp, decorated with three statues of Eros, *Love Found, Love Lost* and *Love Regained.* How meticulously she had cleaned. With thin wooden sticks, with brushes, scalpels and cotton swabs. And, by removing the blue-green patina and taking away the encrusted rust, bit by tiny bit she had painstakingly revealed the shape and the details. It was she, Alma, who had given those gods their faces back, their joy, their rapture and yes, their pain. But it was also as the curator had said, someone must have first treasured the lamp and kept it safe, and then, when that someone was no longer there, all the conditions had had to be right for it to survive the period of neglect.

The room sang with silence. The ribbon fell aside. The letters in her hands, all had the same address, a scribble in Turkish words written alongside.

Turning the first envelope over, she knew what she would find. And there it was, the return address.

Flat 7, Sydney House, 5 Layton Rd, Enfield, London.

These were the letters Sonja had written, letters that always came back, letters that Sonja had held in her hand as she'd leaned against the front door, her face swollen with grief. *Is your mother home, Alma? When she gets back will you ask her to call in?* Letters kept safe, first by Sonja and then unknown to Alma, by her mother. As if it might crumble to dust, she eased the first folded page out of the first envelope and began reading.

Do you think it is possible to inherit loneliness, Meryem? Before you were born, back in those days when I listened to the sound of cows on the television and peeled potatoes at my feet and did not know what day it was, I grew loneliness like rain grows seed. And you too were growing inside me. So I ask again, is it possible to inherit loneliness?

For your sake, I hope that it is not.

Love always, Mamma

Alma closed her eyes, let the letter rest on her lap. A long-forgotton memory rose up. The old kitchen. Sonja weeping, her mother consoling and a young Alma watching. But the young version in this memory was older. Seventeen? Eighteen? There was a suitcase in the hall. And with a rush of goosebumps, she knew that what she was remembering was Sonja returned from Turkey, without Meryem, without Emin. And from a distance of thirty years she could still feel the heat of a grief that had smothered them all, that could not be assuaged. Not her own, not her mother's, not Sonja's.

Opening her eyes, she folded the letter along the exact same lines where it had been folded before and slipped it back into its envelope. Then she took the ribbon and retied the bundle.

If Sonja had kept her returned letters safe, and, after her death, her own mother had preserved them, the idea of handing them now to Meryem left her cold and numb. Which Meryem would read them? The jet-setting hostess hopping on and off private jets? Or the blasé liar who had *left. Left?* Everyone knew that wasn't true! Meryem didn't *leave,* she was *taken.* And whatever her life had been afterwards, it wasn't, Alma was sure, the rose-tinted version she was trying so hard to convince them all it was.

How could it have been, when the world she left behind had turned so black? The shadow must have reached her too. She must have thought about them. She must have wondered what it was like for them. She took her glasses off and pinched the bridge of her nose, her arms loose with a feeling of hopelessness. Because now there was a worse possibility to consider. Meryem might not even read the letters. The casual way in which she had spoken of Sonja... she might not even be interested. And if that happened, it would mean Sonja's letters would go unread *again*, and that would be like Sonja dying *again* and Sonja she *knew* did not drink herself to death. That last, immutable fact had Alma sitting up, untying the ribbon again with hands that were anything but detached. Hands that remembered what it was to be stained with blood, how it felt to touch a lifeless body.

She found what she was looking for easily. A single envelope, with no postage stamp. Addressed simply: *To Mery and Emin.* Taking the envelope aside, she noticed that the flap was open and inside she could see several smaller notes, neatly folded. One by one she took them out, her hands trembling as she unfolded the first one and began to read.

ALMA

Flat 3, Sydney House
5 Layton Rd
Enfield, London

January 14th 1986

Dear Mery,

I'm writing this letter, even though I haven't got your address. Mum says she's sure we'll get one soon. I thought I'd write because otherwise I'm going to forget all the things I need to tell you. It's been twenty-four days already and I miss you.

Gary asked me when you were coming back. I said I thought you'd be back by spring, that's what my mum says. I hope you are, because there's a school trip in April, and we're going to stay away overnight. I don't want to go unless you're going.

We have a new teacher for maths. Mr Edwards. He's very funny. At the end of class, he gets us to tell jokes. He decides whose joke is the funniest and that person gets a sweet. You'd like him. You'd win most of the time.

Everything else is normal. Well, Christmas was strange. Your mother came and stayed with us. I mostly watched TV except when Mum made me go ice-skating with Sammy. She says I have to get out more.

It was okay.

For Christmas I got a Swatch watch.

You were on the news last week. Mum came in and switched it off, but I saw the shopping centre and our flats – it was definitely about you and Emin.

Anyway, I hope it's not too bad, wherever you are. I hope Emin isn't annoying you too much.

I also got a huge bar of Dairy Milk but I'm saving that for when you come back and we can share it.

Got to go now, Mum is calling me for dinner.

Love from Alma xx

PS I'm sorry I didn't come.

ALMA

Flat 3, Sydney House
5 Layton Rd
Enfield, London

April 20th 1986

Dear Mery,

You were in the newspaper again last week. There hasn't been anything for a while, but I've cut out everything so far and saved it. I don't know why. I thought maybe you'd like to see it all when you get back. Also because I still don't have an address. My mum says that doesn't matter. She says I should keep writing anyway, if it helps me feel better. It does. Sometimes it feels as if you're here and I'm just talking to you. Sometimes.

Your mum is feeling better. She's living with us at the moment. Did I say that before? She's in my room. I don't mind. I still keep all my clothes and things in there, but I'm sleeping with my mum.

The police were here again last night. This time no one

made me leave. It's the same stuff anyway. They come in, my mum makes them a cup of tea, they ask your mum how she is and then they tell her that they're doing everything they can, and then your mum tells them again that she knows where you are. She's given them the name of the place and everything. (I can't spell it.) I don't know what they're going to do, the police. I don't know why they don't just go and get you. If I could go, I would Mery. If I was old enough I'd get on a plane and come and get you and Emin back.

And I'm sorry Mery, I had to break into my Dairy Milk. Mum says it won't last forever. I've saved some though.

Everything else is the same. School is boring. It's getting lighter in the evenings, but I just come straight home now. We're getting more homework, but I don't think it will be too hard for you to catch up. I've got all your books, and you can always copy my stuff. I've changed. History is my favourite subject now. I'm thinking of studying it at university.

Oh and you won't believe this. Gary and Sammy are dating. Come back, Mery. I like Sammy, but I'm sure he only asked her because you're not here.

And I still have your hair clip. I washed it last week in, guess what? In Coca-Cola! Mum told me to. It really worked! It looks lovely now.

What's the weather like there? It's still freezing here, but the clocks changed last week. Sammy has started smoking! Can you believe it?

Anyway, that's all for now.

As soon as I get an address I'll send this. There's about ten more waiting for you.

Love from Alma

PS Wham! broke up. Did you hear?

PPS I miss you, and I'm sorry.

ALMA

Flat 3, Sydney House
5 Layton Rd
Enfield, London
Dec 13th 1986

Dear Mery,

Happy birthday. Fifteen! What did you get? How is Emin doing? Everything is the same here. Your mum made you a cake. I did my best, but it was only really me eating it, and I had to throw the last bits away.

I'm sorry I haven't written for a while. Mum took me to Ireland during the summer. She said we both needed a change of air after what happened when your mum came back from Turkey. Did you know she went? There was a collection at her work for plane tickets. Her boss organised it. Your mum was really excited. We helped her paint her living room. She's made new curtains and cushions and it looks really nice. She said she wanted it looking fresh and different for when she brings you back.

But she came back without you, Mery, and I don't know why.

She said she saw the house and everything, where you've been living, but you weren't there.

I don't understand, Mery. I don't understand why someone can't just bring you back.

That's why we went to Ireland really. Your mum had to go into hospital for a couple of weeks. I still don't know exactly what was wrong. My mum said it was a good chance for us to get away. It was nice. We walked on the beach a lot. I love the beach. You would have loved it too, I know you would.

I had to change one of my GCSE courses. I was going to take biology, but I'm changing to art. You know I was never that good at maths and sciences anyway. I wonder what you're doing? Maybe you'll come back for university?

We're looking after your mum, so I don't want you to worry about her. On your birthday she stayed in her room (well my room) nearly all day, except for when she came out and she made the cake. She also lit a candle and put it in the window. She's been doing that a lot. She says it's so you'll know to look for it when you come home.

I hope she's right.

I don't really know what else to say now. Yes I do! Gary and Sammy broke up and then got back together. Gary hasn't been at school much anyway. He's changed. He just looks really angry all the time.

When we got back from Ireland and your mum came out of hospital, the police came round. They haven't been for ages.

I hope you don't mind, but I'm only going to write the next sentence because I don't think you'll ever read it.

I think they've given up, Mery.
Love from Alma x
PS I'm sorry.

ALMA

Flat 3, Sydney House
5 Layton Rd.
Enfield, London
December 13th 1989

5.30pm

Dear Mery,

Today I came home from sixth form and found your mum. She was in the bath. She had cut her wrists and there was a lot of blood and I'm really sorry Mery, but she was dead. I knew straight away.

I'm only writing this because I know you'll never read it.

Happy 18th birthday.

What a stupid thing to write. I'm sorry.

I wasn't supposed to find her. There was a note on the bathroom door saying not to open it. And there was another note on the shelf above the sink, addressed to you and Emin. It wasn't in an envelope. I'm going to put it with this letter. To keep it safe.

I shouldn't have opened the door.

My mum is at work. I rang her. She said she would leave straight away, but she's not home yet. She said not to do anything until she got back. So I haven't.

It's dark outside. I haven't turned the lights on and I'm sitting in the kitchen and I can see the Christmas lights in the street. I've lit a candle, here in the kitchen. I don't know why. For your mum I think. I can smell it now. It is making me feel sick.

I'm so scared, Mery. I'm too scared to stand up and put the light on. I'm sitting with my back against the cupboard and I'm really really scared because your mum is still in the bathroom.

10.23pm

It is ten-thirty, Mery.

I am writing this from my mum's bed. I wonder what you are doing right now, and where you are? I'm glad I wrote everything down earlier. I want to be able to remember, so I can tell you one day.

It's very quiet now. The police were here, and an ambulance. They have taken your mum away. The police made coffee.

My mum is in the kitchen. I can smell her cigarette smoke. Do you want to know something stupid? She's been trying to give up.

I can hear her crying. She's been crying for hours. She thinks I'm asleep, because I was for a little while.

She was in the bathroom with your mum for ages before she called the police. This sounds crazy Mery, but I think she was washing your mum. I could hear her crying and I could hear water running and my mum was talking to your mum and she wouldn't call the ambulance straight away.

I'm sorry, Meryem. I'll always be sorry,
Alma

12

BATTLESTATIONS

Blackpool, present day

THE CEILING of the dining room amplified breakfast, like a cathedral amplifies praise. Spoons plunking, chairs scraping, plates stacking, trays clattering. George Michael on the PA system, and the humming conversation of one hundred and fifty hungry, hungover, middle-aged Wham! fans.

Sammy stood at the entrance, slightly awed, slightly lost, scanning the room for a face she might recognise. Eventually her eyes landed not on a face, but a pair of shoulders. Gary. He hadn't woken her and she hadn't heard him leave, and something about the scenario that presented itself now made her stomach knot. He was sitting opposite Meryem and the two of them were chatting and laughing as easy as old friends.

Swallowing down her discomfiture, she walked across to join them. 'Started have you?' she said as she eased herself into the chair next to Gary. He was already halfway through a huge plate of bacon and eggs.

Mopping his mouth with a napkin, Gary squeezed her thigh. 'I didn't want to wake you,' he said. 'You needed the rest.'

'It was such a good evening, wasn't it!' Meryem smiled. 'I wish I'd slept later.'

Sammy nodded. This was all true. She had needed the rest, and it had been a good evening, because after Alma's abrupt departure which had, for a while, thrown a bucket of cold water over the evening, they had danced for hours. And thank goodness for Meryem! Duran Duran, ABC, Culture Club, Spandau. Even a little bit of Euro-Pop which she'd been far too cool for first time around. The evening wouldn't have been half as much fun had it just been her and Gary left looking at each other, especially as his go-to 80s tunes were Metallica, Metallica and Metallica. Her feet throbbed and her back was stiff, but for the first time in months, she actually had what felt like an appetite. 'Did you sleep well,' she said looking at Meryem.

'Like a tree,' Meryem laughed. 'It was all that dancing!'

'You mean log?' Sammy frowned.

'Yes. Log! I get things wrong sometimes, in English.'

She nodded. 'Did you just have eggs?' She said, looking at Meryem's plate, which apart from a scrape of egg yolk, was clean.

'Oh no!' Meryem leaned back in her chair and stretched her arms up.

'She's eaten a horse!' Gary laughed. 'Well not a horse, but she had a lot more than eggs!'

'What can I say?' Meryem waved a hand at her empty plate. 'I have a healthy appetite!'

Sammy's smile was thinly polite, her own appetite

almost completely diminished. The inadequacy she felt was ridiculous. There was no competition between her and Meryem as to who could eat the biggest breakfast, who had the healthiest appetite, so why did she feel as if there was? She looked across at the fourth empty chair at the table. 'Has Alma surfaced?'

Gary and Meryem shook their heads.

'Okay,' she said, and tugged the sleeves of her jumper down. But she wasn't even cold, she was irritated. Late last night Alma had sent her a text, which she hadn't seen until this morning. A brief, *Sorry I had to bail I really didn't feel good.*

Well, she wasn't buying it and Alma had better not be about to do what she did so well. Cry off at the last minute with some feeble excuse. This weekend was too important for that. Yes, she'd been sceptical when Gary had booked it, but as the weeks had passed since her surgery, and she had begun to feel the first stirrings of something like her old self return, her doubts had faded. And it was true. A change was proving as good as a rest. Even the bacon here wasn't making her queasy. Plus, tomorrow would bring a task she could not quite believe she was looking forward to. Scattering her mother's ashes on Fleetwood beach. Just thinking about it made her feel lighter. It was time to face forward again. Something Alma had been gently persuading her towards for weeks. She could do it on her own. With Gary beside her, she could do it, but she wanted Alma alongside too, and Alma knew that.

'She has to be well for George Mightbe, this evening,' Meryem said, pouring herself a cup of tea. 'It would be such a shame if she missed it. I hope she's okay.'

Sammy nodded, her lips tight. She didn't know why Alma had left so suddenly, but she'd have bet her house on the fact that it was less to do with feeling ill, and more to do with Meryem. Alma's muted response to the tales of private jets and champagne chip suppers hadn't escaped Sammy, although she was sure Gary hadn't noticed, so enrapt was he, asking Meryem all sorts of questions about those bloody jets. Jaw tight, she glanced at him now, but his entire focus was on his last piece of sausage. She wasn't fooled. First of all, he knew she was still simmering over that plane comment. She had been on one! And secondly Gary knew Alma as well as she did. He'd seen, over the years, the many many times Sammy had tried to coax Alma into the folds of their family. Year-round invites to Christmas dinner, or a summer b-b-q. He knew how Alma had pushed the limits of both their patience as she'd cried off at the last minute. A headache, a stomach upset, the beginning of a migraine. As soon as Alma was too far out of her comfort zone, she locked down. Gary joked that she, Sammy, wasn't adventurous enough. But Alma? Alma made her look like Bear Grylls. He'd even pointed out what she had begun to fear herself. The fact that she only maintained the friendship with Alma out of sympathy. The comment had unsettled her, because it contained some truth. It went way back. After Meryem *left* – Sammy flinched – after Meryem *was no longer there,* Alma had seemed so alone. Eating lunch, walking home, in the library, in the classroom, the odd-numbered student who sat as a singleton at the paired desk. And no amount of persuading from anyone, teachers, other pupils, had been able to persuade her to join in. Then, such a few short years later, her mother had died, and she really was alone. So yes, an only child herself, but surrounded by uncles and aunts and cousins, Sammy had felt very very sorry for Alma. It wasn't comfortable for her to understand how close to the mark Gary had come when he'd said that.

To understand that her store of sympathy for Alma wasn't infinite.

Just as she thought this, Meryem looked up, caught her eye and smiled.

Sammy turned away, a whirlpool of emotion whipping up. It was unkind of her to even think like this about Alma. No one had understood better. Since her cancer diagnosis, no one had been present for her so consistently, no one had listened better and no one had done companionable silence better. So much so, that Sammy had acquired a new admiration for her old friend. How, in God's name, had she borne her mother's illness so stoically? She'd been barely twenty-five, with no extended family. It had wrenched Sammy's heart to really understand how utterly alone Alma must have been. It had wiped clean much of the irritation of those last-minute cancellations. Because when it had mattered the most, Alma had shown her nothing but unswerving loyalty and friendship. This was why Sammy needed her this weekend, because if anyone in the world understood what she was going through, Alma did. *Please, Alma. Please don't let me down.*

'Good morning, madam! What can I get you? Tea or coffee?' The shrill voice at her shoulder startled her. She turned to see a waitress, pad in hand, symmetrically tattooed jet-black eyebrows raised in expectation.

'Coffee please,' she said, staring at the eyebrows.

'And will you be having white sliced, toasted, granary, rye or brown?' the waitress sang.

'Sorry?'

'White sliced, toasted, granary, rye or brown?'

'Why brown?'

'*Rye* or brown.'

'Why?'

'*Rye.*' The girl's mouth stretched open to enunciate the word.

'Rye,' Gary barked.

'Alright!' She frowned at him. He was so irritable. If she thought his grumpiness yesterday was fatigue from the journey up, it was looking like she was wrong.

'White,' she muttered. 'Sliced.'

'And how would you like your eggs? Poached, scrambled, boiled, sunny side up, or fried.'

'Oh I don't know.' Sammy picked up the menu, tapping it against the edge of the table as she pretended to study it. So many questions! It didn't matter how the bloody eggs came, she wouldn't be able to taste anything anyway. Although her chemo was finished, the after effects lingered. It made everything taste of wet cardboard, or what she supposed wet cardboard would taste like.

'The fried eggs are great,' Meryem said, delicately mopping the corners of her mouth with a napkin.

'Fried then,' Sammy said, a tight smile in place. 'Is this coffee?' She reached for a pot in the middle of the table. 'Anyone else?'

Meryem looked up. Her thick black hair, loosely pinned, resembled a whippy cone ice cream. She had her phone out, tapping at it. 'No thanks, Sammy. I can't start my day without tea. Every day I tea myself into existence. At home, Nonny brings me lemon tea in bed.'

'Nonny?'

'My maid.'

Maid?

'Don't forget this, Sammy,' Gary said and stretched a small bottle of powder towards her.

'No thanks,' she muttered, pushing it away.

'Sammy.' Meryem lowered her phone. 'Turmeric is super

healthy. Gary was just telling me all about the anti-inflammatory benefits.' And to Sammy's bemusement, she leaned across to push the bottle back to her.

'Okay,' was all she managed, doing a little half turn, patting her pockets. She. Did. Not. Want. The. Turmeric. It only made the wet cardboard of her food look like a dirty-yellow, wet cardboard and suddenly she was enormously resentful of both them. Discussing her health no doubt, chiding her like she was a naughty child, who would not take her medicine. 'Let me just find my...' she stalled. Where were her fags? Not that she could smoke in here, but she certainly could outside. And maybe it would serve Gary right. He'd been so bloody grumpy with her, why shouldn't she have a cigarette! Cancer had happened to her, not him. Why shouldn't she just be allowed to go and stand in a corner and smoke her head off... She glanced up and saw how Meryem and Gary were both looking at her, pushing her into this turmeric corner... 'Okay,' she said, hands raised in surrender. And she took the turmeric and lined it up next to her coffee cup, but she'd be damned if she actually used it.

Meryem leaned back, stretching her arms above her head in a long, easy yawn. 'Tea and a morning bath.' She sighed. 'I'm missing my bath very much.'

'Don't you have one in your room?' she said, as much to push the conversation away from turmeric as anything else.

'Only a shower.'

'Oh.'

'It's not the same. I find it hard to get going without a bath.'

'Well... I mean we have one, if you want to borrow it.' She looked at Gary. 'I'm not going to shower until later?'

Gary raised his palms. They were calloused and pink.

'Fine by me,' he said. Lowering his chin, he picked up a napkin and began folding it, smaller... and smaller. 'Actually,' he said, 'I was talking to the manager... well, Meryem was, and the DeLorean in the car park is available for hire.'

Sammy looked at him. She had no idea what he was talking about.

'It's a local company. It's one of the reasons the owner brought the car along. To drum up some business. There were some fliers at the desk.

Easing the turmeric bottle aside, she shook her head. 'Fliers? Really?'

Now Meryem leaned forward, elbows on the table, her hands folded, the emerald gleaming. 'He does weddings with it, Sammy! And birthdays. Lots of fortieth and fiftieth birthdays.'

'Makes sense,' Sammy murmured. She was looking at Meryem's ring. It was huge.

'So I called. I asked if we could rent it.'

'*We?*'

'Yes!' Meryem laughed. 'Gary thought it would be fun too!'

'Did he?'

'I did,' Gary said, looking like a kid caught with his hand in the sweet jar. 'I mean, yes, I thought it would be fun. For all of us.'

'Are you asking me?' Sammy said.

'If you want to.'

She narrowed her eyes. 'How many does it sit?'

No one answered. Gary looked away and Sammy picked up her coffee. She wasn't sure what she was hearing. A ride in a rented DeLorean. It wasn't her idea of fun, and Gary knew that. 'I think I'll give it a miss,' she said. 'Alma and I had planned on going to the spa anyway.' And when she looked at her husband, and saw how two dots of pink had appeared on each of his cheeks, her heart began a gentle hammering. There was one thing she hadn't added to her List to Live For, because it belonged on a different list. A List to Die For, which everyone had told her she didn't need to think about, but she hadn't been able to stop thinking about. And right at the top of that list would have been, *Let Gary be happy.* They weren't so old. He might have many years left. *Let Gary be happy.* Yes, it was exactly what she would wish for him. But with Meryem Saylan? Oh no. Meryem Saylan wasn't for the likes of her husband and before that thought could fatten up, Gary's hands were on her shoulders, large and warm. A feeling of profound discomfort started, deep in the pit of her stomach.

'You sure you don't mind?' he said.

Shaking her head, Sammy managed an almost silent, 'No.'

'You and Alma should visit the spa,' he said.

Meryem nodded seriously. 'Yes, I think it's a good idea. You and Alma should go to the spa. Alma definitely – it would do her good. I have one in my apartment complex back home. I'm there every week.'

Sammy looked at her. *I bet you bloody are*, she thought.

Meryem smiled. 'Well,' she said, 'this is something I never thought I'd do! Is it okay if I take a quick bath first?'

'Bath?' She'd forgotten. 'Yes,' she managed.

'And you're alright with this?' Gary asked.

So many questions... Her nod was small and tight. Yes, it was alright. *It was alright.* It was just a bath... It was just a car ride.

13

LIKE A BABY

Blackpool, present day

'NOW THEN! Let's see what I brought with me.' Sammy's voice was brittle with sudden nerves as she went into the bathroom. Why on earth had she suggested this? No one would have noticed if she hadn't taken the bloody turmeric, no one needed to mention baths... She could still be at breakfast, taking a last peaceful coffee, enjoying a secret cigarette, not here, with Meryem, who was standing in the doorway, wearing nothing but a fluffy yellow towel that the morning sun had touched gold. It was impossible not to see. Her skin was the colour of sunlight on freshly stripped bark, her hair was silken black and her eyelashes, her natural lashes, were thick as brooms. Every part of her was full and ripe. And it seemed to Sammy, in her headscarf and lumpen mastectomy bra, that Meryem's beauty was both bountiful and earthly, there to be consumed. She was like a juicy fat blackberry. *Why, why, why,* she thought as she turned to the mirrored cabinet, had she gone and opened her big big mouth?

The sudden and unavoidable sight of her own face, reflected back, kicked her legs from under her. Oh God. *Oh God...* Her hollow cheeks... the bruised lilac under her eyes and the single odd eyelash, like a surviving blade of scorched grass... If the specimen of womanhood in the doorway was a big ripe blackberry, she must be its shrunken winter cousin, hollow on the inside, grimly hanging on. It was better not to see this. Flustered, she opened the door and the huge white tub of her medicine showed itself. TAMOXIFEN.

'How about this?' she said brightly, retrieving a small bottle, and closing the door as quickly as possible. '*Invigorating Pineapple and Lime*? It's supposed to be refreshing.' She handed it to Meryem who sniffed at the open bottle, wrinkled her nose and handed it back.

'I can't say I disagree!' Sammy forced a laugh. 'Gary says I smell like a salad if I use it.'

Meryem smiled. 'Don't worry,' she said. 'I'll just use a few drops of my perfume.'

'Perfume?' she said and watched as Meryem went to her handbag, lying on the bed.

In another moment, Meryem was back, holding a dark, voluptuously curved bottle. She stretched her hand out and let several drops fall into the steaming water.

'Good idea,' Sammy murmured.

'Do you like it?' Beaming, Meryem turned to her, one hand wafting the newly perfumed air upward. 'I bought it in Harrods yesterday,' she said, and inhaled deeply.'Here, smell!' And she thrust the bottle under Sammy's nose. 'It's for the woman who loves luxury! Who chooses her own destiny! It has the scent of vanilla pops and coffee and woods.'

Looking up from underneath the bare dents where eyebrows had once lived, Sammy held Meryem's eye. No, she wasn't joking. She was still holding the bottle an inch from Sammy's nose and it was clear that Meryem was *the woman who loves luxury, who chooses her own destiny,* or she wholeheartedly believed this perfume would make her so, and if the situation hadn't been so surreal, Sammy might have laughed. She couldn't smell a bloody thing! So there would be no choosing her own destiny then! Nostrils wide as a stallion's, she tried again. Nothing! No vanilla pops. No coffee. No woods. 'Very nice,' she lied, straightening up.

'Isn't it!' Meryem popped the lid back on, turned to the bath and let her towel drop.

'Oh...ooh... I....' A long wobbly sound whistled out of Sammy as she began backing out of the door, in a clumsy criss-crossed movement. 'I'll... I'll leave you to it then. I...'

But one leg over the bath, Meryem stopped. 'Wait!'

'Wait?'

'I forgot my eye mask.' Meryem was pointing towards the bed. 'It's in my bag.'

'I'll get it.' Sammy thrust her hand forward in a stop sign. 'I can get it!' she repeated, mustering as much authority as she could, because now Meryem was stepping back out of the bath, coming towards her, and her breasts were so alive! Full and swinging, and she couldn't stop, her eyes kept switching back to them, no matter how hard she tried to look away. God it was embarrassing! So embarrassing!

'It's okay. I know where it is. Oh! Look at that!' Naked as a baby, Meryem had stopped to turn and look at her reflection in the mirrored cabinet. 'Look at my eyes!' she exclaimed. 'I knew I should have slept later!' She shook her head. 'This is what one late night can do nowadays!' And she stretched forward to see more closely, and, as she did, Sammy flattened her spine back against the wall, as if Meryem was a walking bomb.

'Puffy puffy puffy,' the bomb was saying, patting her fingertips to her eyes as she walked out of the bathroom to collect her eye mask.

And pinned against the bathroom wall, Sammy could hardly breathe. Meryem's tits were perfect. Far better than any of the pictures in the reconstruction brochures she'd been given. Far, *far* better. They would do fine thanks. Perhaps she should just take a photo of them and take it in to her next appointment. *Here. I'll have these please Mr Reconstructive Surgeon.*

Meryem came back and slipped into the bath. She placed the mask over her eyes and slid deep into the scented water. 'Oh, that's better,' she breathed.

'Okay. Well, I'll leave you to it,' Sammy said, peeling herself off the wall.

'It was such fun last night wasn't it?'

In the doorway, Sammy paused. Meryem's voice was small, her question almost childlike in its obvious need for affirmation. 'Yes,' she answered. 'Yes, it was.'

'I can't remember when I had so much fun.' Meryem sighed. 'I hope Alma is feeling okay for tonight. I really do.'

'Me too,' Sammy whispered and eased the door shut.

Safely out, she stood very still. There she was again, reflected back now in the wardrobe mirror. Small, dumpy, headscarfed. The room was so quiet she could hear the thump of her own heart, see the cloud of dust mites that floated high above. She turned sideways and looked at her reflection. She wasn't even on speaking terms with her nudity. In fact, since the operation, they had become complete strangers, Sammy going out of her way to avoid any kind of confrontation. She got dressed, and undressed, as quickly as possible, in as little light as possible: no witnesses. And yet here was Meryem, the same age, living in her skin in a way that Sammy could not conceive of, comfortable and unashamed.

Socks sinking into the carpet pile, she walked across the room until she was inches from the mirror, paused and took a deep breath. Then in one decisive move, she tugged her jumper over her head, reached for her bra strap and undid it.

Outside a car engine revved. It felt horribly close. Sammy turned to the window. The engine died away. She turned back, and as she did, she kept her hands pressed to her chest and let the bra fall away.

The skin felt flat and ridged, hard and dead. Nothing like the dense, miraculously living flesh that anyone feeling Meryem would feel. One knee buckled. She felt a warmth between her legs, as if she was going to wet herself and panic overwhelmed. Panic that someone might see, panic that she looked like this, panic that she had survived such a mutilation. Yanking her sweater back on, she stumbled to the bed, folding herself into a curl, knuckles under her chin, her face already wet with swift and silent tears. Sometimes she was just too scared of this disease. Sometimes was now. She pulled her knees tighter and closed her eyes and her breath was ragged as her body convulsed with grief and she gasped air. It felt an age, but the moment was brief. Emotion ebbed as swiftly as it had arrived, leaving her in a pocket of calm so sacred and deep she did not hear the bathroom door ease open, and she only knew someone was close when she felt the mattress beside her shoulder sink. There was an arm around her shoulder and a brush of towel on her arm, a tumble of hair in her face.

'Don't cry,' the voice said, and Sammy turned her face into Meryem's towelled bosom and cried. And Meryem rocked her and said, 'Don't cry, Sammy. Don't cry.'

Enough time passed for embarrassment to seep in. A minute? A few seconds? Pushing herself upright, her hand under her nose, she whispered, 'I'm sorry.'

But Meryem, shook her head.

So did Sammy. 'You didn't need to see that,' she murmured. 'I'm sorry.'

'Sammy?' Meryem put her hand on top of Sammy's. 'Have they taken them away?' she said, her face serious as she drew a line across her own chest.

'Taken them—' A laugh escaped her. It was the ridiculousness of the situation – Meryem Saylan, after all these years, the two of them sitting on this bed. She laughed again. 'Yes,' she said, 'They've taken them away to a better place.' But, seeing Meryem's uncomprehending frown, she batted the joke away. 'I had a double mastectomy last year.'

Meryem nodded. 'I'm sorry.'

Sammy's smile was weak. Her shoulders rose as she breathed in. When she breathed out, she shuddered.

'Are you cold?'

She shook her head. She wasn't cold, she was nervous. An idea had come to her and although it was making her anxious, it wouldn't go away. She *needed* to show someone. She hadn't done that. In the weeks that had passed since her operation, no one, not even Gary, had seen this new version of herself. Now, suddenly, she knew that she needed to share it. And she also knew that if anyone could take it, Meryem could. 'No one has seen,' she said quietly.

Meryem smiled. 'Do you want to show me?' she said, as if she'd just read Sammy's mind.

'You won't be shocked?'

'I've seen many things, Sammy.'

And that, Sammy knew, holding Meryem's eye, was true. 'Okay,' she said. 'Okay.' And she began removing her sweater.

Meryem did not look away. Not once. Not even when the sad hollow of Sammy's chest, puckered and mottled, was there, exposed in all its ugly reality. Instead, she lifted her hand and asked, with her eyes, if she could touch, and Sammy, with her eyes, answered *yes* and Meryem touched her fingertips to the delicate pink scars that stretched across Sammy's chest and said, 'You are alive though.' And Sammy nodded, her eyes burning tears, her lips pressed hard together. Meryem reached forward and put her arms around Sammy's neck, touching her fingertips together across Sammy's pale and freckly shoulders. And again she said, 'You're alive, Sammy. You're alive.'

'Oh fuck!' A tear escaped, and then another. 'I'm sorry,' she whispered. 'It was just seeing you before, naked, like that... It made me...' She shook her head.

Meryem pulled back, her hands on Sammy's shoulders. 'I made you cry?' she said and frowned.

'No. Not you exactly. Just...' Shaking her head, she reached for her sweater. When she was safely covered again, she looked down at the flat expanse of her chest, and then at the swell of Meryem's.

And Meryem, too, looked down. 'These,' she said, pointing to her bosom. 'These made you cry?'

A warm embarrassment swept through, reaching even the tips of her ears. 'I mean...' Sammy started. 'Well they are...Oh God, Meryem, I'd be happy with anything right now!'

Meryem smiled. 'You know, Sammy, they've done many things, my tits, but they've never made anyone cry.'

'No?' How was she supposed to respond to that? 'Well!' she said, her voice artificially light. 'There's a first time for everything I suppose.'

But Meryem didn't respond. She sat, one leg tucked under the other, hands folded in her lap as she stared out of the window.

And Sammy too, didn't move. On the floor, where she'd left it, her mastectomy bra lay in a soft-mounded pile.

'If I tell you something,' Meryem said, without turning, 'will you promise that *you* won't be shocked?'

Sammy looked up. 'I've seen a lot of things too,' she said, trying to maintain the lightness, feeling that, somehow, she'd just stepped off a cliff.

'Do you know what usually happens when people... when men see my tits?'

Lips clamped tight, Sammy shook her head.

Meryem leaned forward. 'This!' she said, groping the air between them with claw-like hands.

'Oh!' The movement was instinctive and swift as Sammy flinched backward. 'That must be...' She stared at Meryem. The conversation wasn't making sense. 'They can't just touch you,' she said. 'That's not—'

'They can if they are paying,' Meryem said, and her words sliced the air between them clean as a guillotine.

'Right.' She didn't move, and she didn't look away, even though every nerve and sinew yearned to. She couldn't, because the look on Meryem's face was an unspoken challenge. *I dare you,* it said. *I dare you to keep looking at me.* Meryem was a prostitute? She had said she wouldn't be shocked, or she had let Meryem believe that she wouldn't be shocked. Or she had let herself believe she wouldn't be shocked. But she was. She really was. 'Right,' she said again, and then a third time. 'Right.' And when, finally, Meryem looked away, Sammy knew it was for her sake.

'They make me good money, Sammy,' Meryem said, her voice as steely light as titanium, her chin lifted defiantly. 'I am an escort and they make me *very* good money.' Slowly, she turned back. 'Are you shocked?'

'No.'

'You are shocked.'

Sammy didn't speak. She was shocked rigid and she couldn't help it. She tried not to, but again she looked down at Meryem´s tits.

'Alma doesn't know.'

'Right.' Sammy nodded. She had no idea what to say. She could feel Meryem watching her and she knew she was being tested and she had no idea what the penalty might be if she failed.

'You're surprised?' Meryem said, breaking the tension.

'No!... Well, yes...'

'You've never met someone like me before?'

'No,' Sammy whispered.

'Me neither, Sammy.' Meryem shrugged. 'Before me, I hadn't met an escort either.'

'Right.' Sammy laughed, but it was pathetically unconvincing, and if she could just find another word... but she hadn't ever met a prostitute before, never mind sat down and had a chat with one.

'I'll tell you something else now,' Meryem said.

Sammy's fingers folded around the edge of the duvet cover. She had the strangest feeling, like she was in the front car of a rollercoaster, chugging up to a point of no return.

'For a divorced woman in the UAE, it's very hard to find work. Impossible actually, especially as I'm not even a citizen.'

'Right.'

'And it is expensive living there, Sammy. *Very* expensive.'

'I imagine it is,' Sammy whispered. Words. She'd found words.

'And when my husband divorced me, he lied. So he could keep his money, he lied. His brother came to the court to swear that he had already provided enough money for me to live on. I was left with nothing.'

Sammy shook her head. 'And they believed him? Just like that?'

'Of course,' Meryem said, her voice humming with bitterness. 'They are men. The judge was a man. Of course, he was believed.'

Sammy stared at her. 'But he can't do that!'

Meryem looked at her. 'He can, Sammy, and he did.'

And when Sammy didn't speak, Meryem shrugged. 'After I went to Turkey, I didn't go to school anymore. And then when I was sixteen—'

'Wait!' Finally, the rollercoaster had stopped. Or at least slowed enough for her to get off. 'You didn't go to school?' she said.

Meryem nodded.

'After fourteen?'

Again, Meryem nodded.

And Sammy had to put her hand on her chest just to keep her heart in place. A well of emotion surged, filling her eyes with tears and sending blood to her pallid cheeks. Meryem had been the smartest girl in the class! In maths, in science... No one got marks like Meryem's, except perhaps

Alma. 'What did you do?' she managed. 'If you didn't go to school.'

Meryem smiled. 'I did what all the girls did. I looked after the sheep, and the goats. I cleaned the house and prepared the food.'

Sammy nodded, but she was thinking of her own daughter, Sarah, at fourteen. The goofy teenager in braces and the young woman she was now. A bossy manager, with a smart uniform and a fantastic social life.

'When I turned sixteen, I was married,' Meryem said quietly.

'You *were* married?'

'Yes. That was how it worked. For me, there was no choice. I didn't get married. I *was* married.'

Sammy didn't speak. There wasn't anything she could think of to say.

'I had my first child at seventeen, Sammy. I'm not like Alma. I don't have an education. I don't have any qualifications. I had to find a way to live. Not just survive, but live.'

Again, Sammy couldn't find a response.

'And now I invest my money.' Meryem shrugged. 'I don't know if you remember, but I have always been good with maths.'

'I do,' Sammy whispered. 'I remember very well.'

'And the men...'

Sammy winced. She didn't want to know. She *wanted* to know.

'They are okay.' Meryem smiled. 'Mostly,' she added, 'they are just lonely. In fact, the older I get, the more lonely people I seem to meet.' And she turned away to stare out of the window.

Lonely? Sammy looked at her. That was the word she would have used to describe Meryem herself. And suddenly, for the first time since they had met again yesterday, she had the feeling that they did still inhabit the same universe. That for all her glamour and money and international lifestyle, Meryem woke up to the same fears they all did. Perhaps worse. Because what kind of fears did a forty-something *escort* wake up to?

'How old are your children, Sammy?' Meryem said, without turning.

Her children? What did they have to do with this? 'Twenty-five,' she murmured. 'The oldest is twenty-five and—'

'So you were a young mother too?'

'Well...' She looked down at her hands. 'Yes,' she said. 'Yes, I was.'

'How old?'

'Nineteen,' she said. 'Just nineteen.'

'Nearly the same as me.' Meryem nodded. 'You're not a career woman, like Alma?'

Sammy snorted. 'No. I work, but I wouldn't ever have called it a career.'

'Then we are a lot the same, Sammy,' Meryem said, turning now to hold her eye. 'A lot the same.'

But Sammy didn't answer and the sound of the silence between them grew loud, and she watched, as eventually Meryem stood up and turned away.

'I'll get dressed now.' At the bathroom door, Meryem stopped. 'Alma doesn't know,' she said, and it was, Sammy understood, less a statement and far more a threat.

SONJA

Flat 7, Sydney House
5 Layton Rd
Enfield, London

27th January 1988

My darling Meryem,

Do you remember the play-school you and Alma went to? The curtains were yellow and white, and if the windows had been left open overnight, they might be moving when we opened the door. It used to scare you, Meryem. We were the first to arrive. You would hold onto my jeans and hide behind my leg. Sometimes I dream of that, you holding my legs and me able to protect you. But this is only when I don't take my sleeping pills. The doctor says it is better if I take them all the time, that way I will sleep. Kathy says the same. I understand. If I don't take them, I know I will dream, but what I don't know is if it is going to be a good dream, or a bad dream. Mostly they are bad, and I can see in Kathy's face how bad. She is tired. I am a lot of trouble for her and Alma.

But sometimes the dreams are good and I see your faces again and it makes every nightmare worth it.

The play-school was my first job. When you were sure it was safe, when you understood the curtains were just curtains, you would let go of my legs and run to the kitchen. Get the cups and line them on the bench. Orange, then yellow, then orange again. You had a special order because this was your first job as well. You were four, nearly ready for school, and you and Alma were amongst the oldest. You were like two mother hens, bossing all the younger children around. It was good practice for you because, although you didn't know it, I was expecting Emin. You always were such a good little mother to him and that gives me comfort, knowing that he still has you.

Kathy got me the job and I was grateful, but it was hard. The children pulled at my headscarf and the other women said nothing to stop them. Then when they learned that I could not read the words in their storybooks, they stopped coming to me. But at least the children were honest. The adults were not. They smiled to my face and stopped talking when I went into the kitchen. I watched as toys were re-sorted after I had tidied up. And I saw them pour away coffee I had made. Why didn't they just tell me they didn't like it? Yes, it was hard at first, until the day you slapped another child!

Oh Meryem! I am laughing as I write this. Good memories, like good dreams, make me happy, so I'm going to tell you, and maybe you will laugh too when you read it? If you read it. I have had all my letters to you and Emin returned. Many came at once, in a bundle. Now they come back one by one. I send them, they come back. But I won't stop writing, Meryem. I promise you, I won't stop.

The child you slapped was a boy called James. I

remember so well. He called me stupid. There was no one else to read to him and I knew he didn't want me, but there was no one else. So I pointed to the pictures, and said the words I knew – house, boy, ball. It wasn't enough. He was frustrated. He turned around and said it again, You are stupid! Stupid! Oh, you hit him hard, Meryem! You were playing next to me and you stood up and slapped his face and he cried and ran away to the lady in charge. Wendy.

I remember squatting back on my heels and looking at you with your chin pushed out, as Wendy told you off. You didn't care and you were not afraid! After that I hardly heard what Wendy was saying. I was thinking of you, and what the future would bring you. I still see it now – the way you blinked at Wendy and lifted your little chin and looked away from her, out of the window. I understood then that the future would bring nothing *to* you, because you would decide for yourself. I thought you could be a teacher! Like Pinar in the village. Before I came to England, she was the woman I admired most in the world, and the idea that you too might one day become a teacher and know all the things that Pinar did filled me with such happiness. But even as I looked at you my mind became a house, shuttered too long. Window after window was thrown open to the sun, Meryem! Yes, you might become a teacher, or you might become a nurse like Kathy. Or you might even become a doctor. You were still looking out of the window, and Wendy was still talking and I was understanding, in a way I never had before, how you had the chance to be anything you wanted to be.

And when I heard Wendy talking again, I realised she was talking to me, and she was holding a leaflet.

Later, your father laughed when I told him how you had hit the boy. But when I told him why, and showed him the leaflet, he became serious. He read it through. It is better than dreaming about water, he said, because he knew how I dreamed of going to the well in the early mornings, when the lanes of the village are empty and the only sounds are those of the sheep on the hills. He did not understand why I would dream of this when I had taps. But how could I tell him how lonely the echo of running water in empty rooms still made me feel?

And he was right. Learning to read and write was better than dreaming. He encouraged me to go to the classes. Sometimes I wonder if he remembers that?

And this, Meryem was how I too started to choose my own future. My plans were simple. I will tell you them. A house with a garden, where I could grow vegetables again. School for you and Emin, and perhaps even university for you both, because the shutters in my mind kept opening and opening. Maybe it was the English summers, stretching days longer than I could ever have believed possible. I too felt stretched. We could do anything!

We had neighbours, Jo and Danny. You won't remember them. They left the flats when you were small and moved away to their own house. We passed them one day, Kathy and I, fixing the roof of their new house. Jo was wearing a bikini and this was the most astonishing thing I had ever seen. A woman, fixing a roof, in a bikini!

Everyone was moving forward. Jo and Danny had a garden, and Kathy had finished her training now. She was earning more money. Sometimes Alma would come to stay overnight, and I would tell your father that Kathy was working a nightshift. This wasn't always true, Meryem, but I had changed. I was no longer the woman who hid in hall-ways, and I wasn't angry or ashamed for Kathy. I was happy for her, because she was happy. Life was good.

The playgroup building is still there, but the curtains are blue now. Sometimes I sit on the bench in the garden outside and watch them move in the breeze.

You have been gone nearly three years.

Love always, Mamma

14

EVERYTHING SHE WANTS

D*ecember 13th 1989*

Dear Meryem,

I cannot carry on. The only thing I brought to this country was my youth and that is gone and I am so tired. I am not a dreamer. Rivers do not run back from the sea to the hills. For me, it is over. I hope, in time, you will forgive me. For that to happen, I need you to understand that I didn't leave you. I just couldn't find a way of staying.

I tried. I tried for so long.

I have walked for hours in the rain so I could feel it fall on my face, because to feel something meant I was still alive.

I have written to you. So many times. They all came back unopened.

I have talked with good people. Men and women who wanted to help, who thought they knew how to help but couldn't because the one thing that would help was the one thing they couldn't do. They could not bring you back to me.

And I have begged those who could have done that. Who should have helped me.

I had no family of my own. My brother and his family had moved away. Your father's father closed the door on my face.

Afife told me she had not seen you.

The neighbours told me they had not seen you and the house your father built, the biggest house in the village, was silent as it told me it had not seen you. It lied. They lied.

Why did he build the railings around the house? Who was he keeping out? Who was he keeping in?

I stayed as long as I could. I came from Ankara every day, until there was no more money. Everyone told me to go home. Go home to England and wait, they said, because they knew, as I did, England was home for me now. They told me that you would come back one day and this is what I held onto. I believed you would come back.

And then a year later your father wrote to me. I was excited to get the letter. I thought he was writing to tell me that you had decided to return. You were so nearly an adult by then, Meryem.

I could not have been more wrong.

He was writing to tell me that you were married. That you were living in Saudi Arabia now. No address. No telephone number. Only the age of your husband. And so now your youth is over too.

The police said there was nothing they could do. Why? Why was there nothing they could do? You were seventeen. If you were Alma, it could not have happened without her mother's consent. I did not consent to your marriage, Meryem. I want you to know this. I did not consent.

When I read this, I knew you would not be coming back. How could I find you in a country like Saudi Arabia? My mind will not even allow me to imagine you there, you will be a bird in a cage and I cannot set you free.

And then your father told me it was time for me to stop writing. He said that he would never show you or Emin my letters, because talking about me upset you both. He said that I had brought this upon myself. You had a new life as a wife now and that Emin did not want to see me. He did not want to hear about me. He was so much younger than you, Meryem. Perhaps this is true?

So, forgive me, but the anger I once had has gone – it needs an energy I no longer possess. I don't want to wake up any more.

It is very quiet. Today, Meryem, you will be eighteen years old and I remember so clearly the doctor who brought you into this world and how he told us that although the space between life and death can be finer than a human hair, there is always time for human hands to intervene.

It is because I remember so well that I have made sure that there will be no time today for human hands.

Kathy will find me. She will know what to do. She will wash me, the way she washed me the day you were born. I want to tell you how. I want to tell you how I found my friend, because my greatest wish for you in this life, Meryem, is that you too, find such a friend.

It started with the day she washed me, the first hour of your life...

When she led me to the hospital bathroom, her hands were gentle as a child's. She did not let go of me. I was so weak that I would have fallen and she knew that. She tucked my hair behind my ear. She turned the shower dial and, together, we watched the water pour down through my hair and my empty stomach. She wiped the blood from my thighs and held my legs because they were shaking, and she knew I would fall. I did not stop watching her. I was afraid she would disappear if I looked away. She asked if I was okay. She pressed her flannel against me like the soft petal of a flower, until the whiteness was black with blood. She did this again and again, and as she did I cried because never in my life had anyone shown me such kindness as this stranger did now. Never had anyone touched me so tenderly or spoken to me so gently. I cried with relief, and Kathy soaked and rinsed and soaked and rinsed. And then I tried to tell her but she did not understand the word: Isemek.

She thought I was in pain.

I said it again, and this time the word ended as I emptied my bladder and it splashed up Kathy's arms and I remember the mirror above the sink, how we looked at each other through it, and Kathy laughed and I laughed.

She was the first person that I had shared laughter with since I came to live in England but I haven't seen her laugh in so very long now, and I cannot be a burden any longer.

Please forgive me.

We will all meet again.

Love always, Mamma

SAMMY'S HANDS shook as she folded the three pieces of paper in half and returned them to the envelope. Her face was ashen with shock. Slowly she handed the envelope back to Alma.

They were sitting side by side on the bed, in Alma's room. Dressed in towelling robes, toilet bags beside them. Spa treatments booked.

'I hope you can see,' Alma said quietly. 'I had to leave. When she began talking about her mother, I had to leave. And this morning...' She shook her head. 'I wanted to speak to you first. I couldn't face ... I'm sorry.'

Sammy squeezed Alma's hand. 'You never told me. All these years, Alma, and you never said a word.'

'I ...' Alma shook her head.

'Why didn't you ever say?'

She didn't speak. She looked down at her dressing gown cord, her fingers working themselves. through the knot, loosening, then re-tying it. 'I've tried not to think about it,' she said quietly.

'You were seventeen, Alma.'

'I was,' she whispered. 'I was seventeen.' Alma took a napkin and wiped her hand clean. When she was done, she folded the napkin in half and then half again. A chill had started, spreading from her stomach to reach up her spine, the back of her neck. She was seventeen. She was too scared to stand up and put the light on. Sitting with her back against the cupboard because Sonja was lying dead in the bathroom. And it didn't matter how many years passed, in the eye of this memory, she would always be seventeen. The body remembered, which is why the only way was for the mind to forget. This is what the therapist had told her. This is what her mother told her. 'We didn't talk about it,' she said, looking up at Sammy. 'My mum and me. We never talked about it and – I don't think Meryem knows.'

Sammy waited.

When she didn't speak, Alma took a deep breath, trying to find the words to answer the question that had haunted her all night. 'If she knew, why would she have said what she did?'

'What did she say?'

'She said...' Alma pulled a breath in. 'She said that Sonja drank herself to death.'

'I don't know. I don't know, Alma. I never really knew

what happened at the time, and I can't imagine...' Looking at the letter in Alma's hand, Sammy's mouth hardened. 'I don't understand,' she said. 'If they knew where Meryem and her brother were, why didn't the police just go and get them? I don't understand why they didn't do that!'

'Meryem's father wasn't a British citizen. They didn't even take it seriously at first. That's what my mum said, later. They thought it was an argument between a husband and wife.

Sammy snorted. 'Wow.'

'They did issue an arrest warrant, eventually. I remember that.'

'Fat lot of good that would have done! How did he even get them out of the country?'

And Alma's smile was as sad as it was small. 'It wasn't like it is now, Sammy,' she said. 'Children didn't have their own passports.' She took her glasses off and laid them on the table. 'We used to go and visit Sonja's grave every year. She's buried in Edmonton Cemetery. I think we were the only visitors. There was never any sign. My mum arranged it all and now they're next to each other.' Alma shrugged. 'It's what they would have wanted. Both of them.'

For a long moment, Sammy didn't speak. Then, reaching for her handbag, she took her cigarettes out, re-tied the knot of her headscarf and said, 'I really need a smoke.' And she went to the window of Alma's room and opened it. 'It it okay?' she said.

Alma nodded.

'What are you going to do?'

Alma sighed. Substitute that window for the kitchen window of their old flat, she thought, and it could be her mother, taking a quick cigarette break from life. It could so easily be her mother, leaning out of the window. She looked at the letters, in a pile on the bedside table. She wished she'd never found them. She wished her mother had destroyed them, thrown them away with the bloody towels that had littered the bathroom floor that night. Sammy's question wasn't hard. She could hear the answer, but her own thoughts were louder. Her mother had expended all her energy on keeping Sonja alive. A gargantuan effort that had, in the end, failed. And now it felt to Alma that Sonja, even in death, remained too vulnerable to be saved. The woman Meryem was today was not and never could be the fourteen-year-old who had disappeared. But she had no choice. She had no control over how Meryem might respond to her mother's letters. Just as she had no control over how Meryem remembered her mother. Picking up the ribbon, smoothing it between forefinger and thumb, she said, 'I have to give them to her. I have to.'

Sammy turned to look back at Alma. Her shoulders hunched against the cold. 'Did you ever try to find her?' she said. 'You know, through Facebook? Email?'

'A few times. When Facebook started. And after she rang the other day I looked. I never found anything. I don't think she uses social media.'

'So why now?' Sammy said. 'Why did she get back in touch now?'

It wasn't the questions that had Alma hesitating to answer, it was the tone of Sammy's voice, laced through as it was with suspicion. 'Her father told her something,' she said. 'He was dying. She'd gone back to see him. She asked if I remembered her mother, talking about her. And if I did, what she had said.'

'And did you?'

'No.' Staring down the tunnel of thirty years, Alma shook her head. So many whispered conversations, so many times she'd walked in and the room had gone quiet. 'My mother and Sonja talked all the time,' she said quietly. 'But not in front of me.'

Sammy looked at her.

'I didn't know what to say,' Alma whispered. 'They didn't talk in front of me and I didn't know what she wanted to hear.'

'Of course.' Sammy nodded, then, 'And you didn't discuss it? On the way up?'

'No.' Again, Alma shook her head. 'Everything happened so quickly.' Everything had happened so quickly. After Sammy had bought her jeans and Meryem had bought her dress, Meryem had zipped back to her hotel to collect her bag and within the space of an hour, Alma had found herself driving along the M40, Meryem beside her, plugged into a pink wireless headset, texting and calling and re-arranging work commitments. Although she could have been planning a trip to the moon for all Alma had understood, because she really did switch languages the way other people switched shoes. Conversation, as long as it had stayed on the surface, had been smooth enough. Emin was well. No, she didn't see her grown-up children much. They were busy! *So busy, Alma.* 'I tried,' she said quietly. And she had, but her questions had been swatted away like flies, and Meryem had launched into an unstopabble, and, it had seemed to Alma, nervous stream of chatter. On and on about nothing at all. How she loved Harrods, and Harvey Nichols! Black taxis and red buses. How she missed the red buses! How for years she'd hadn't learned to drive, even once the ban on women driving was lifted, because why would she bother, when she had her own personal chauffeur! And the London Eye! Had Alma been to the London Eye? No? Well now they were back in touch, she would make sure she came to London again soon and they could do it together! If Alma could stand heights that was? In Dubai there was a rooftop with a balcony made of glass. Glass kept so clean that it was easy to believe there was nothing between your glass of champagne and the sky. She loved it! There were always free stools because most people were too scared to sit there. Not, her! No, not her! Amazed anew at the fact that she'd spent three hours in a car with Meryem, and had gotten no closer to finding out a single real thing about her, Alma picked up her cup and drained her coffee. 'Meryem,' she said now, 'is very good at talking only about what she wants to. Don't you think?'

Sammy threw her stub away and came and sat back down. 'Oh yes,' she said. 'I definitely think so.'

'I'm amazed she's here at all to be honest. She seems to have such a busy life. She was re-arranging work appointments all the way up.'

'Work appointments?'

'I think so. It was mostly in Arabic. I didn't understand and I wasn't going to start asking.'

Sammy didn't speak.

'I'm so sorry,' Alma whispered.

'For what?'

'For all this.' Alma lifted her hand and waved it limply at the letter. 'For this. This was supposed to be your weekend.'

A stitch of a frown formed across Sammy's forehead. 'None of this is your fault,' she whispered. 'Surely you don't think that?'

'*I* invited Meryem to join us.' Sammy's voice snatched her back. 'Not you. *Me*. Remember?'

'I do,' Alma murmured.

'And I don't regret doing that.' In one swift movement, Sammy twisted down for her handbag, lifted it to the bed, dug deep inside and took out a piece of paper.

Silently, Alma watched.

'Number one, Sammy said, unfolding the paper and laying it on the table between them. 'Be blonde. Number two, scatter Mum's ashes...' She paused, nodding to herself. 'Number three...'

'Your List to Live For?' Alma's smile was small.

'Yes.' Sammy folded the paper back in half. 'I've been so lucky,' she said finally. 'I've been so happy, for so long, and not everyone can say that.' Looking down at her hands, she said, 'Gary always thought Sean was born a month early. I never told you that did I?'

Alma frowned.

'I lied, Alma!' Sammy's voice was both urgent and hoarse. 'All those years ago, when I fell pregnant, I waited weeks before I told Gary. And when I did, I told him that I was further gone than I was. That it was too late to do anything about it and, because he is a good man, he believed me.' She looked so small and so sad, it hurt Alma to see. 'I loved him so much. I was eighteen years old and I couldn't wait to be a mum! It was all I ever wanted. I know I'm not supposed to say that, I know I'm not ambitious but...'

'Sammy.'

'There I was, dreaming of what colour wallpaper I'd have in the little house of my dreams, with the man of my dreams! What we'd call the baby of my dreams! Never stopping to think about what Gary's dreams might have been. I trapped him! I know I did, and now... Now I think I'm paying for it.'

'No.' Alma reached her hand out. 'No. Don't say that. Gary is happy.'

'Is he?' Slowly, Sammy turned to her. 'Is he, Alma? You've seen him, since the kids left. He's a lost soul. She pressed her hands to the ruby pinpricks spreading across her cheeks. 'I don't think we want the same thing anymore. I'm not even sure he wants me anymore.'

'Sammy.' Squeezing Sammy's hand, Alma said, 'That's not true.'

'Isn't it? I don't know. Do you know why I put this Eighties thing on my list?'

Alma shook her head.

'I wanted to go back. I remember dancing to 'Club Tropicana', feeling like there really was enough sunshine for everyone, and I just wanted to go back to that feeling.'

Alma nodded. Her eyes were hot with tears.

'I wanted to pretend that I was fourteen. Starting out again.'

'I understand,' Alma said.

'No, I don't think you do.' Urgent now, Sammy leaned across the table. 'I think that's why Meryem is here too, Alma. I really do. I think she's trying to find a way back to a time when she was happy as well. I think, Alma, that she is a very unhappy person.'

Truer than a tuning fork, clear as a bell, the words reverberated, and it shamed her to realise that Sammy had picked up on something she hadn't. In the scant time they had spent together, Alma hadn't scratched beneath the surface of what Meryem's life was really like now, never mind all the years in between. The tiny glances she'd snatched were enough for her to know that it hadn't been good, and she didn't doubt what Sammy was saying.

'It's George Mightbe tonight.' Sammy's smile was small. 'She's really looking forward to it.'

Alma nodded.

'We'll go to the spa. Have the afternoon we planned. And...'

'Let Meryem have tonight,' Alma finished.

'Yes. Let her have tonight.'

15

JESUS TO A CHILD

Blackpool, present day

'STAND BACK! The door, it's going to—'

But Meryem had already pulled the handle of the DeLorean and the gull-wing door swung upward, not outward, missing her by inches.'*Oh!*' she cried as she twisted away.

'Are you okay?' Gary was in the driver's seat and when she didn't answer, he leaned across. 'Did it hit you?'

'No, I'm fine.' Meryem climbed in, reached up and pulled the door closed. Then she sat a moment, palms together, forehead lowered, as if in prayer. 'I forgot,' she whispered, and shook her head.

'It's not too late,' he said quietly. 'If you're uncomfortable.'

Clicking her belt into place, she smiled at him. 'I'm fine. I just forgot about the door.'

'Okay.' Gary started the engine and its low hum filled the silence between them. They pulled out of the car park and onto the exit road and as they did, he lowered his window and Meryem did too. The car filled with all the sounds of the passing world. The rush of wind, the whoosh of oncoming traffic, seagulls circling high above. She rested her elbow on the rim of the window and looked out at the avenues they passed, the school playground, a supermarket car park... and the growing distance from where she was now, and where she had been an hour ago, was a reassurance. It was too late, because Sammy hadn't understood, and she'd been a fool to think she might. Sammy of all people, whose life had stayed so small. One night dancing to 80s pop did not make her a confidant. Even now, she could be telling Alma... Well, she would be ready. If it came, she would be ready. She would be prepared in a way she hadn't been when Hassan had phoned. *Is it true, Mamma? Tell me!* Her mouth turned down hard as she looked down and twisted her emerald ring. *I demand you stop!* His young voice on the end of the telephone line, so confident and self-important, echoing the language of his father: *I demand... You must.* It had been hard to take him seriously. Her little boy, who had once followed her from room to room, who could never sleep unless she was lying alongside, laying down ultimatums like a toy soldier. That was four years ago. He'd stuck to his word and persuaded his sister as well, more resolutely mature – and cruel – than she could have anticipated. She pulled her sunglasses down and tilted her chin to the fresh air. If she'd known, if she'd been made aware of the cost in advance, would she have made the same choice? Despite having had years to consider, the answer was further away than ever, because what she had told Sammy was true. She enjoyed her work. Many of her clients were just lonely, and it wasn't onerous to to ease that burden for a few hours. On the contrary, it would have astonished Sammy if she'd said what she really felt. She took pride in her work. Making herself beautiful for them, talking through their problems and worries. Sex was such a small part of the process. They left happier and lighter of soul, and she was proud of that. Over the years she had made good money and invested it well. She didn't need to carry on with the few that she chose to, but she did because the companionship of those hours was mutually beneficial. Arms holding her, were arms holding her. The transaction behind it more open, more honest and more mutally consensual than any that had gone before. What should she be doing? Scrubbing toilets in a rich Arab woman's house? The idea almost made Meryem smile, cementing as it did the customary determination that she would continue to live the way she chose. For as long as she had left, she would allow no one to dictate. Not even, as painful as it was, her children.

'So, how does it feel to be riding in a time machine?'

Gary's voice startled her. She turned and looked at him and for a brief moment had no idea who he was, and where she was going, and the déjà vu that brought back the feeling of being driven somewhere unknown, the terrifying powerlessness, was so overwhelming her fingers gripped the window rim, and she had to concentrate on his face.

'Are you okay?' He frowned.

Meryem nodded. 'Time machine,' she said weakly.

'Feels good, doesn't it?'

She turned back to the window. Now wasn't then and the fresh wind on her face was an anchor. And this was a second-hand sports car, not a time machine.

The space between the DeLorean and the car behind

grew bigger. The wheels rolled faster, and green fields began to replace avenues of terraced housing. Above, what had been a clear blue sky was now dark clouds. She took off her sunglasses, stretched forward and pressed a switch on the glove compartment. It flipped open. 'This is the ashtray?' she said, sliding the lid open, then closed, then open again. 'I don't smoke though. And you don't need it now either?'

Gary's cheeks bloomed pink. 'No.' He kept his eyes on the road ahead, and she took the chance to look at him.

The discomfort she knew her presence was causing felt familiar. She'd seen it so many times before, back in those early days of her work, when her clients had been strangers. She knew all the faces of a man caught up in a situation he could not control. Those who couldn't look her in the eye, those who'd remained angry throughout, those whose public bravado vanished the moment the hotel room door closed, leaving them rabbits caught in headlights. But Gary Collins had been her first and only consensual kiss and she didn't want a single thing from him, except that he be easy in her company. Tapping the arm of her sunglasses against her lips, staring blankly ahead, she smiled. How to make a man easy in her company was something she was paid to do, but this was not a professional situation. Behind closed doors her husband's attitude to her had at first been one of greed, then entitlement and finally indifference. So being a woman, in the company of a man, with no expectations on either side, was as alien to her as the stars. She was almost lost. As lightly as she could manage, she stretched down to the row of switches on the centre console and as she pressed the switch, said, 'What does this button do?'

'Woha!' Yanking his arm back just in time, Gary's window shot up.

'Sorry.' Meryem re-pressed the switch and his window

rolled down again, and she leaned back, lips twitching. It was funny. She wanted to laugh.

He turned to look at her and, just as he did, she turned to look at him.

'Sorry,' she said again and the corners of her mouth turned up, and then she laughed.

And he did too. His chin dipped as he stretched his arms forward, palms on the wheel. 'It is kind of fun, isn't it? The car?'

'It is,' she said, relaxing back in her seat.

Rain began to fall, and as he switched the wipers on, they beat a steady rhythm against the windscreen.

'It's so green,' Meryem sighed, looking out at the fields. 'I'd really forgotten how green England is.' And turning away, she looked down at the console, the image of Emin's tiny model car, all those years ago, coming back as clear as if the toy were in her hands now. Her hand edged towards the gearstick. Almost instantly Gary's hand shot out, brushing hers away.

'Sorry.' He blushed.

'It's okay.'

'I didn't mean… It's just best not to touch,' he finished.

'Of course.'

For a while they didn't speak. High above, the sky had lightened again and the drops on the windscreen became scarce. The wipers scraped as he flicked them off. Meryem turned back to the window, watching as the rooftops of tiny houses flashed by, as they passed people walking dogs and trees coming into leaf. Here they were, a grown man and a grown woman, neither of them wanting anything more from the other person than their presence, and it was such a wonderful and rare moment in her life she couldn't stop herself from smiling.

'The door didn't put you off then?'

'The door?'

'The gull-wing door. You said you'd forgotten that it swung upward.'

'No.' Meryem shook her head. 'I did just forget.'

'Most people wouldn't have known in the first place.'

'Oh I knew.' Resting her chin in her hand, she continued. 'When my brother was small, he had a toy model. I remember him lying on his tummy, opening and closing the doors. And then, I must have forgotten. Swoosh!' she said, sweeping her arm up. '*Take me back!* That's what he kept saying. *Take me back!* He kept it under his pillow when he went to sleep and *this...*' Like a stick underfoot, her voice broke. She put a hand on her chest and breathed in.

Gary glanced sideways at her, back at the road and then back at her.

'*This*,' she managed, 'this is why I couldn't believe I forgot how the doors worked.'

For another long moment, neither of them said anything, and then Gary said quietly, 'Does he still like them? DeLoreans?'

'I don't know,' Meryem said flatly. 'I don't see him much to ask.'

TEN SILENT MINUTES LATER, they had turned into Fleetwood, passed The Mount and the museum, and were making a final turn onto the road through the town, when the engine suddenly spluttered and the car began to jerk.

Reacting quickly, Gary pressed his foot to the accelerator. In response the jerking became more violent. He tried again, and when the same thing happened, he flicked the indicator on and manoeuvred the DeLorean to the side of the busy dual carriageway where it came to a silent, subdued stop.

'What?' Meryem said as she turned to him. 'What is it?'

'I don't know.' He reached forward, and put the hazard lights on. 'I don't know.'

16

IF YOU WERE THERE

London, 1985

THE LOUD THWANG of a guitar burst through the PA system, followed by a deep base. A riff so infectious, so joyously alive, so instantly recognisable it bounced off the walls of the school gymnasium and had Mrs Jackson, the drama teacher, bobbing along. 'And... click one, two!' she yelled.

Jitterbug!

'Three, four.'

Jitterbug!

'Five, six'

Jitterbug!

'Seven, eight. Let's go!'

Hips swaying, ponytails swinging, hands clapping, Alma and Meryem burst into life as they went through their dance routine.

A WEEK HAD PASSED and although there had been no more talk of going home, Sonja did not feel at ease. On the contrary, as she stood now to clear the dinner table, the discomfort she felt, the creeping realisation that something had started that she might not be able to control, had only grown. The chicken she had prepared had gone uneaten and twice now, with no warning, Arslan had arranged to start his shift later. He was testing her, she was sure. So far, she had passed. They all had. But today Meryem had rehearsals, and all through dinner, as the clock had ticked the minutes away, she had watched her husband's sullen anger deepen, his eyes constantly flicker to the empty space at the table.

'Are you finished,' she murmured, her hand on his plate.

He didn't answer. His eyes had glassed over, trance-like.

'Have you finished—'

Fast as a snake, his hand shot out, cutting off both her words and the blood supply to her wrist.

'*Arslan.*' Her cry was a yelp, like a wounded dog.

Next to his father, Emin slipped off his chair and ran to the doorway.

The movement broke Arslan's trance. He withdrew his hand. 'Did you think I didn't mean it, when I said she must come straight home, Sonja? Did you think I didn't mean it when I said that if you don't make it stop, *I* will?'

Sonja eased herself back into her chair. So, it hadn't gone away. The tomorrow she'd refused to believe in really was here and, to her surprise, she felt unnaturally calm. Even hopeful. As if, now that she could see this new horizon, she could also see how there was, as there always is, a path forward. 'Meryem is a good girl,' she said. 'She works hard, Arslan. You know that.'

'Do I?'

'Of course you do.' She smiled. 'You—'

'How do I?' he cut her off. 'It is you who has raised them, Sonja. You who has allowed this behaviour.'

She blinked. 'What behaviour?' The comment was a stone thrown into a mirrored lake. Any fragile hope she might have been nursing, shattered. In its place anger rose. Fifteen years she had been by his side. Dutifully filling the role of his wife and his lover and his friend. She kept the house clean, she kept the children fed. It was he who had turned away from her in bed, now she didn't even try. Meryem was doing well in school. She had friends and she was happy. Emin the same. What more did he want? What more could, should, she have done for this man?

But he didn't answer. He ignored her. He picked up the last piece of meat with his hand, wiped his plate clean with it, and began chewing.

'It was a study group, Arslan,' she said, watching his plate. 'And if you are unhappy with the way I have raised them, maybe you should have spent more time with them.'

'I was working,' he said quietly. 'So you could spend money. I was working.'

'As I was too!' Elbows wide, Sonja leaned forward. 'You could have changed shifts. Tariq did. I don't like the man, but at least he changed to days, so he could actually see his children.'

'Tariq,' and Arslan's lip curled, 'is under the thumb of his wife. And before that, he was under the thumb of his mother. All his life, he has been under the thumb of one woman or another.'

Sonja leaned back, her arms folded. She didn't like Tariq

at all, but there was no doubt that he had been more of a father to his children than her own husband had been. Even then, it wasn't as simple as that. She knew where Arslan's derision came from. And it was like poking a bear, but she did it anyway. 'You're jealous,' she said. 'He got promoted ahead of you and you've never forgotten that. And now, he's buying land back home, and filling your head with all sorts of stuff about my daughter... Yes, *my* daughter. You're jealous, Arslan.'

Springing to his feet, his hand flung out, squeezing down on her throat, his eyes dilated with anger.

And he had moved so quickly. She was pinned in her chair. She couldn't breathe. One moment she could, and now she couldn't. *Please...* She used her eyes... *Please.*

His fingers relaxed. She gasped a breath, turned, doubled over, and coughed. 'Don't,' she started, but there was no sound to her voice. She put a hand to her chest and breathed deeply and looked at him, looking at her. And there was no fear now and she had a moment in which to think that she had been wrong. That the courage she had always admired in her daughter came not from Arslan, but from herself. She was Sonja. Illiterate and orphaned teenage bride, she was Sonja, a woman who answered transatlantic telephone calls, on the front desk of a transatlantic company. She was Sonja, and she would raise her children the way she saw fit. Her voice was back. She knew this before she had even opened her mouth. 'If you ever—'

But she never finished. The pressure from his hand back on her throat cut her off. She saw silver stars. She saw Emin, in the doorway, pulling the sleeve of his jumper across his face, turning and running. One slippered foot stumbled over the other, every sinew strained, as she clawed at the table, desperate to escape.

And then he let go, and she fell, her scrabbling fingers flipping Emin's discarded dinner plate, peas spilling across the floor.

~

'AND LUNGE TO THE LEFT, twist and turn! Move it now!'

Meryem jump-turned.

Alma mirrored her. A move they had practised so many times, it was almost perfect.

'Jump-kick back, turn it round...' Their teacher, Mrs Jackson, standing at the side of the hall called out.

And on they danced. Fingers clicking, legs kicking, bouncing, jumping, spinning, and the music reverberated and everyone who watched was smiling.

~

THE TABLE RUNNER was on the floor. Sonja saw it in flashes of yellow and red as she held onto the table, steadying herself. Her hair swung loose. '*Arslan*,' she gasped, and turned into the broad slab of his fist.

Nothing held. Her knees folded, her bladder emptied. She crashed back, spine to wall. Her chin flopped down, bounced up, dropped down again and in her hand she felt a strange warmth. Looking down, she saw an offering, a pool of her own dark blood in her open palm. The floor between her legs was wet, her slipper had come loose at the heel.

~

ALMA'S LEGS were were lead. Hands on hips, she stood, catching her breath.

'One more time?' Meryem laughed.

She looked up. Mrs Jackson had left. Rehearsals were over. Everyone else was leaving, and that was exactly what she wanted to do too.

'Come on, Alma!' Meryem barked. She was walking backwards, clapping her hands together. 'One more time? We have to be perfect!'

She glanced at the clock. She was tired. She needed to get home to make a start on dinner. Her mother was working long night shifts. Most days it was Alma putting a pie in the oven, vacuuming the living room, doing her homework. And lately she'd found herself waking on the settee, schoolbooks scattered, the *Nine o'Clock News* starting. She was very tired, and Meryem was very bossy and although it had been her idea that they dance in the show, she was beginning to wish they weren't. 'Okay,' she sighed. 'Last time.'

Meryem pressed play. The guitar twanged out. Alone in the gym, they resumed their positions.

'NEVER CALL me jealous of a man like Tariq,' he whispered. '*Never.*' Arslan took a strand of Sonja's hair and pushed it behind her ear. He cupped his hand under her chin, and raised it, so they were eye to eye.

She tried to nod, to make him understand that she understood now. But as she moved her head, a metal spasm of pain sliced through it.

His hand was on her cheek, stroking her hair and it was the tenderest caress, a touch to turn toward, to rest and lie down upon. 'Maybe you are right,' he said, and his lips turned up in a thin, unsmiling smile. 'Maybe I should be spending more time with the children.'

This time she kept her head still. If she tried to move it, it would, she felt, fall apart like the halves of a sliced apple. She didn't move. Long after she had heard his footsteps cross the room, long after she had heard the bathroom door close, she remained, back against the wall, unable to move.

'Get this cleared up,' he said when he came back in. And he took his keys from the table and left.

AS SOON AS Meryem turned her key in the door and walked into the silent hall, she knew something had changed. The perspex dial of the telephone had the same numbers, in the same order. It still sat on hall table, on top of the red-and-white cloth her mother had embroidered for Christmas, but something *had* changed. She went into the living room. The tapestry cushions were piled neatly on the settee, the lid was down on the turntable, the blown glass ornament was still on top of the TV... Then she saw the crumpled runner on the floor, a flash of yellow stitching, a curved tail of peas and the upside-down plate. She turned and with a pool of pure cold filling her stomach, walked soundlessly along the corridor to Emin's room.

He was asleep in bed, fully dressed, his face blotchy against a dark wet stain on the pillow. Her parents' room was empty. The bathroom door locked. She knocked three times before her mother responded.

'Your dinner is in the oven, Meryem.'

'Mamma?'

But Sonja didn't answer again.

Silently Meryem went to the kitchen and got her dinner

from the oven. She took a knife and fork and went into the living room and sat at the table by the window. The same place she and her mother had sat in the moonlight the week before. Every mouthful stuck. Every mouthful she had to force down. When she finished she took her plate, and the plate from the floor, and washed them. She picked up the peas with her fingertips, one by one, so as not to crush them. And she smoothed out the creases of the runner as she pressed it back on the table. She worked quietly and slowly. It was only as she spread the dishcloth over the edge of the sink that she realised her mother, still in the bathroom, might be waiting for her to go to her bedroom. So she picked up her schoolbag, went into her room and closed the door. A few minutes later she heard the bathroom door unlock and then her mother's soft footsteps along the hallway.

THE NEXT MORNING, she woke to the smell of fresh bread. In the kitchen, her father was slicing a loaf, freshly bought. There was cereal on the table, and chocolate spread. Emin was eating. She sat down opposite and stared at him. He didn't look up.

'Where is Mamma?' she whispered to Emin.

He didn't answer. Keeping his head down, he spooned methodically.

'*Emin?*'

'Your mother isn't feeling well,' Arslan said. 'I'll be taking you to school. Now, who wants fresh bread?'

Meryem stared at Emin. His eyes were still down, but he was shaking his head in a small and silent, *No.*

'We walk,' Meryem said as she picked up the cereal box. 'With Alma.'

The sudden bang made by her father slamming the

bread board onto the table sent a shock through her that had her hand trembling as she tried to open the plastic and pour the cereal.

'I will take you to school, Meryem,' her father said, his voice slow and calm. '*Do you understand?*'

In the car her father put the radio on. The only time he spoke was when she opened the door to get out. 'Straight home tonight, Meryem.'

She looked at her shoes.

'Do you understand?'

'Yes.'

The car tyres scrunched ice and grit as he pulled away. Emin went ahead and Meryem stood. Around her, the world passed in a blur.

Do you understand?

Not completely she hadn't, but enough to know that what had happened at home yesterday, had continued into today.

What's wrong? Alma asked, at the end of every lesson, the beginning of every break. Gary she avoided completely. When school finished, she went straight home.

And then she understood.

Her mother's swollen face, the eyelid that drooped as if it were dying, the delta of broken veins across her cheek and red-blue blotches at her temple. No explanation was needed. Meryem couldn't look, a ball of nausea stuck in her throat. Beside her Emin moaned, his thin little legs crossed tight at the knees.

In one movement her mother crossed the room and caught them both in her arms. 'I'm okay,' she whispered. 'It doesn't hurt. Not at all. It looks worse than it feels. I fell.

Against the table. My slipper came off and I tripped but it doesn't hurt.' On and on she went, stroking their hair, talking to them, answering a stream of questions neither of them had asked. Emin's small back jumped with each sob. And, cheek pressed against her mother's chest, Meryem was silent, her toes itching in fear. 'Go,' Sonja whispered, easing Emin gently away. 'Go to the toilet.'

As he left, Sonja put her hands on Meryem's shoulders. 'I'm okay, Mery,' she said. 'I'm okay.'

'Pappa said I had to come straight home.' Meryem looked at the floor. She could not look at her mother's face, it repulsed and terrified her.

'I know. I think it's best for now if you do as he says.'

'But what about rehearsals?'

Sonja didn't speak, she smoothed her hands over her jumper, stretching down the fabric.

'Mamma?'

Water flushed and the bathroom door flung open. Emin ran back into the room and wrapped himself against Sonja's leg.

'I'm making köfte for dinner,' she said, stroking his hair. 'Who wants some?'

'Me! Me!'

And as if everything was normal, they went into the kitchen, Emin chatting about the goal he'd scored at lunch, Sonja laughing too much. And as Meryem watched she remembered the peas. How easy it would have been to crush them, to leave a stain on the floor. But she hadn't. She'd picked them up carefully, one by one. So *why* was her mother telling them it was a slipper? She wasn't a child. Not like Emin. Swinging her bag over her shoulder she went into her room, slamming the door behind her.

17

HAND TO MOUTH

Blackpool, present day

'TRY IT ONE MORE TIME,' the mechanic called. He was bent over the DeLorean.

In the driver's seat, Gary turned over an unresponsive engine.

A few feet away, Meryem sat on the roadside barrier, behind which rose a steep embankment. The sea breeze tumbled her hair as she pulled her jacket tight. She'd lost count now of how many attempts there had been to get the engine started. Her fingers were numb with cold, as were her toes. She couldn't remember ever being so cold. 'What are we going to do?' she called, trying to keep her voice level.

'Nothing we can do, love.' And wiping his hands with a cloth, the mechanic straightened up and closed the hood. He turned to Gary. 'I'll have to take her in.'

Meryem watched.

Gary slumped back, arms stretched out, hands on the wheel. 'This is all I need,' he muttered.

'I'll give my partner a call,' the mechanic said.

Gary nodded.

'Right-oh.' And pulling out a phone, the mechanic walked away to make the call.

Meryem stood up. The air was so tangy with salt she could almost taste it. It would already be in her hair, matting it to knots. Her face felt dry and weather blown. 'What's going on?' she said as she walked back to the car. 'Who is he calling?' She felt a rising irritation, at the wind, and the situation. At Gary, and the mechanic. Making decisions as if she wasn't even there.

'His partner.' Gary said. 'We need a tow.'

'A tow?'

He got out of the car and closed the door. 'It won't start. It's going to have to go into the garage.' And turning to look out at the expanse of beach, he said, 'I hope it doesn't take long. Sammy's going to kill me.'

'Why?' Meryem shrugged. 'It's not your fault.'

'I know that,' he said. 'But she's been looking forward to this weekend. I don't want to spend the whole afternoon here.'

Hands deep in her pockets, Meryem looked at him closely. 'Neither do I,' she said. 'I don't want to miss the show tonight!'

'Oh.' His face relaxed. 'We won't.' And when she didn't respond, he added. 'It's hours away, Meryem.'

'It's going to be a while I'm afraid.' The mechanic was walking back, head lowered against the wind. 'There's a café about a hundred yards further on, if you want to wait somewhere warmer.'

Meryem turned to him.

'Just keep on this road, past the roundabout and you'll see it.'

But he wasn't talking to her, he wasn't even looking at her. In fact, she realised now, since he had turned up, he hadn't once addressed her directly. She hadn't been driving, but she wasn't invisible either. A cold slow fury started. This was how her husband had behaved towards her. In those last years, he didn't even bother to pretend she existed. Ignoring her in front of their children, their servants, even guests.

'Any idea what *a while* might be,' Gary said amiably.

The mechanic stuck his bottom lip out, palms to the sky. 'Your guess is as good as mine, guv. The truck's on another call at the moment. Over Preston way.'

Gary nodded. He turned to Meryem, 'Shall we wait in the café?'

'Where is Preston?'

And for the first time, the mechanic turned and looked at her.

'Where is Preston?' she repeated.

He laughed.

Her eyes narrowed to slits. Slowly, she turned to Gary. 'Call another one.'

The mechanic stopped laughing. 'Is she serious?' he said, looking at Gary.

'Why,' Meryem said, 'are you asking him, if *I'm* serious.'

'Now look, love—'

She stepped forward. He was nothing, and he was all of them. All the men in her life who had routinely ignored her, spoken over the top of her, or not spoken at all to her. Who had made decisions for her, who had never asked her, who had belittled and abused and worst of all, taken her for a fool. 'I asked you where Preston was,' she said, 'and you laughed at me.'

'I wasn't laughing at you—'

'Call another one.' She turned to Gary.

The mechanic's face narrowed in anger. 'You can try, love, but Dave won't be happy. There isn't a garage in a hundred miles he'd trust with this car.'

Twisting to him, her voice was a hiss of anger. 'Stop calling me, love. I am not your love.'

'Woah.' He thrust his hands in the air, an exaggerated gesture of surrender, his voice mocking as he said, 'Touchy.'

Meryem glared at him. Her heart was pounding and he was twice her size, and if Gary hadn't stepped in between them, she was almost scared of what she might have done. 'Call another one,' she said quietly, her chin level with Gary's shoulders.

'I can't,' he said, equally quiet.

'Why not?'

'Because he's right. The guy who owns the DeLorean only uses this garage. It's not a Volvo, Meryem.'

'I'll pay.'

A few feet away, she thought she heard the mechanic laugh again. 'I'll pay, Gary. There must be someone else.'

'No.' He shook his head.

'But it might take hours!'

'It won't. Trust me. We'll get back in time.'

Pressing her lips together in anger, Meryem turned and took a step away. The easiest thing in the world would be to just trust him. The concert was hours away, they would probably make it.

'You need to listen to him, love,' the mechanic said. 'You'll get back in time.'

You need, you must, I insist, I forbid.

Hair flying, face white with anger, she turned on her heels and walked away along the roadside, the words in her head, a silent and ruthless pace-setter. Hadn't her money bought her the freedom never to have to listen to them again?

'She's hysterical,' the mechanic said.

The same words, just a different man...

'Women, eh?'

Meryem took a step closer to the edge of the dual carriageway.

'Meryem!' Gary called. 'Step back.'

Her mouth was moving as she turned to him, her hair whipping, but anything she might have been saying was obliterated by the ground-shaking noise of a huge double-trailered lorry.

'Come back!'

Another lorry sped past. Meryem dragged her hair from her face and the wind blew it straight back, blinding her. As she stumbled forward she could see the yellow of her sleeves, billowing outward. *You need, you must, I insist, I forbid.* She shivered, and then the shiver was a shudder, and her breath was sticking in her throat and her hands were freezing.

'*Meryem!*'

And all she could see was her sleeves, yellow as sunbeams, blackened edges, that expanded, pooling inward from the edge of her vision, tipping her forward. And all she could hear was *You need, you must, I insist...*

'*Meryem!*'

It felt like an age, it felt as if she had stepped into a void, but finally her hands met with something solid and she stopped tipping and stood holding, her entire body shaking.

'Meryem!'

It was nothing more than a scrap of sound, a whisper in space, but it was enough. Keeping the grip on the solid thing she had found, she raised her eyes. Across two lanes of traffic, Gary stood. He had his hands either side of his mouth, calling to her. In response, she tried to straighten up, but the sudden bellow of a blasting horn, sent her teeth rattling. She was in the middle of the dual carriageway. Two lanes of traffic thundering past in one direction, two in the other. Horns blared, faces loomed, ugly, pink and angry. Her hair was streaming loose, and as she tried to pull it back her hand shook desperately... Her hair might get caught, she might get dragged. Like before. The day she had tried to run away. Getting nowhere on that dust road, her father catching her by her hair. And her wedding day, dragged backwards by him, through her grandparents' house, because she had dared to fight. Had begged and pleaded, and then refused to go through with it. He'd taken a fist of her hair and wrapped it around his knuckles and wrenched her backward, towards her future husband who had stood silently, arms crossed over the mound of his stomach, eyes dead. Emin had been there too, curled up, crying in the corner. Her grandmother and her aunties, watching from the shadows. And her mother? Not there. *Never there. Never ever there.* Meryem blinked, her eyes sore with the grit that spewed from the road. She could not let go of the barrier and she could not move. With a tiny movement, she raised her chin and saw, in the windscreen of an approaching lorry, a red face, one arm stretched rigid, fist on the horn. Another memory thrust itself forward. The driver's fist was her husband's, coming toward her face.

A heaving started in her stomach. She grabbed at her hair again and retched, hurling bile and fluid to the broken pitiful grass. Why was everyone always so angry with her?

And then suddenly, there was a hand upon her back, and it wasn't a memory, it was real and it was warm and it stayed. It didn't try to move her, and it didn't move. It was the steadiest hand she had ever felt and she knew it was Gary's. She straightened herself an inch and the hand became two, and then they became arms that wrapped around and held her very tight and very still.

PART THREE

18

EDGE OF HEAVEN

Blackpool, present day

INSIDE, giant paper stars, in warm orange, hung above the dance floor. Outside, transformed by the sun's last rays, the evening was golden. The oily trickle in the car park gutter, as darkly iridescent as frankincense. Meryem waited at a window table. The only other person in the room was a middle-aged man, moving across the raised stage as he set up a sound system.

Gary had insisted.

He was at the bar now, buying them both a drink. They needed it, he said. And it was all he had said. From the moment he'd steered her back across the central reservation, and all through the hours they had spent in the café, sipping hot tea, watching Volvos and Fords travelling through nothing more than a suburban Saturday afternoon. Cars filled with children and dogs, grandparents and grocery bags, driving to football training and supermarket shopping. Ordinary people, in an ordinary world, that felt to Meryem as alien and out of reach as the hidden depths of the deepest ocean. A world that she would never be a part of, that even a DeLorean could never take her back to. She leaned back, scooped her hair into a loose knot and smiled. A rented DeLorean? What had she been thinking when she'd rung the number on the flier and booked the car. That it could take her back? Nothing could, and now she wasn't even sure that she should stay here. Sammy had not understood. And Alma? The distance between them felt insurmountable to Meryem. The closeness they had once shared lived only in memory, and the deep sadness she felt as she considered this was that it was better left alone. Safe to revisit perhaps for the duration of an old pop tune heard on the radio. But not like this. Not this deep dive into something that no longer existed for either of them. And wasn't this true of her reasons for coming back in the first place? The overwhelming disappointment that had felled her yesterday returned, filling her eyes with hot tears. Why had she come? What had she been hoping to find? The fact that her mother had written had been such a revelation, had been clouds parting after a lifetime of grey, it had dazzled and blinded her, carried her so quickly, and so thoughtlessly, to where she was now. But what did it matter? Now that she had had time to think it all through, what did it matter anyway? Because there was still a cold and hard truth that she could not pass. Her mother never came.

She hadn't believed everything she had been told. Of course not. Neither her father's increasingly angry, and increasingly exaggerated, explanations as to why her mother hadn't come to join them. Nor her female relatives' sadly resigned confirmations. But with nothing else to fill the void, what choice had she had other than to accept what she was being told?

None.

A burst of thin, tinny music floated across the empty room. Meryem turned. The man on the stage had stopped what he was doing to slouch-sit on a speaker, shoulders hunched, as he scrolled through his phone, his jeans slipping low to reveal grey underpants. As he stood again, he looked up and caught Meryem's eye and smiled, and it was such a sad smile she wondered what kind of message he'd just read, or if was always this sad. She didn't have time to decide. Gary was halfway across the dance floor. A glass of wine in one hand, an orange juice in the other. As he walked towards her, she noticed, in a way she hadn't before, the thickness of his silhouette.

'It's not quite champagne,' he said as he gave her the glass, and slid into the seat opposite.

Meryem smiled. 'It doesn't have to be.'

'Sammy is resting.' Gary leaned forward to tuck his shirt in.

'That's good.'

'I just popped in to see her.'

Meryem nodded. 'We were gone a long time I think.'

'Yes.'

For a moment, she held his eye. Then, looking away, her hand went to her phone, turning it through one half turn, and then another. When she looked up, he was still looking at her, and his face was open, his blue eyes filled with such tender concern, she could see all the way back to the boy with the flop of hair. 'Gary,' she said and smiled. He had grown into a good man, showing her in one afternoon more kindness and patience than she'd received from her husband in all the years of marriage. 'I'm sorry,' she said. 'The way I behaved was very wrong.'

Gary leaned forward, both hands cupping his glass. 'You don't need to apologise.'

Meryem looked away, across the empty dance floor. 'The last person that called me hysterical was my brother. It wasn't so long ago.'

'Not all families are perfect,' he said. 'Far from it.'

Meryem turned to him. 'The family you made with Sammy though, that was good.'

'Yes. It was... It is good.'

She looked down at her phone again, her fingers tracing the edge. 'When was the last time you saw your son? The one in Australia?'

Taking a deep breath, Gary leaned back. 'Two years, I think. I'm not sure.'

'Don't lose touch with him.'

'I won't.' He started. 'We try to—'

'I mean it,' Meryem said, looking at him. 'Don't let him go.' Her voice was thick with emotion, and it came trailing an echo, *Don't let me go, Mamma. Don't let me go.*

Holding her eye, Gary didn't speak, and before he could, the room was plunged into darkness.

Above their heads, the paper stars lit up and the first syncopated downbeats of 'Careless Whisper' burst through the speakers. On the stage, the man in the jeans, George Mightbe, picked up a plastic saxophone. He looked across, smiled and raised his palm to them as he offered up the empty dance floor.

Gary stared at him.

'He wants us to dance,' Meryem smiled.

He turned to her. 'Shall we?'

His face, he had such a kind face... and it would, she

thought, be so nice to held for a moment by someone with such a kind face.

'For old time's sake, Meryem,' he winked. 'That's all.'

SHY AT FIRST, they moved together clumsily, his hand holding hers, warm and heavy, the rough callouses across his palm revealing a lifetime of manual work. George Mightbe sang and under paper stars, leaning against a boy she had once known, it felt to Meryem that the lyrics had been written especially for her. There was no comfort in the truths she had been told, and there never had been. It was better now to leave it all alone, to leave it behind. And as the music flowed around them like water, he pressed her hand to his chest and when he spoke, his lips brushed her ear. 'I never forgot you, Meryem. I want you to know that. I never forgot.'

Meryem stiffened.

He pulled back and looked at her. 'How could I? I'd never met anyone like you. You were brilliant.'

'Don't.' She put her hands on his chest and tried to push out of the embrace. And as his arms relaxed and she eased back, he looked so bereft, so childlike in his misery, that she took hold of his hands and squeezed them. 'I was good at maths,' she said, laughing. 'That's all, Gary. That's all.'

'No.' He shook his head. 'No, Meryem. You were a star, and we all knew it. You were in a different league. I don't know where you did go, but back then you could have gone anywhere. You could have done anything!'

'Gary...'

'And I hope you did!' he continued, his voice breaking, his eyes fierce with tears. 'I *really* hope you did go somewhere great.' He put his hands on her shoulders, gripping them. 'The trouble is I thought I'd be going with you. Up and out of Enfield. I was *so* ready for that, Meryem. I didn't have it easy at home, and I looked at you and thought that if you could do it, I could too.'

'You—'

'I didn't.'

'Gary.'

But he wouldn't look at her, his head had dropped. 'All my life,' he said quietly. 'I've always tried to do the right thing, not always the thing I wanted, but the right thing.' He stopped talking, thrust his hands deep into his pockets and looked at her. 'You wouldn't have done that, would you, Meryem? You wouldn't have wasted your time, or your life. You never wasted time.' Tears had filled his eyes again, and in a clumsy move to blot them away he brought his arm to his eyes and held it there. It was a move that made Meryem think of Emin as a small boy. The way he'd tried to hide his tears for weeks and months, until eventually his tears had run dry and he no longer needed the comfort of her arms. Her heart swelled so, she thought it might burst. 'Gary,' she said and put her arms around him. 'I don't understand how you can say this. Sammy and you have something wonderful. All these years and you still love each other. Not many people can say this. And your children.' She pulled back, tears in her own eyes now. 'You created a family. A family that want to be together. That love each other. Don't you see? Don't you understand how special this is?'

He kept his hand at his face and he sobbed.

And again, Meryem stepped forward and put her arms around him and held him, and it could so easily have been Emin, and for a moment she didn't know who it was that was crying in her arms. Emin? Or one of her children, when they were tiny? It didn't matter. She was needed, and she was wanted, and that was all.

'I've been so scared,' he said as, pulling back, he regained his composure.

'Of losing Sammy?'

'Yes.' He nodded. 'I don't know what happened. I was terrified for her and... this is selfish, but I was terrified for me as well. Of all the things I hadn't done. We hadn't done. I don't know. One minute you're a kid, catching the bus to school, the next you're looking out the window on a Saturday morning, in an empty house, wondering what the hell happened. And then you turn up and it's like...'

'Me?'

Gary gave the smallest of laughs. 'Yes you, Meryem. You obviously did what none of us had the courage to do. You went out and grabbed life with both hands. You...' He shook his head. 'I don't know. You're doing so well. Private jets and—'

'I'm an escort, Gary.'

Gary's mouth stayed open as he looked at her, confusion making a statue of him.

The only thing that moved was the working of his mind. So clearly she could see it all. The desperate de-scrambling of her words going on, the befuddled attempts to put them together in a different way, to make them say something else. 'I am an escort,' she repeated, and it was like the thud of a vault closing for eternity. 'And yes,' she whispered, softer now, 'my work involves what you are thinking, Gary. I'm sorry. *That's* where I went.' And she watched as his face drained.

'You said hospitality,' he whispered.

'It is.' She smiled. 'It really is. But it's also a very long story, and one day I may tell it to you, but this is my life. This is my life now.'

A moment passed. Behind them, footsteps sounded across the dance floor, a door squealed open and then closed. She lowered her head so it came to rest on his shoulder, the fabric of his shirt cool against her forehead. 'I'm sorry,' she said, because she was. She was sorry for the way her words had hurt him, sorry for the unhappiness he so obviously felt in what looked to her like a good marriage, a good life. And she was sorry that he had allowed himself to think he had wasted his life, when he so clearly hadn't. And she was thinking something else. *I never forgot you.* That's what he had said. And then she was thinking of Alma and her head pressed heavier against his chest. Alma had been closer than anyone. Alma would have taken the brunt of the fallout. What had it done to Alma? It wasn't a question she had ever asked.

Music began again, a generic tape of 1980s covers, floating softly over the sound system.

Gary straightened up, opened his eyes and looked at her. 'I'm sorry,' he whispered. 'I'm so sorry that happened to you, Meryem.'

You can't. I won't allow. I forbid.

Holding his hands in hers, Meryem stepped back to see him clearer. Light had entered her heart, she could feel it spreading through her body, lifting every fibre. There wasn't a trace of judgement in his face, not a shade of condemnation. No narrow anger, distorting it, no pious pity flattening it, no thin disgust twisting it beyond recognition. She kept men company, because she had chosen to. She sold her body, because she had chosen to. Her life, after all, had been decided by the sale of her body. It continued now on her terms. She was who she was. She wasn't ashamed or embarrassed and although she thought she never had been, it was only in experiencing his response that she knew she never had been. 'Please,' she said and squeezed his hands. He looked so sad. 'Please don't feel sorry for me. I don't feel sorry for myself. So why should you?' And before he could speak, she added, 'You can go anywhere, Gary. You still can. You and Sammy can go anywhere.' And slipping free, she turned and walked back to the table.

'THAT'S GOOD, GARY.' She nodded, but she was only half listening. She was thinking of Alma, and all her thoughts were coloured with a fragile excitement. Maybe there was still a chance to rediscover the friendship they had once shared.

Out in the foyer, Gary called the lift. 'It's ironic,' he said.

'What is?'

'That you asked about my son. I was planning to go and visit him. *We* were planning to go. Sammy and I... And then she got cold feet.' He shrugged. 'I'd even started thinking I'd go by myself.' He stopped talking, his hands pushed deep into his pockets as he stared at the ground. 'And then she got sick. And I couldn't leave.'

Meryem looked at him. 'It will be okay,' she said.

'Will it?'

'Sammy's going to be okay, Gary. And then you can both go to Australia.'

'She doesn't even have a passport, Meryem.'

'She can get one.'

'Yes,' he said sadly. 'Yes, she can.'

The elevator arrived. Smoothing down her blouse,

Meryem stepped in. 'You know,' she said as she pressed the button. 'On the way, you could both stop by and see me in Dubai?'

'Yes,' he said, his shoulders rising as he took a deep breath. 'We could do that. We could definitely do that.'

19

FLAWLESS

Blackpool, present day

Opening the door to her hotel room, a cloud of perfume hit the back of Alma's throat, just as it had the day before, dense and musky, irritating.

'Alma!' Meryem cried. 'George Michael! Finally!' She was dressed in the sapphire- blue bandage-dress of yesterday. Jewels at her ears and her neck. Her bosom piled over the neckline. Her cheeks were buffed, her brows highlighted, her lips glossed, her skin gleamed, her eyes shone and against the pedestrian fittings of the pedestrian hotel, she stood exotic as an un-mined diamond. 'Are you excited?'

Instinctively Alma took a step back. She hadn't seen Meryem since last night. Since she left so abruptly and since... her eyes went to the closed door of the wardrobe, inside which she'd placed the box of her mother's possessions. The box that contained such a small but essential part of Meryem's mother's possessions. She had no idea what to do. Should she give the letters to Meryem now? She'd promised Sammy that she'd wait, and at the time that hadn't been difficult. But it felt wrong. It felt very wrong.

'And you're better now?' Meryem swept into the room. 'Thank goodness! I was worried, you know. You did look very pale last night. Gary has reserved a table for dinner and the show starts at eight.'

'Yes, I got the text.' Pressing her damp hair against the towel in her hands, Alma watched as Meryem walked across the room. Sammy had texted. Sammy had texted several times. More than several times.

Where are they?

Has Meryem called?

Gary's phone is going straight to voicemail.

What's taking them so long?

WHAT is taking them so long?

'It took a long time,' she said. 'To get back and everything.'

Standing at the window, Meryem turned. 'It was a nightmare, Alma! First, as you know, the car breaks down! Then the repair man had to call someone, but the person he called was on another job and he couldn't make it. And we didn't have any choice, you know? The man who owns it won't use any other garage.'

'I see.' Alma looked at her.

'It did take a long time,' Meryem sighed. 'Hours.' She

turned to look out of the window. 'You have a nice view up here. All I can see is the car park.'

Alma didn't answer. Fleetwood was half an hour away. Car problems or not, Meryem and Gary had been gone for most of the afternoon and with each text Sammy had sent, Alma had sensed her unease increasing

Don't worry.

she'd texted back.

Meryem says they are waiting for a tow-truck. Try to relax. Have a nap.

'I'll dry my hair. She slipped into the bathroom. A moment later she was out again, opening the wardrobe door to double check that the box was where she had left it, that the lid was closed, that... what? That Meryem hadn't found them? Surely the best thing to have done was to have given them to her straight away. To not have hidden away in her room all morning like a frightened rabbit, waiting until she knew Meryem had left with Gary. Yes, like a frightened rabbit waiting to cross the road.

'I am so exited!' Meryem turned, her hands pressed together. 'If he sings 'Wake Me Up Before You Go-Go', we have to dance the Jitterbug after all. Promise you'll dance, Alma?'

'I need to get ready,' Alma said and once again slipped into the bathroom. But the towel stayed limp in her hands as she stood looking at her reflection. Jitterbug? Meryem was like a child who still believed in Father Christmas. And it was so fragile, this bubble of an evening she had invested so much in. The thin skein wrapped around so much hope and anticipation was as vulnerable as a snowflake. Rather than look at herself a moment longer, she closed her eyes. If she gave the letters to Meryem tonight, or tomorrow, what would be the difference? Don't answer that, she whispered. The difference could be everything, or nothing at all, and in between everything or nothing at all, was Sammy, who had pleaded that Meryem needed tonight, never acknowledging her own needs. Sammy needed tonight. And, she had to concede, Meryem too, because the discomfiture she felt, the anger at Meryem's blithe indifference to the wreckage her disappearance had caused, was tempered by something else. She opened her eyes and once again looked in the mirror. Only now she was looking at a reflection that she couldn't see. What she saw instead, what she hadn't stopped seeing since she'd found them last night, were the four handwritten notes she had forgotten about. Every one of them ending with the same apology. And what she could hear, what she hadn't stopped hearing all through a long and sleepless night, was Mery's voice, playing through the speaker of her mother's answerphone, one whole day too late.

Alma? Pick up Alma... Alma, please, if you can hear me, please, please, pick up... I'm scared ... If you're here, it will be alright. I know it. Alma...

Memory had come back, piece by shattered piece. And Sammy had been right when she said that what had happened last night wasn't her fault. It wasn't. She didn't know why, Meryem talked that way about Sonja, but she did know something else. She knew it in her bones, so long had she lived with it. When she was most needed, she hadn't been there. She knew why she hadn't answered Meryem's call, and she always had. *You owe her,* she whispered. *You owe her tonight.*

'Who owes?' Meryem leaned around the door.

'I... It...' Panicked, Alma reached for her toilet bag.

'George Mightbe, Alma! Finally!'

'You look so glamorous.' Alma forced a laugh. 'I was saying I should make an effort. I owe it, for George.'

Meryem nodded. 'Don't be long. We don't want to miss him.'

Alma took out a bottle of ancient foundation, and a dried-up mascara. There was nothing else. 'You go ahead,' she said, pretend-rummaging. 'I'll meet you there.'

'I'll wait,' Meryem said and disappeared.

She put the toilet bag back on the shelf, turned to the mirror and dropped forward, forehead against the glass.

'Alma!' And then Meryem was back, standing in the doorway holding a small blue tube that she tapped with fuchsia-pink nails. 'You should try some of this serum before you put any make-up on. It's magic.'

Alma looked from the tube of serum to Meryem's nails. Yesterday they had been gold. 'I really don't use—'

'Is that it?' Meryem stared at the botttle of foundation, half used, cakey with age.

'I—' And Alma, too, turned to look at it. 'I don't use much—'

'Never mind!' Meryem was at her side, interrupting her, looking at her in the mirror, so close they were almost cheek to cheek. 'I have everything you need!' She disappeared, returning less than a moment later with her handbag. 'Mascara!' she said triumphantly as she took out a gold lamé cosmetic purse. 'Concealer, blusher. Lipgloss. Contour stick.' Holding up a brown-coloured stick, she said, 'Have you seen the YouTube videos. It's amazing, Alma. You can totally change the shape of your face!'

'I'm not sure I want to,' Alma said.

'No.' Meryem put her head to one side. 'But you must

have a bit of mascara. Every woman needs mascara. If I was on a desert island, I would take mascara.'

And before Alma knew what was happening, Meryem's face was inches from her own.

'Close your eyes,' Meryem commanded.

Alma stiffened, but she didn't resist. What was the point? It would be quicker to simply... and suddenly she felt the tickly sweep of a mascara wand on her lashes.

'Keep them closed!'

So she did. And Meryem swept and dabbed and swept and dabbed, and Alma's mouth twitched and twitched, and finally broke into a smile. She was remembering something. Her and Meryem in front of the dressing table, in her childhood bedroom. Standing just like this, Meryem sweeping make-up across her closed lids, strips of black-and-white photo-booth pictures tucked into the mirror frame behind them. Her mouth twitched again, breaking into a small smile.

'What?' Meryem pulled back, smiling herself.

'I just got a really clear image,' she said. 'You doing my make-up, at my mum's old flat. Dressing up I suppose, for something.'

Looking down, Meryem's smile was small as she screwed the lid of the mascara back into place.

Look at me, Alma wanted to say. Because if she did, if Meryem would just stand still, just *be* still long enough, everything else she wanted to say would surely follow: *I'm sorry. I let you down. I've missed you.* 'I'm looking forward to this,' was all she managed, her voice barely a whisper.

'Me too,' Meryem answered, quietly, as she concentrated upon the next coat of mascara. 'Me too, Alma.'

20

CLUB TROPICANA

Blackpool, present day

AT THE END of the huge semi-circular bar, Sammy sat next to Gary, self-consciously crossing and re-crossing her legs. She was wearing her new Versace jeans, and he hadn't said a word! Not as they had gotten changed and not through dinner, which had been a stilted affair that she'd struggled to get through.

Meryem had done most of the talking. Wearing that dress she'd bought yesterday, and holding court like a queen, she'd babbled on about Dubai and how they must all come and visit, never once addressing the fact that she and Gary had been gone nearly the whole afternoon. Was she just supposed to swallow the story about the garage? About having no charge left on his phone? Nearly three hours for a ten-mile trip to the beach? They could have walked back quicker. But then Meryem didn't do walking, did she? Well then, he could have put her in the driver's seat and pushed the bloody car! She didn't know what she was more angry about. The fact he'd been gone so long, or the fact that he hadn't explained it. Not to her satisfaction anyway. And it was definitely anger she felt, fuelled by an emotion that was as alien as it was new: jealousy. She was jealous. Her marriage had been the safest, the happiest place in her world and now it wasn't. Maybe it even went some way in explaining her reluctance to seek out new horizons. Travel was for those who wanted to be somewhere else, when all she'd ever wanted was to come home to Gary. To fall asleep next to him, to wake beside him. The idea that the bedrock of her life might be cracking, that she might be losing him to someone like Meryem, terrified and enraged her. Couldn't he see what he was throwing away? And for what? Women like Meryem ate men like Gary for breakfast.

Wham! was playing through the sound system. A warm-up she supposed for the main act to follow. 'Club Tropicana' now, of all things. Meryem and Alma were in the ladies. She had, she guessed, five minutes to coax him round, to bring him out of the withdrawn mood he'd been in since he got back. To find out what was going on... or what had gone on.

'Club Tropicana?' Sammy snorted, trying to raise a smile out of him.

He didn't look up.

She leaned back to look out of the window. 'Don't think so,' she muttered, tilting her head at the rain-soaked car park.

'What?'

'Club Tropicana. The sea and all that? I thought this place was supposed to be next to the sea?'

'It's close enough, isn't it?' he muttered and turned back to his tomato juice.

Sammy let out a long low breath, and the feeling of dread that had nestled in her stomach all afternoon turned over once again. Her fear felt as deep as the ocean. This wasn't her husband. This rude and irritable man, hunched over the bar. This was so far off from the man she thought she knew as to be a stranger. And the irony was this had been his idea! This weekend, the whole 80s thing. She wasn't sure what had happened, but she was absolutely certain it began with an M and ended with an M. *Meryem.* Jaw set, nails digging into her palm, she picked up her drink. 'Living with you right now, Gary Collins,' she hissed, 'is like living with a bear with a big sore head.' And she raised her hands, spacing them either side of her ears, to demonstrate just how big the head she was thinking of was. He didn't respond, he didn't turn, he didn't smile, he didn't move.

Gary picked up his plastic stirrer, chin on hand as he stirred... and stirred.

Sammy stared straight ahead. Me-r-y-e-m. Who sold herself for money. Whose moral compass pointed any which way but north. Her mouth turned down hard. What a bloody fool she had been encouraging them to go off together.

Shadows stretched across the polished wood of the bar, and at the far end a young bartender stood, her shoulders rounded over, the phone in her hand a blue rectangle of light. A group of four stood on the other side, all rosy cheeks and sweaty hairlines. The men wore floral shirts over paunchy stomachs, the women had honey-blonde high-lights and clear drinks. Steadying herself, with one hand on the bar, Sammy took another sip of wine. Maybe, just maybe, it had been as Gary had said. Maybe the delay had been nothing more than an overlong wait for services. Sadly, she looked across at him. George Mightbe needed to be better than good. At this rate, he needed to be a miracle-worker. 'So,' she said, cheerfully, 'the guy who owns the DeLorean? He was okay about things?'

'He said so.'

'And we'll be able to stick to our plan for tomorrow?'

He looked at her. 'Yes.'

Sammy nodded. Something about the way he wouldn't hold her eye stirred a panic, needle-thin. She wanted to know. She needed to know. Alma and Meryem could turn up any moment, but she needed to know, *now.* Turning to Gary, her voice artificially light, she said, 'Do you remember much about Meryem before she left. Her family I mean?'

He shrugged. 'I know her father took her and her brother back to Turkey.'

'Alma found some letters, Gary,' she said. And when he didn't respond, she continued. 'I wasn't going to say anything, not tonight anyway, but that box we had in the loft? There were letters in there, that Meryem's mother wrote. They got returned. All of them.'

Slowly, he turned to look at her.

'Her mother committed suicide.' Sammy's voice faltered. The words, spoken aloud, were far, far colder than when nursed in her head. 'It was awful,' she said, looking down at her glass. 'Alma doesn't think that Meryem knows. That's what yesterday was about, why Alma—'

'Why she left so suddenly?'

Sammy nodded.

'How can she *not* know, Sammy?'

'I don't know. She thinks it was to do with alcohol. That's what Alma said. You heard her, last night.'

Gary folded his arms and tilted his chin to the ceiling. He didn't speak.

'She never saw her mother again, you know. After her father took her, Meryem never saw her mother again.'

'I didn't know that,' he whispered. 'I did not know that.'

'No.' Sammy pressed her lips together. She could hardly hold her glass, the shock at the depth of emotion in his reaction, the dismal guilt she felt at even speaking about Meryem's mother... She swivelled on her stool and turned away herself. Towards the room, which was full of women her age. Women in glittery tops, who leaned in to talk to each other, and threw their heads back in laughter, whose arms and stomachs jiggled and swayed. Women having a great time. The kind of time she was supposed to be having. Her arm felt tingly and light, but she managed to get her glass back down on the bar to fold her arms across her chest, across the dense padding of her clumpy bra. On lockdown, because she couldn't cry, she *wouldn't* cry.

'What?' he said, turning. 'What's the matter?'

What was the matter? Because she didn't trust what she might say, she pushed her lips together and shook her head.

'What is it, Sammy?' This time his voice was kinder.

What was it? It was everything. It was Meryem's poor mother, whom she couldn't get out of her head. It was Alma, living with that and never telling a soul. But mostly it was him! Her husband and the way he'd changed and the thought of what might have happened this afternoon. She looked at him now, his face as darkly serious as she thought she'd ever seen it. As it was the day they told her she had cancer. He didn't laugh anymore. Or, more to the point, she couldn't make him laugh anymore. The truth of this last thought struck her like a bullet. That was it. She wasn't the same person, either in her head, or in her body, and the one thing that the old Sammy had never failed to do, this new Sammy couldn't make happen to save her life – or her marriage. She couldn't make him laugh. And wasn't it just last night that Meryem had him roaring with laughter! Crying with it!

And it was so obvious, she was stunned. How could she have expected to still make him laugh, when she'd stopped laughing herself? Her sense of humour had packed up and left the day of her diagnosis, and it had taken Meryem to show her this. Meryem, who was the strangest person she'd ever met, whom she wasn't even sure she liked, but who squeezed fun from life like other people squeezed pips from fruit. It was barely a day since Harrods and the kind of legs-crossed, bladder-challenged laughter she hadn't experienced in years. What had happened to her? Sadness draped her. Because wasn't that what Gary had always loved about her? Her sense of fun? There were things he said, she'd never forgotten. That she was lucky. That she'd been made exactly the right shape for the life she led, not too small for it, not too big. Very few people, he used to say, were so content. He'd been right as well. She had been content. Her house, her kids, even her job had given her joy. She was Sammy – who never left the house without a smile on her face – and not everyone could say that. And he had been her troubled, restless boy. Her Irish rover, who'd settled with a girl who was born settled... except now, neither of them were, and that was as painfully clear as the paper stars above their heads.

'Gary,' she murmured, but she didn't get any further. Her head turned to watch the group at the end of the bar, just as their heads had turned to watch something, someone else.

FOLLOWING THEIR LEAD, Sammy glanced first across the room, and then down at her blouse, her jeans. Versace or not, there was no comparison, and she knew it. Not with Meryem, flashing smiles and spilling flesh as she walked towards them now, Alma close behind as they made their way back from the ladies. The dress was a triumph and Meryem was stunning. A cyclone, the focus of the room. She turned to Gary, noted immediately how he was *not* looking, and her guts swirled anew.

'I hope we haven't missed anything!' Meryem called as she drew near.

Gary stood, frowning at his empty glass of tomato juice.

A step behind, Alma caught Sammy's eye and managed a small smile. 'I don't think he's started yet, has he?' she said.

'Not yet,' Sammy echoed, her face a mask.

Now Gary turned. 'I'll get some drinks in,' he said, his voice tight. 'The usual champagne?' he joked.

No one laughed, except Meryem who shook her head and said, 'Wonderful! Yes, but I'll get a bottle, for everyone.' And stepping forward, she put a hand on his shoulder, moved to the bar and called the bartender over so quickly that Sammy and Alma were left looking at each other.

'Everything okay,' Alma said quietly, looking at Sammy.

'I hope so,' Sammy said, and her voice was so small she might have been speaking to herself.

Meryem pulled up a stool and sat down, her hand on her chest as if the exertion was too much. Smiling she reached across, patted Gary's arm and took a deep dramatic breath. 'I have an apology to make to you, Sammy,' she said. 'I should have said so earlier.'

Sammy didn't speak. She was looking at Meryem's hand, on her husband's arm, this over-dressed, over-made-up, over-confident woman. Sailing in like a cartoon goddess, swallowing up minnows in her net, including her own husband. 'No need,' she said her jaw tight, her eyes still on the hand.

'If I hadn't booked the car, it never would have happened,' Meryem continued, as if she hadn't heard Sammy, or as if Sammy hadn't spoken.

Gary shifted his weight from one foot to the other.

'So I wanted to apologise. I hope it hasn't spoiled your weekend.'

Alma looked at her glass.

Sammy looked at Meryem.

'Anyway!' Meryem finished and turned her palms to the ceiling. 'Let's have some champagne.'

Exactly on cue, orange and violet light began strobing the dance floor, and a gloriously handsome man sprang onto the stage. He was naked from the waist up, save for a sleeveless leather gilet, silver cross earring and aviator sunglasses. He was George Mightbe, and his voice instantly filled the clubroom.

'Oh I love this one!' Meryem slipped off her stool, hands clapping, hips swaying, lips syncing.

No one else moved.

The bartender pushed a loaded tray towards them. Meryem turned and reached for it. 'Gary and I were talking,' she said, as she picked up the champagne bottle and began pouring. 'He's thinking, when you're better, Sammy, that it would be good for you, if you were both to come and visit me in Dubai.'

'Meryem.' Gary's voice was low.

'And Alma!' Meryem added, turning now to Alma. 'You must come too!'

Alma paled. 'I'm not sure that's—'

'You can!' Meryem interrupted. She patted Alma's arm. 'You can do this. I know you can!'

Seated at the edge of the group, Sammy flicked her eyes back to Gary. He looked as uncomfortable as she hoped he felt. Something *had* happened this afternoon, she was absolutely sure of it now. A moment ticked by. *When?* she wanted to say to him. *When* were you talking about me, like that, with her? *How could you,* she wanted to scream. How could you talk about me, like that, with her, She watched Meryem pour another glass and her fury grew. Another moment ticked past. The question erupted. 'Did you say that?' She turned to Gary. 'Did you *really* say that?'

He pushed his hands deep in his pockets. 'Not now,' he mumbled. 'I didn't mean now. You're not well enough—'

'Not well enough?' Sammy laughed, short and brutally hard. She had obviously been discussed, the hopeless invalid that she was. They had obviously spent the afternoon discussing her illness. Maybe even her deformit... Her stomach clenched. She felt lighter than air, the boundaries between herself and the world dissolving, as if she might collapse into a million pieces of nothing. What if Meryem had told him? What if she had told him how deformed she was now? How ugly it looked? Her hand went to her mouth. Oh God, she could just imagine it! Meryem's consoling hand on Gary's arm. *I've seen, Gary. I'm sorry, Gary.* Her hands came together, fingers entwined in a desperate prayer. 'Don't use me, or my cancer as an excuse, Gary!' she whispered. 'Don't use me as an excuse for anything.'

'I'm not using you as an excuse.' He stopped talking and looked at her, his eyes pleading.

Meryem had reached the third glass.

Shaking, Sammy leaned forward and thrust a hand over it. 'Not for me, thanks.'

'No?' Turning, Meryem said, 'The sunshine would do

you good, Sammy. When you're better it will be fun. Life should be fun!'

'Fun!'

Gary reached a hand to her, but she brushed it off. The lightness had vanished, replaced by an anger that rose so fast, it was unstoppable. She didn't need someone she hadn't seen in thirty years telling her what life *should* be! Meryem, with her perfect tits! Meryem, who solved everything with her Platinum Amex card! Meryem who was a prostitute! Not an escort, whatever that was supposed to mean. A prostitute! And suddenly she reached a level of fury she would never have believed possible. White-hot incandescent, and not just with Meryem. With Gary, for going along with it, for betraying her like this. 'Fun?' she hissed. 'Do you think it will be fun for Alma to travel halfway around the world to find out what you are?'

Holding the bottle over the last glass, Meryem's hand betrayed the smallest of tremors.

George Mightbe was on to his next song, the strumming from his guitar suddenly quieter than the bubble of silence that had filmed around them.

Then Gary said, 'It's just a trip, Sammy. Calm down. People go to New York shopping.'

She snapped her head to him. *Shopping?* The least this had to do with was *shopping*. And when had he ever talked about people going to New York, to go... shopping! Meryem had made an utter fool of him. Again, he tried to put his hand on hers, and again she threw it off. 'Do you know where she gets her money from?' she said, and her voice was far louder than she knew. '*Do you?*'

'Yes.'

'She's a...' Sammy stopped, glanced at the group of four

at the end of the bar, leaned closer to Gary and hissed, 'She's a prostitute, Gary. A prostitute!'

In the vacuum that followed, everything happened in slow motion. The way Gary lowered his head, the delayed clatter as the bartender dropped her phone, and Meryem's hands shaking, holding the champagne bottle mid-air, its thin bubbly, trickle the only thing that seemed to move in real time.

Except for something else. Another movement, just as real, close by her side. Alma reaching out for a stool. Sammy turned. 'Alma?' she whispered.

Alma didn't speak, she shook her head, opened her mouth, but again didn't speak.

Meryem put the bottle back on the bar.

The bartender stooped for her phone.

Another moment passed and then Gary looked up and said, 'I know. She told me, Sammy.'

'Right,' Sammy snorted. But she wasn't even looking at him. She was looking at Alma. 'I'm sorry,' she said, because Alma's face was frozen with shock.

'I know, Sammy,' Gary said again, and this time Sammy heard.

'*You knew?*'

'Yes,' Meryem tilted her chin. 'He knew, because I told him, Sammy. Just like I told you. In confidence.'

'You...' Sammy's mouth made a soft round shape. She held Meryem's eye and as she did, she felt the heat of a deep flush. Meryem had told her in confidence.

'If,' and Meryem's voice chipped the air between them like a chisel chips marble, 'Gary or Alma want to come to Dubai, then it's *their* choice, Sammy. They are adults. They can decide without you.'

'They... the...' The air left her voice.

'*If* they are okay visiting a prostitute, you can't stop them.'

Sammy blinked. She put her hand at her throat. It was hard as rock, she couldn't even swallow.

'You don't like the idea?' Meryem continued, lining up the champagne glasses. 'I'm not good enough for you? Or your husband? Or even my own friend?' she finished, looking at Alma.

And finally the rock dissolved. 'No,' Sammy said quietly, swallowing down a painful, burning lump of emotion. 'I don't like it. I don't like it at all.'

Meryem turned to her. 'Sammy,' she said and smiled, and leaned in, and her hiss was so close, Sammy felt it move the hairs on her cheek. '*You* don't get to tell me I'm not good enough for anyone! Alma was my friend. *Mine.* And your husband?' Pulling back, Meryem turned and picked up her glass. 'Because of you, he's never even been to see your son in Australia.'

'*Stop!*' It was Alma. Her fingers limp on the bar.

'Australia?' Sammy whispered. 'Sean?'

'Ask him!' Meryem flicked her hair back. 'Ask him!'

Her face white, her heart hammering, she turned to Gary. 'What is she talking about, Gary? What does she mean?'

'He was going to Australia.' Meryem answered. 'Except he can't now because you wouldn't let him go.'

Wouldn't let him go. The words winded her. She put her hand on her chest. 'Are you?' she gasped. 'Were you? I thought we'd decided...'

'It's not the way it seems, Sammy—' Gary started.

'*Stop it, Meryem. Stop now!*' Alma's voice was so commanding, everyone turned to her.

Meryem didn't speak. She nodded, picked up her glass, and turned her back to the group.

Chin wobbling, eyes blinking, Sammy turned away. Across the room, in the middle of the dance floor, a group of women had linked arms as they swayed together, the sheen of sweat upon their cheeks and the glow of orange stars above giving them a youthful aura. They looked younger than she could imagine ever being again. Her vision narrowed. She sat, aware of nothing apart from the women. She didn't see Alma step forward to put her champagne glass back on the bar, she didn't see her turning square now to face Meryem. She was stranded, deaf and dumb to everything but those three words: *Wouldn't let him go.*

'It's enough, Meryem!' Alma said. She was trembling with nerves but Sammy was wounded and it had to stop. She had to make it all stop.

The corners of Meryem's mouth turned up. 'A-a-a-l-ma,' she said, and smiled. as if she were talking to a child, as if... as if they were fourteen again.

Alma looked at her. The astonishment she felt was paralysing. It wasn't as *if* they were fourteen again, for Meryem she *was* fourteen. Thirty years had passed, but if she hadn't understood before, she did now. For Meryem, she was still that little girl, the shadow, the sidekick. It was why, from the moment they had reunited, Meryem had steamrollered over every conversation she had tried to instigate, and why, she understood now, Alma had allowed it. Even the way Meryem had applied her make-up was nothing more than a re-enactment, a role-playing with them both in the same pre-designated roles. And she had been complicit. Once again she had allowed herself to fall under Meryem's spell. She looked at Sammy, at her pale face and her hands balled to fists. Sammy, whose life had been so ordinary, like her own, and whose friendship had been so constant. Turning, she said, 'Sammy is sick, Meryem, and you're hurting her. Can't you see?'

'*Hurting?*' Meryem shrank, her hand gripping the bar in support.

'Yes, hurting! It's not fair, Meryem. Sammy isn't well.'

And then Gary was taking Sammy's arm, easing her off the stool, his arm around her back.

'Did you say that?' Sammy whispered, as she looked up at him, her face white, her eyes full of tears.

He didn't answer. Keeping his hand on her back, he turned to Alma. 'I'm going to find a quiet corner.'

Alma nodded.

Meryem took a deep breath, the line of her jaw set hard. 'What do you know about hurting, Alma?' she hissed, as she watched Gary and Sammy disappear into the shadows. 'Tell me, what do you know about *fair*?' On the bar, her hand had curled tight.

'I know enough,' Alma said quietly.

'You know *nothing*!' Meryem hissed. '*Nothing*!' She lifted her glass and held it at her lips, but she didn't drink. When she put it down, her hand came to her mouth, as if she was trying to smother herself. '*You!*' she hissed, and twisting, jabbed her finger to Alma's face. '*You were the lucky one, Alma!* You got to do all the things that I wanted. You got to finish school. Go to university. You got a career! You got your house by the water. Remember? You weren't forced to marry a man twice your age. A fat man! An ugly man! You weren't cheated out of your whole life, Alma. It wasn't you that all this happened to, and you know *nothing* about what's fair in life! *NOTHING!*'

Alma didn't move. Her mouth opened as if she might speak, but nothing came out.

'That *hurt,* Alma. To have everything taken away. Even my language! I wasn't even allowed to speak English. For years! And my mother...' Meryem gasped and the gasp became a sob. 'Your mother...' She pressed the back of her hand to her mouth and held it there. 'You had a mother who wanted you.'

Caught in the deluge, still Alma didn't move. The wall was down, the dam she'd been chipping away at since they'd first met again. She wanted to reach out and touch Meryem, but it didn't feel possible. That first step, that first movement... 'Your mother,' she whispered, 'she wanted you, Meryem.' It was all, and everything she could do.

'My mother?' Meryem shook her head. 'The last time I saw my mother, Alma, I was fourteen years old. I didn't even know she'd died, until my father told me. I didn't even cry.'

'It wasn't drink.' The words fell out.

'*Who cares!*' Meryem cried, waving her hand in the air. '*Who cares, Alma!* It was a long time ago. Twenty-seven—'

'Twenty-six.'

Eyes wild, Meryem stared. 'What does it matter how many years! What was the point in crying? She wasn't there for me.'

'Whatever you remember,' she started. 'Whatever else you remember... Your mother *did* want you, Meryem.'

'*Then why did she let us go?*' Meryem exploded. '*Why?*'

'Let you go?' Alma shook her head, stars and people blurring at the edge of her vision. 'Your mother didn't let you go. Your father *took* you, Meryem. *He took you!*'

Slowly, Meryem turned. 'There are things you don't know,' she said threateningly.

Heart pounding, blood running canyons in her ears, Alma said, 'And there are things you don't know.'

'She was divorcing my father, Alma. He had no choice. You don't understand the culture. He had no choice.'

Alma didn't hear. She was looking at Meryem, they were a foot apart and everything she had wanted to say from the moment they had met again was ready now to be said. 'Your mother wanted you, Meryem. It broke her heart when your father took you. It—'

'She could have come. Why didn't she come for us?'

Wasn't that enough? *Your mother wanted you.* It should have been enough. 'Why?' she echoed, and from the pit of her stomach a horrible warmth took hold, creeping up to her chest. 'She *did come,'* she choked, and now she could almost see it as a physical thing – the abyss of knowledge that Meryem lived with. She didn't know any of it. 'Meryem,' she pleaded. 'She *did* try. Your mother went to Turkey. She tried to get you back!'

Meryem shook her head. 'We weren't hard to find, Alma.'

'But she did! I was there! I know. I—'

'You know nothing! Why do you keep saying this? Suddenly it is different? Suddenly my mother is the perfect mother?'

'She did all she could!'

'It wasn't enough!' Meryem's voice was ice. 'She left him with us! He ruined my life and she... she left us there!'

But it had been enough. It had been too much, and this was the truth. Alma grabbed the back of her stool, her balance failing as the memory she had spent much of her life trying to suppress rose again. Fully formed, rich and alive with detail. Blood so dark, it was black. The thin line of it, running down the bath. The tear-shape of it, pooled on the floor. Sonja's hair limp against her colourless face. And the note. The note on the door. Releasing her grip she took that step forward, one hand reaching out. 'She cared, Meryem. She cared so much.'

'She cared so much, she drank herself dead!'

'*No!*'

'*Yes!*'

'Who told you that?'

Meryem flinched.

'Your father?'

'What does it matter?'

'It's not true, Meryem. Who told you? Your father?'

For a cold moment, Meryem held her eye, then turning back to the bar, she lifted her glass. 'Yes,' she said, 'he told me.'

Everything narrowed. 'Your mother committed suicide, Meryem,' she said, her voice clear as a raindrop on a window. 'It wasn't drink.'

Meryem held the glass at her lips. Steady.

'It wasn't drink!' And only now did Alma's voice waver. She had moved in closer, as close as she dared. Speaking to a cloud of Meryem's hair, her ear, the perfect line of her painted brow. She had kept those words buried perfectly. But now they had surfaced, they were no longer hers. They belonged to Sonja. And they would, finally, be heard. 'Your mother killed herself, Meryem. And it was me that found her. She put a note on the door, telling me not to come in, but I did.'

Meryem was a statue.

'She did it,' Alma whispered, 'because she couldn't live another day without you, or Emin. She couldn't work and she couldn't sleep. She cried every day, and she tried. She tried so hard to get you back.' The words, Sonja's words, brought themselves to an end. Alma swallowed and it was swallowing razor blades. 'In the end,' she rasped, 'it killed my mother too.' And now she was rocking. She could feel it. Back and forth, back and forth. And Meryem's face loomed close, black with mascara, pink lips, black mascara, pink lips. Then a sweep of hair and she was, Alma understood, gone.

21

LAST CHRISTMAS

L*ondon, 1985*

SONJA STOOD BY THE WINDOW, fingertips meeting around the cup in her hands. She watched as a car made its silent way along the street, imagining the soft crunch of the tyres on snow but hearing nothing. The street was deserted, the snow silenced everything, and there was still no sign of Meryem, or Alma. The steam from her coffee rose, stinging her upper cheek. She lifted her hand and tapped the skin at her eye gently. It was still tender. Still sore. From behind came the sharp sound of canned laughter. She turned.

'Emin, time to turn it off now.'

'It only has five minutes, Mamma.'

Sonja smiled as she looked at her son. He was curled into a ball on the settee, one sock hanging loose, his jeans slipped low to reveal red underpants and a belt of smooth brown skin. The finest line of black hair had begun to grow in the valley of his spine. Last week she'd noticed how the hair on his legs had darkened. 'When it finishes then,' she said gently. 'Straight off?'

Emin nodded, his eyes on the screen, his hanging arm clutching the remote control.

She turned back to the window. Across the street a rat appeared from behind a bin, scurried toward the road and stopped. *Which way will you go, little rat?* And as if it had heard her, the rat looked up. *Make a move,* she whispered. And it did. Running behind a row of dustbins. Smiling she glanced again at the clock, and again at the road. *Where are you, Meryem*? She closed her eyes, put the pad of her fingertip on her eye again and let it rest there. He'd be back from the club within half an hour. *Half an hour.* Her stomach flipped.

Music filled the room. She turned and saw Emin slip off the settee to turn the TV off. He came to where she was standing and leaned against her leg and she wrapped her arm around his shoulder, bent down and kissed his hair.

'Mamma,' he whispered. 'If I write to Father Christmas, do you think he'll bring me a Mr T?'

'Maybe.'

'Pappa says I can't write to him.'

Sonja closed her eyes.

'He says there isn't a Father Christmas.'

The heat from the cup burned her fingers. She changed hands. 'Well,' she said. 'What do you think?'

'I think there is one.'

'Then you should write to him.'

'But if I do, will I get one?'

Mr T was already wrapped and hidden in a box under her bed. 'I should think,' she whispered close to his ear, 'that if you write very politely, in your best writing, that you will get one. But we'll keep the letter a secret.'

'Okay.' Emin let his weight drop against her leg, and threw his arms around her waist.

'Are you tired?' she said.

'Noooope. Is Meryem home?'

'She will be soon.'

Releasing her leg, Emin moved forward to lean on the window shelf. 'Will Pappa hit you again if Meryem isn't home, Mamma?'

Her hands went limp. The cup slipped and she only just caught it, coffee splashing over her hands. It took all her effort to shape the words. 'Pappa doesn't hit me, Emin.'

'Yes, he does.' He had his nose pressed against the window, his perfect little fingers spread wide. Then suddenly, he turned and flung his arms around her waist again and she bent and lifted him. His little arms were around her neck now, his little legs around her hips, clinging onto her as if she might stop existing. She swayed him, her hand cradling the back of his head as he cried into her neck, and she cried into his. He'd seen. Of course he had seen it all.

Pulling back he lowered his chin, looking seriously at her through his eyelashes.

She reached out and pulled his bottom lip down, once, and then again and again, both of them laughing at the funny vibrating sound he made.

'It's okay,' she whispered. 'It's going to be okay.'

'Mamma!' He cried, slipping from her arms easy as silk. 'They're coming! They're coming!' And he raised his hand and pointed.

Heart thumping, Sonja leaned to look. At the far end of the street she could make out two small figures, arm in arm, heads down against the driving snow. 'Are you sure?' she said and took Emin's shoulders and turned him to her. 'Are you sure it's Meryem and Alma?'

He shook himself free. 'Ouch Mamma. Yes, it's them. It's them.'

'Go then. Go and get your pyjamas on.' But she was moving before he was, almost running to the bathroom, as her stomach unclenched itself.

After, as she studied her face in the mirror, the decision she had been trying to make since the moment Arslan had walked out and left her on the floor decided itself. Emin had seen. Maybe for herself, she could have carried on. But Emin had seen and if there was one thing Sonja could not bear to happen, it would be that he grew up accepting that his father hit his mother. *It wasn't okay,* Kathy had said. *I can help you with a solicitor,* her boss had said. And he had. She hadn't asked, but he had given her a phone number and waited as she had dialled the number. And Kathy had taken photograph after photograph of her obscenely puffy face, and now it was all there, hidden away in Emin's sock drawer. All the paperwork the solicitor had asked for. Her hands pressed deep into the pile of the towel as she turned sideways and looked again at her swollen eye. She felt different. Lighter, stronger. The fear had gone. Divorce would be hard, but no harder than those first lonely months in England. And she would be spoken of with disgust back home, condemned by all who heard. But what would that matter now? She never went back. Meryem and Emin were more English than Turkish. Their future, and hers, was here. She put the towel back on the rail, smoothing the creases, until there were none left to smooth, a deep sadness holding her still.

She was leaving him. The boy who ran up mountains.

How could this have happened? Lifting her chin, Sonja stared at her reflection and as she did, the answer to her question stared back. He wasn't the same man anymore, that was true. But more than that, she wasn't the same woman. And it wasn't that she couldn't control Meryem the way he demanded, it was that she didn't want to

'PLEASE COME IN. *Please.* I'll help you start the science project if you want.' Meryem leaned back against the heavy glass entry door, her schoolbag swinging between her legs.

'It's not that bad, Mery.'

'It is!' Meryem cried, lifting her chin and looking hard at Alma. 'It is, Alma and it's so unfair.' It's been two weeks, and I showed you Mrs Jackson's letter! If I can't come to rehearsals, I can't be in the show.'

Alma looked down at her hands. She was tired and cold, she wanted to go home, to her own home, make toast and watch TV. She didn't want to start the science project and even if she did, she had an idea for it that she was happy to start alone. It was irritating that Meryem always thought she needed help, when she didn't. And yes, it was true. If Meryem missed one more rehearsal, she wouldn't be able to participate in the end of term show. Which meant that Alma wouldn't be able to either, because their dance was a duet. The part that neither Mrs Jackson, nor Meryem knew, was that secretly, she was relieved. The dance rehearsals had become something she dreaded. Just one more excuse for Meryem to boss her around. Why had she expected anything different?

Meryem threw her shoulder against the door. '*Please,* Alma. Everything is so boring now! Emin just watches *The A-Team* all the time. I can't do anything. Please!'

Meryem stared down at her bag.

'Okay. But...' Feeling the heat in her cheeks, Alma stopped talking.

'What?'

'I'm tired, Meryem,' she stammered. 'I... really want to go home.'

'Fine!' Meryem said. '*That's fine!* ' And she turned and pushed the door open.

Alma didn't follow. For a long moment she stood, staring through the door, watching Meryem disappear up the stairs. She didn't know if she was relieved or scared, and she didn't know if Meryem would reappear, bouncing down the steps, brushing off what had just happened. When enough time had passed for her to understand that Meryem wasn't coming back, she pushed the door open and made her way home. Turning the key in the lock, switching the light on in the hall – it all felt different. She felt different and although she was scared, she was also deeply relieved. She had said no. For the first time, she had said no.

As Meryem took her coat off, she saw the handbag and keys on the table. Her mother was home. Early. Probably just to check that she was coming *straight home*. Well, she needn't have bothered. Emin was already doing a great job of that. Every morning he asked the same stupid question.

Are you coming straight home today, Meryem?

No, I'm flying to the moon first, Emin, then I'll come back.

This morning, she'd been so rude, she'd made him cry, which had made her mother angry and, it seemed to Meryem, there was nothing she could do right, and none of it was her fault! Why didn't her mother say something? Why didn't she tell them what was happening, instead of lying about slippers. If she told them, they could just leave. Emin and her mother and her – go and live somewhere else and she wouldn't have to keep coming *straight home* and she could get on with her life.

'Hello.' From around the corner of the hallway, her mother appeared, her face still bearing a faded bruise.

'I'm home,' Meryem said. '*See.*'

'I see,' Sonja nodded. 'I'm... I'm just cleaning Emin's room. Why don't you go and watch TV?'

But Meryem didn't move.

'*Go and watch TV, Mery.*'

Frowning, Meryem flung herself onto the arm of the sofa. Emin was sprawled across the cushions, remote in hand. Something was definitely going on.

'My turn,' Meryem snapped, lunching forward to grab the remote.

But Emin was too quick, shoving it under his tummy.

And suddenly Meryem couldn't be bothered. Everyone was against her! Alma, her mother, even Emin now. 'I'm don't care anyway!' she said and stalked out. If she could, she would have taken her coat and left. That would teach them.

The light at the end of the hallway was coming from Emin's room, and it was instinct keeping her light on her feet that meant her approach was a silent approach. She couldn't have said why, only that she knew... She just knew that what her mother was doing in Emin's room wasn't anything to do with cleaning. As she came closer to lean around the doorframe, she saw how the top drawer of Emin's dresser was wide open. How her mother was standing next to it, a brown envelope in her hands. She was reading a sheet of paper that she'd pulled halfway out. It was clear to Meryem that she hadn't been heard, and already the moment was too long to pretend that she hadn't seen anything. She took a silent step backward, and then another, and another, all the way back to the living room.

LATER, when Emin was in the bath and her father was safely at work, she walked into the kitchen, the letter from Mrs Jackson in her hands, a world of questions on her tongue. It had been an agonising wait, all through dinner, but this letter was her lifeline. Incontrovertible proof that she needed to get back to rehearsals. A letter from a teacher was something she knew her mother would never ignore. She would read it and see. And then she would have to explain what was going on.

'I have a letter, Mamma,' she said. 'From Mrs Jackson.'

Sonja turned. She looked first at the envelope, then at Meryem.

'I'm not in trouble!'

'I didn't think you were,' Sonja said and her face softened. She dried her hands and took the envelope. As she read, she did not change expression, and when she'd finished, she put the letter on the table and turned back to the dishes.

'Well?' Meryem flushed with anger. She'd nurtured that letter all the way home. For her mother to simply put it aside like an unwanted party invite was inexplicable. 'Everything's getting worse!' she shouted. 'And I won't be able to do the show now!' As she turned, her ponytail whipped like a rising snake. She hadn't reached the door before her mother's voice caught her. 'Mery?'

'Yes,' she sulked, glowering bright as an ember.

'Do you trust me?'

Meryem shrugged.

'It's important.' Sonja turned. 'There will be changes. Big

changes, because I'm doing something. But right now you must keep coming straight home. Do you understand?'

Meryem nodded. The expression on her mother's face subdued her. There was an intensity in her eyes she hadn't seen before. 'I do,' she whispered.

'Can you rehearse at lunchtime?'

Meryem shrugged.

'I'll write to Mrs Jackson to ask.' And Sonja turned back to the dishes.

Meryem didn't move. Half of her was willing her mother to turn and tell her what she already knew, the other half was terrified in case she did. That her father had hit her mother was beyond doubt. That she was ready to hear her mother say that was a different thing because that would make it real, this terrifying black cloud she had lived under since it happened. It was everywhere. Filtering through the crack of light at the bottom of the closed bathroom door, when she'd lain in the bath, listening for his footsteps along the hallway, escaping from the kitchen cupboard when she'd opened it to get breakfast cereal. He appeared now at any time of the day, or the night. The father who had never been to a parents' evening, who hadn't even known she'd had, and loved, a Sindy doll until her mother had packed it up in a box for the local secondhand shop. A long time ago, she had a memory of sitting on his knee, pointing at an elephant. They would have been at the zoo. But that was years ago, and between then and now there was nothing to fill the gap. Only an absence she had barely noticed. Alma didn't have a father either. She'd never felt she was missing something. 'Mamma?' she said now. She was thinking of that brown envelope she'd seen in her mother's hands. Big changes, her mother had said.

Sonja turned.

'Mamma!' Emin cried, as he ran in brushing past Meryem's knee. 'Come! Come!' He grabbed Sonja's hand to drag her out of the kitchen. 'They're trying to get Mr T on an aeroplane.'

Sonja laughed. 'I'll be back,' she said as she allowed herself to be pulled.

'It's okay,' Meryem said. 'It can wait.'

~

THE NEXT DAY

SO MUCH SNOW HAD FALLEN, it had blurred the space between earth and sky, and all afternoon the world had rested under low cloud. But with dusk, the grey had gone, replaced by a rich violet sky, studded with silver stars. Every window shone with bright Advent lights, the snow bloomed white and the air was sharp and clear.

Together, her gloved hand in his, Meryem and Emin trudged along, their boots marking out tracks in the new-fallen snow. She was on her way *straight home* again, and she had offered to walk with Emin, something she never did. When school had finished, she hadn't been able to find Alma, who was, Meryem suspected, avoiding her. Never mind. Her mother had promised that she was doing something. Today was much better than yesterday, and as soon as she could, she'd make it up to Alma. 'You have to follow my tracks,' she called now, as she strode ahead. She'd make it up to Emin as well!

They made a game of walking only where no one else had. Two adventurers together. Along the edge of the kerb, zig-zags across the path, and best of all into the park where they stopped and she watched him play on the slide.

Down he came! Boots bulldozing snow that sprayed into his face. Up and down, up and down countless times and he would have continued but Meryem was cold. 'You can have the remote control,' she called, 'if you come now.'

'You have to promise, Meryem.' Emin stood at the top of the slide.

'I do.'

'And you have to keep your promise.'

'I promise, I'll keep my promise,' she said.

'Okay. But you *have* to keep it,' he said, whooshing down.

'Emin.' Meryem bent so they were eye to eye. 'I will keep my promise to you, and Mamma will keep her promise to me.'

His face darkened. 'What has Mamma promised?'

Meryem put her hands in Emin's and pulled him up. 'She's promised she's doing something that means I can start doing things again. Like rehearsals for the show. You know Alma and me are dancing.'

'No!' He snatched his hands away so quickly she almost laughed. It was only the fear in his eyes that stopped her. That turned her stomach over.

'You can't dance with Alma,' Emin whispered. 'Ever, Meryem. *Ever.*'

And now she did laugh, because she was scared herself. 'Why not?'

'If you do, Pappa will hit Mamma again.'

'Emin.' Meryem squeezed his hands, pulled him towards her and hugged him tight. His face had paled whiter than the snow, his eyes little pools of terror. 'It's going to be okay,' she breathed. 'Mamma is doing something. It won't happen again. He won't do it again.'

'No, Meryem, you don't understand!' Emin's muffled voice pushed through. 'You can't! Pappa will hit Mamma if you go back to dancing. He said he would.'

She felt the pavement slide away. She felt sick. 'What,' she whispered, 'are you talking about?'

But Emin only pulled out of the embrace, staring miserably down at the ground.

'Emin!' she said and shook his shoulders. 'Emin!' And again. '*EMIN!*'

'They were arguing about you. Pappa hit Mamma because you weren't home, Meryem!' Huge tears rolled down Emin's cheeks. His mitten was stiff with cold as he tried to wipe them clear.

And although Emin's voice was tiny, the force of his words rocked her back on her heels, leaving her slumped in the snow. 'Did you hear this Emin?' she said. 'Did you hear them?'

Staring at his boots, Emin nodded.

WHEN THEY GOT HOME, and she had settled Emin in front of the TV, Meryem went into his bedroom and straight to his chest of drawers. Her mother had promised, and she knew now whatever the promise was, it was something to do with that brown envelope. It was still there, hidden under a pile of socks.

She took it out and opened it. It was full of documents, mostly in English, two in Turkish, which she couldn't understand. There was a packet of photographs which she took out as well. All of them were of her mother, looking horrible with her bruised eye. Meryem shoved them back in the wallet. The last letter she picked up was from a solicitor. It was very clear. Her mother was divorcing her father.

Two hours later

Sitting in the back of her father's car, Meryem looked across at Emin. He had Mr T in his hands, moving the figure to a tune that only he could hear, his lips shaping a stream of mumbled instructions. In the front seat she could see the dark of her father's outstretched arm, his hand on the steering wheel and the top of his head, his hair streaked grey.

She couldn't settle.

Where had Mr T come from? Her father said it was a surprise early Christmas present, but he never got involved in Christmas and she knew he hated Emin even watching *The A-Team.*

She wasn't excited.

Why wasn't he working? He'd come home from the Turkish club as usual and then instead of going to work, he'd said he had a surprise. He was taking them to the cinema. To see *Back To The Future.* But he never took them anywhere, and Emin was too young, and she couldn't say she didn't want to go. She couldn't say that a boy from school had promised to take her. She couldn't say anything because she was too scared. And she'd tried to tell Alma. She'd gone straight to the phone, because she knew that if Alma came up, if Alma was with them, it would be okay. Her father wouldn't take them anywhere.

But Alma hadn't answered, and she hadn't rung back, even though Meryem had left a message, pleading for her to do so.

Alma? Pick up Alma... Alma, please, if you can hear me

please, please, pick up... I'm scared. My dad says he's taking us to see Back To The Future. I... I don't believe him... If you can hear me, please come upstairs now. If you're here, if you come, it will be alright.

And then, when she'd put the phone down and tried to dial her mother at work, to let her know they were going, her father had come into the room and stopped her.

Her stomach gurgled. She bit down on her lip feeling sick. She had an idea that would not go away: it would have been better if she had called her mother first.

Outside, the high-rises of Enfield flashed by. Meryem pulled her headphones up and switched on her Walkman. She looked down and pressed the FF button. There would only be time to hear one track before they got to the cinema. A high-pitched warble whistled through her ear as she released the button and pressed FF again and watched the sliver of brown tape whiz through. It took three attempts before she got to the track she wanted. She leaned back and looked out the window, watching street lamps float by. By the time the song ended, the gurgle in her stomach had moved up to the back of her throat, because now there were no street lamps. Now the car was travelling much faster. Now, they were on a motorway. Suddenly she felt very cold and very weak and it took a massive effort just to lift her arms and take the headphones off. 'Pappa?'

He didn't answer.

'Baba, where are we going?' It was barely a whisper.

'We have to see a friend first.'

Never had her father taken them to see a friend. Something was very wrong.

'What friend—'

'*Sit back,* Meryem.' That was all he said.

Later that night

THE NOTE WAS WRITTEN in Turkish.

Sonja read it three times before she understood. He had taken Meryem and Emin to see *Back To The Future* at the Odeon. Then he would take them for a hamburger. They might be late. She shouldn't wait up.

It didn't make sense.

Arslan had never taken the kids anywhere. Her stomach clenched and released with a fear so sudden she had to run to the toilet. When she came out, she went straight to Emin's room. The first thing she saw, like a broken limb, was his top drawer hanging open. The next thing she saw was the empty brown A4 envelope. All the papers had been laid, face up, covering the dinosaur faces of his quilt. Two neat rows stretched all the way across her boy's bed.

'He knows.' Somehow, her legs had bent at the knee to carry her out to the hallway, and somehow her fingers had managed to dial Kathy's number.

'We're coming,' Kathy said, and put the phone down.

Sonja went to the front door and opened the latch. Then, leanng against the wall of her home, her legs gave way as she slid to the floor.

22

YOUNG GUNS

Blackpool, present day

THE STAGE WAS EMPTY, but the show wasn't over. George Mightbe was taking one last break. Harsh fluorescent light lit the room, and an announcement over the PA had dozens of women looking through handbags. *Would the owner of a set of keys, with a Best Mum Ever keyring, kindly collect them from reception.*

Sammy looked around. The lights had stripped away that ubiquitous youthful glow. Everyone, she could see now, was as softly contoured, as finely wrinkled, as widened by gravity as she was. She didn't know if this made her feel happy or sad. She didn't know what she felt. She felt as drained of energy as the room was drained of magic.

'Sammy?'

Turning to Gary, she said, 'Tell me then. I want to hear.' And she did. She was ready now.

In those dreadful moments after Gary had eased her away from the bar and sat her down at this secluded table, she'd been too shell shocked to resist. He'd even bought himself a pint, his first in months. And then he'd sat down opposite, and asked her to listen. He had something he wanted to tell her. And although she had no idea what was coming, she *did* want to hear, if only to stop herself thinking about those words, *You wouldn't let him.* 'So, tell me,' she said again. Anything was possible this evening.

'1988,' he said. 'May the twelfth. My technical drawing exam. GCSE.' He crossed his arms, looked down at the table, and smiled such a smile, she felt as if her heart had been sliced. It hurt, that smile. It was loaded with, and shaped by, regret and she wondered if she would be able to bear what was coming.

He looked up. 'I can still remember the day. It was sunny. Warm. I made breakfast for me and my brother. Took a cup of tea into my dad. He was on a late shift. Then...' Gary shrugged. 'Then I went to school, and I never told you this, Sammy.' He paused.

'What?' she whispered.

'I wanted to be an architect. I wasn't much good at school, but I was good at the drawings. Technical drawing.'

Thirty years and she hadn't known that. 'I didn't know,' she said quietly.

'No.' He leaned forward and wrapped his hands around his glass. 'Anyway, I went in for the exam. I had a plan. It wasn't much of one, but it was a plan. I'd be an architect. I'd already made this drawing of a house we could all live in. My dad, me and my brother.' He stopped talking.

'What happened?'

'I saw my mother on the way to school. She was sitting

on the kerb. She had no shoes on. Been out all night, I guessed.' He shrugged. 'She was a mess.'

Sammy reached across the table and wrapped his hand in hers. The feel of it, every callous and joint, was familiar. 'What did you do?'

'I went to school,' he said, letting her hands go as he leaned back. 'I went to school, sat down at my desk in front of the exam paper, stared at it for ten minutes. And then I left.'

'Gary...'

He smiled. 'It was simple really, Sammy. I needed to get home to my dad before she did. I knew that was where she would be heading to next, and I knew my dad was weak. He would have let her back in. We hadn't seen her for a long time by then, and we were doing okay. Really okay. If he'd let her back into his life, she would have destroyed him. Maybe all of us. I did what I thought was right.'

'I...' But she didn't know what to say next, so she stopped trying. This was her husband's story. One he'd never told before. 'You didn't take the exam then?'

'No.' He shook his head. 'And as you know, I didn't become an architect. But I did meet my mother, halfway down our street. And I stopped her.'

'Couldn't you have taken it later?'

'Sammy.' He looked at her as if he was waiting for her to answer her own question. When she didn't, he said, 'We'd had Sean, eighteen months later. Someone had to pay the bills. I did what I had to do.'

Sammy pressed her lips together. She didn't know what he was trying to say. 'Is that what this is all about?' she said, resentment rising. 'That you wished you'd had a different life? Because it's never too late, Gary. It's never—'

'No.' He was shaking his head. 'No. That is not what I'm saying. This isn't even really about me.'

'Well what then?' But she knew. If this wasn't about her husband, she knew who it was about.

'I was lucky, Sammy.'

'Lucky!'

'Yes. I haven't been easy to live with lately. I know that. I've been short-tempered and grumpy. And––'

'Miserable,' she added. 'Don't forget miserable.'

He laughed. 'I know. You're right. Like a bear with a sore head. And I'm sorry. I really am. But you?' He smiled. 'You've always been so easy to live with. Even with everything that's happened.'

Eyes smarting, she looked at him. 'Have I?'

'Yes, Sammy you have. And I *was* lucky.'

'How?' she whispered. 'How?'

'I didn't plan what happened to me. Marrying you. The kids. And for a long time I've let that matter too much, when actually it didn't matter at all.' He reached across the table and took her hands. 'Because it worked out. And I'm happy. It's not like that for everyone. There are so many people living a life they didn't plan, or want. That they can't escape from. That they're not happy in.'

Her face darkened, her voice was tight. 'You mean Meryem?'

'I do. Yes.'

Sammy's lips were a thin tight line. She leaned back and crossed her arms. 'You make it sound simple, Gary. But the choice she made... She chose to do what she's doing.'

'Yes, she did. And maybe, Sammy, maybe that was the first time in her life that she got to choose.' He shook his head. 'I'm not going to judge her. I won't do that. I won't.'

Sammy reached for her drink, took a long sip and sat

back. She looked at Gary and he looked back at her and then, suddenly, her head dropped and the back of her hand was at her eyes, soaking up hot swift tears. 'I didn't mean what I said before,' she whispered, tears rolling over her hands. 'I was just angry.'

Gary nodded. 'I know.'

'And jealous.'

'I know.'

She looked up at him. 'Gary,' she murmured, readying herself to say words she thought she'd never, ever say. 'I would understand, if you wanted... If you needed some space.' And although the effort was super-human, she stayed calm and held his eye, as he held hers. 'Things have obviously changed.'

'What are you trying to say?' And his voice was as careful as if he had tiptoed to the edge of a canyon.

'It's just...' A baby wisp of new hair escaped the side of her headscarf, her hand trembled as she tucked it back in. 'It's ironic,' she said. 'I was hoping this trip might help us get closer, but it seems to be doing just the opposite.' She smiled. He was so handsome. For her, he was as handsome as the day they had married. 'You're still young,' she managed. And she took a deep breath and blurted it out. 'You might want a whole woman.'

Sure as if a fist had swung past his nose, Gary flinched. His cheeks coloured and he sat up straight. For a long moment he didn't speak, then he reached out and grabbed her hand. 'I have a *whole* woman. Right here!'

She tried to pull away, startled, embarrassed, but his grip was stronger, much stronger and the feeling she had was almost that of fear. She didn't think she'd ever seen him so furious. With her? Himself? She didn't know.

'*Look at me!*' he whispered.

So she did.

'I'm not going anywhere, Sammy.' His eyes fixed on hers. 'You know that? *Do you know that?*'

If she hadn't before, she did now. She nodded, a small up and down, and before she could do anything else he had leaned to her, his nose pushed against hers, forehead to forehead. And then his hand was on her cheek. 'You are my wife and I said, I'm not going anywhere.'

Flustered, Sammy put a hand on his chest and eased him away.

He lifted his glass and drank. When he put it down, he rubbed his hand across his eyes.

'Are you tired?' she said quietly.

He shook his head, eyes still hidden by his hand. 'I wanted to be there for you, Sammy.'

'You are!' She stared at him. Did he think he hadn't been? 'You have always been there for me. From the beginning.'

But Gary only shook his head again. 'I feel I've let you down.'

'How could you have let me down? You've done everything.' And now she was crying. 'Sometimes it was too much. And I'm sorry. All you wanted was to help, when sometimes all I wanted was to hide. Or forget. Or... I don't know, pretend it wasn't happening.'

Letting his hand drop, Gary looked at her. 'Is that why you're still smoking?'

'Yes!' Tears streamed down her face. 'Yes, that's why I'm still smoking. I can't help it. I'm sorry, but I can't help it.'

'Sammy.' In one movement, Gary was on his feet, his arms around her, pulling her up and into an embrace, holding her as close as he ever had. 'I'm sorry,' he whispered. 'I got scared. You were the one with cancer and I got scared.'

'You never showed it.'

'Well I was. I was terrified of losing you. And I couldn't help you. To watch you go through what you've been through. And what could I do? Make a bacon sandwich? I felt useless.'

Smiling, Sammy drew back. 'You researched turmeric pretty well.'

'Is it that bad?'

'Foul.'

'But it's also—'

'I know, I know,' she said, leaning into him again, laying her head against his shoulder.

'I think,' he said, 'I just wanted to escape, and I can't explain why because what we have is the most special thing in the world. The most ordinary, and the most special.' He pulled back, his hands on her shoulders as he looked at her. 'We have a family, Sammy. A family that works. We made that happen. Every day for the last thirty years, we made that happen.'

Sammy nodded. 'You don't still want to then,' she said, her voice small. 'Escape.'

Gary put his hands on her cheeks, leaned forward and kissed her forehead. 'Only with you, Sammy. Only with you.'

23

YOU HAVE BEEN LOVED (1)

Blackpool, present day

STANDING AT THE HOTEL ENTRANCE, Alma clutched the ribbon-tied bundle to her chest. Although Meryem was only twenty yards away, sat on a bench, turned away from the light, she might as well have been back in Dubai, or Turkey, or Saudi Arabia, or any of the places she had been hidden for so long. The distance between them was that far.

When Meryem had fled the bar, so had Alma – straight back to her room to get what she needed. And then on to Meryem's room, her heart full of dread. And as she had stood and knocked, and waited, and knocked and waited, panic had seeded itself as she began to understand that it could already be too late. That Meryem could already be gone, as quickly and as permanently as she went before. The panic had swept her back along the corridor and down the stairs, to here, the front entrance of the hotel. She bent her head and tried to clear her throat, but it wouldn't clear. Nothing would clear, nothing would calm until she had done what she needed to do. 'Meryem.' It was only a whisper.

Alma took a step forward. And then one more, and then one more. 'Can I sit?' she managed, as she came close enough. And when no answer came, she edged herself down.

Meryem had neither moved, nor spoken.

'These are for you.' Her voice was small and her hand was shaking as she stretched the bundle of letters to Meryem. 'I... I found them last night.' And maybe she imagined it, the tiniest movement, the smallest turning of the head from Meryem... Real or not, it was enough. 'Sammy brought a box of mine up. They're letters your mother wrote, Meryem. To you and Emin. My mother must have kept them.'

And then it was real, the movement. The slight uplift of the chin, the change of light on Meryem's face as she turned.

'I haven't read them... I wouldn't do that.'

Meryem looked at the letters, her face blank, her hand inching forward.

'I'm sorry.'

And then suddenly, the hand wasn't inching forward, it was at Meryem's mouth and her eyes were huge with terror, staring back at Alma as her body convulsed and she lurched forward, hands spread, vomit spewing between her fingers.

'Meryem.' Alma was at her side, scooping back handfuls of hair.

Another retch, another spill.

From across the car park, someone laughed. *Too much of the bubbly stuff!*

Alma moved in closer, wrapping an arm around

Meryem's bare shoulders, making of herself a wall. 'I'm here,' she said. 'I'm—' But her voice failed as Meryem's shoulders heaved, and her arms shook, and her body spewed out all it could no longer contain. And when it was over, when she had fallen onto the pavement, half-sitting, half-slumped against the bin, Alma too sat down. And the time they sat could not have been measured. It reached back too many years. It covered a lifetime of loss, an eternity of grief. It was as long as they didn't know they needed it to be, and it only ended when, in a gesture as weary as that of a dying man, Meryem lifted her head from her knees and turned to Alma, her eyes empty.

'She asked me to trust her, Alma,' she whispered. 'My mother asked me to trust her. It's one of the last memories I have.'

'You didn't know, did you?' Alma looked down at the bundle she still protected. 'You didn't know,' she whispered, as if she were speaking to the letters themselves.

Meryem dipped her forehead to the cupped palms of her hands, her head shaking. 'I told myself she would come. Every day I believed she would come. And then I didn't. I don't know when. I don't know when I stopped believing.'

'She never gave up,' Alma whispered. She looked down at the curve of Meryem's back. She wanted to hold her. It was all she could do not to reach out and touch her.

'My father,' Meryem said, her voice muffled by her hands, 'only told us she had written when he died last week.'

'He told you?' Alma breathed. Her heart began pounding. *He said something before he died. Something that has brought me back here.*'This is why you're here,' she whispered. 'This is why you came back. Were you looking for them?'

Meryem didn't answer. Lifting her head, she turned to look at Alma. 'He called us to him, Alma. Emin and me. He called us to come to him, in his big empty house in the village. And he told us that she had written. That he sent all the letters back.'

Alma's mouth dried. The tips of her fingers tingled.

'He wanted forgiveness before he died. I didn't.'

'Forgive him?'

Meryem nodded, her face open, her voice soft as she said, 'I looked into his eyes and I said, I do not forgive you, Baba.' Her mouth turned up in a smile that did not reach her eyes. 'This is another reason for my brother not to talk to me. You know the first. You know what I do. For money.'

'I don't care what you do for money!' Holding Meryem's eye, Alma mirrored her. Lifted her chin to the same angle, set her jaw at the same line. 'I don't care what you do, Meryem.'

'I think you do, Alma.'

'*No.*' Alma shook her head. 'I don't, Meryem. I don't.' And, as she heard herself say it, Alma knew it was the truth. She didn't care because what Meryem did, didn't take away Mery. Her best friend. The most ambitious girl in the class. 'In a way,' she started and paused. The words... what word was the right word? 'Impressed,' she said, testing it. Then a little surer, 'Yes, I'm impressed.' Alma nodded. She meant it. Of course it was the right word. For Mery, it had always been the right word.

'No, Alma. There is nothing to be impressed—'

'You're brave, Meryem! You're so much braver than me!' Alma put her head back and laughed at the stars. The relief of the honesty of it! Mery always was, always had been, and always would be, far far braver than she could ever hope to be. 'Why *shouldn't* you choose how to survive?' she demanded. 'Why *should* you forgive your father? Why *should* you?'

'Tradition?' Meryem said sadly.

'*Fuck tradition!*'

Meryem laughed.

So she said it again.'Fuck tradition! Fuck fuck fuck it!'

'Me too,' Meryem smiled. 'That's what I think, Alma. Fuck tradition!'

For a long moment, neither of them spoke. Meryem tucked her legs to one side, and using the back of her hand, wiped away spittle from her face. 'He was an angry man,' she said, looking down at her lap. 'And after he took us to Turkey, he just became angrier. Everyone said it was because my mother wasn't a good wife to him.'

'That's not true, Meryem.'

But Meryem only smiled. 'Everyone told us, Alma. My father's family. My aunts. Even my mother's best friend. Afife.'

Alma shook her head. She could hear her heart thumping. 'What did they tell you?' she whispered.

'That if she was a good wife, a good mother, she would come.'

'Did you believe them?'

Meryem shook her head. 'No. But I knew that my mother was divorcing my father. Before we left, I knew that and—'

'You didn't leave. You—'

Meryem put her finger to her lips, the gentlest gesture, a request for silence, which Alma complied with. 'Some things are too difficult to say, Alma.'

Chastened, Alma nodded. 'I understand,' she whispered. She hadn't, but she was, she thought, beginning to.

'In my father's culture, in the village, if a woman chooses to divorce her husband, she chooses to divorce her whole family. The children as well. That was how it worked.' Meryem's eyes were half-closed now, as if the world beyond the veined skin of her eyelids was too much to witness. 'There was a woman,' she sighed, 'who had chosen this. She lived on her own in a house, furthest away from the square. No one talked to her. Her children lived on the other side of the village, and she never saw them. Once I watched as she waited outside the school. When her children came out, another woman took them away. They didn't even look back at her.' Meryem sighed. 'I didn't want to believe what they were saying,' she said quietly. 'And neither did Emin. But if this was what her life would have been like...' She stopped talking, staring blankly ahead. 'I just wanted her to come and take us back.'

'Meryem—'

'He was playing with us, Alma. Emin, me, my mother. He tried to torture her into coming to him. But she was strong, wasn't she?'

Alma didn't speak.

And suddenly Meryem looked at her. 'Is it true? Is that how she died?'

Nodding, Alma put her hand to her chest and forced air into her lungs. It was true. As true and as distant as galaxies above them, as real and present as the ground beneath them.

Meryem looked up to the black black sky.

And Alma tried to catch a memory, a thread to wind around her friend, and pull her back to safety. 'Your mother went to Turkey,' she said. 'Twice. She went to the police. Even her boss at work tried—'

But Meryem shook her head.

'I'm sorry. I just want you to know the truth.'

'Me too,' Meryem answered, her eyes black glass. 'Me too, Alma. And one day you will tell me everything, but...'

Tears fell into her upturned hands. 'Please not now. I can't hear it now.'

And looking down at the letters, Alma nodded.

'There was nowhere to go,' Meryem said. 'There was one road to the village and nothing else. And I was never allowed to leave the house on my own. I tried once. I tried to run away, once.' Turning to look at Alma, she whispered, 'Can you understand? There was nothing else I could do, Alma. I had to believe what they were saying, otherwise how could I have lived? How could I have carried on?'

'I do.' Tears streamed down Alma's face. 'I do understand.'

'I let her down. My mother asked me to trust her and I let her down.'

'You were fourteen, Meryem. You had no choice.'

Meryem shivered. 'No choice,' she said, 'is still a choice. And I chose to believe them, instead of her. I chose to believe that she didn't want us, and it wasn't hard either, Alma. It wasn't hard for me to do that.'

'You were a child, Meryem.'

'No.'

'Yes.'

'No!' Meryem grabbed Alma's hand. 'It wasn't hard,' she said, 'because I deserved it.'

Alma stared in astonishment.

'I had so much time to understand. And I deserved it. I deserved what had happened to me. I deserved to be the kind of child a mother wouldn't want.'

'*No!*' Alma's voice was hoarse. 'Why would you think that?'

But Meryem didn't answer. She fell forward, her arms wrapped around her body as she rocked back and forward.'

'Why, Meryem?'

'It was my fault! That all of this happened, *was* my fault.'

And because it was clear to Alma that Meryem meant every word, she didn't even try to speak. Instead, she moved closer, placed her hand on Meryem's back and waited.

And a long moment later, Meryem lifted her head and took a deep breath and her words, when they came, were fluent and easy. As well preserved as a treasure that has been lovingly protected, and when finally unwrapped, is perfect.

MERYEM

London, 1985

With Emin safely absorbed in the TV, Meryem sat on his bed, her heart thumping and looked again at the documents she'd seen her mother hide in the drawer the other evening. The last letter she picked up was from a solicitor. It was very clear. Her mother was divorcing her father.

Was this good news or bad news? Either way it wasn't meant for her eyes, yet. Very slowly she piled the documents together and began sliding them carefully back into the envelope. As she was doing so, the telephone rang and she jumped as the sudden shrillness cut through the quiet room.

It was her mother, ringing to say she would be working an extra hour – and also, Meryem suspected, ringing to check that she was straight home. She listened to her mother talk and felt no resentment or anger. She promised that she'd look after Emin until their father came home from the club. Her mother was wondering about food. 'I'll make toast, Mamma,' she said and her mother had laughed and said, 'Thank you.'

And she did. She made toast, and then made some more. After that she cleaned the kitchen and vacuumed the living room. She kept busy because if she didn't she would start thinking about her mother's eye, and what Emin had said in the park. It was better not to think of it. Better just to keep busy and not think of anything.

YOU HAVE BEEN LOVED (2)

Blackpool, present day

'And I did, Alma,' Meryem whispered. 'I kept myself so busy. I made Emin toast. More and more toast. I wanted to make things right. I was trying to make things right.' Her voice broke. She slumped forward, head in hands.

'Meryem.' Alma inched her hand forward. 'You don't have to say anything. It's—'

'I do! I have to! I have to tell you.'

And making the smallest of nods, Alma inched her hand back.

'I kept busy. I cleaned the flat. I made toast.' Slowly, Meryem raised her head and looked at Alma. 'I even remember thinking that after the divorce, my house might be like your house.' She smiled. 'That made me happy, Alma. So happy I forgot about the envelope I left on Emin's bed. The solicitor's letter. The photographs. I forgot all about it.'

Alma didn't move. She felt numb. Her fingers felt numb,

her face felt numb, only her heartbeat was traceable, steady and loud.

'It was still there when my father came home. So I know, you see. I know.'

'What,' Alma managed. 'What do you know, Meryem?'

'I know he saw them, Alma. I know he went into Emin's room and he saw what she was planning to do. I've always known. Do you see now?'

'No.' Shaking her head, Alma stared back. 'No... See what?'

'It was my fault, Alma. What happened was my fault.'

And again, Alma tried to reach out, but her hand wouldn't move, not a finger. She felt unnaturally calm, like the mirrored surface of a bottomless lake. It was unfathomable. What Meryem was saying, the guilt she carried, was unfathomable.

'I came to England to talk with your mother, Alma.'

There was a warmth on her hand that she couldn't determine. And when she looked down, it took a long moment to understand that the warmth was Meryem's hand, holding hers.

'When he told me, I thought I would come back and talk to her. I thought if anyone knew the truth, it would be your mother. They were good friends, your mother and mine.'

'Yes,' Alma said. 'They were.'

Meryem took a deep breath. 'I never expected to...' And as her words drifted off, she looked down at the bundle in Alma's lap, and Alma did too, and although neither of them spoke, another voice was loud, whispering across years, restless, finally, to be heard.

My darling Meryem, You were born on December 13th 1971... I ask again, is it possible to inherit loneliness? For your sake, I hope that it is not... Perspective is everything. Now that I have it,

I can see clearly the moments of my life in which I made choices that hurt us both.

'These,' Alma whispered, and her hand was shaking as she picked up the letters. 'These are your hope, Meryem.'

But Meryem didn't move. 'I'm scared,' she whispered. 'Too scared.'

Alma squeezed her hand. 'Your mother would never have wanted you to blame yourself. And if my mother were alive, this is what she would have said too. All you have to do is read the letters. Read them and you will know it too. She wanted you, Meryem. She loved you.' And she pressed the bundle into Meryem's lap. 'Read them,' she whispered. 'Promise me, you will read them.'

Meryem looked down at the letters.

'And I will be here. For as long as you need me, Meryem, I will be here. I won't...' Alma couldn't catch her breath. 'I won't let you down,' she said. 'I let you down, Meryem. If I had come with you that night. If I—'

'No.' Meryem's whisper was a door brushing closed. 'No,' she said. 'You mustn't think that. The only person that should feel any guilt is dead now.'

And the weight that Alma hadn't understood was constricting her eased. She spread her hands out and leaned back, tipping her head to the stars. She felt light-headed. She felt drained. She felt a sadness as immeasurable as the stars above. Guilt. She'd carried it for so long, she'd grown layers and layers over it. And it hurt to understand how Meryem had been similarly weighted. What had happened to them? Those girls with plans? With dreams? With light hearts? Urgently, she turned now to Meryem, took her hand and pressed it to her own heart, holding it there as if it were the only thing that kept it beating. Because she *had* to. She *had* to make Meryem understand.

'Your mother,' she whispered, 'did not blame you, Meryem. *Ever.*'

Meryem looked at her.

'Do you believe me?'

A moment passed.

'And I never blamed you, Alma,' Meryem said. '*Ever.*'

'So we're free of it?' she whispered.

Meryem nodded. 'We should be. We should be free.'

Alma lifted her chin to the sky. Her eyes filled with tears. For everything that had been lost, everyone who was gone. Meryem was speaking now, her words opening themselves up to Alma like flowers in the sun.

'I never had friends in the village, Alma.' Meryem looked at her. 'You were my best friend. You always were.'

A band tightened around Alma's chest. 'Me too,' she scraped. 'You were my best friend too.'

24

FREEDOM

Blackpool, present day

SAMMY SAT at the same breakfast table as she had the day before. She was wearing her Versace jeans and a white t-shirt, with *Choose Life* emblazoned in large black letters across her chest. On the empty chair next to her, she had placed two plastic bags. 'I suppose everyone is hung over,' she said, looking around. The dining room was quiet, only half a dozen having made it to breakfast.

'I guess so.' Opposite her, Gary was halfway through a plate of bacon and eggs.

'Do you think they will come down?' She looked at the bags.

Fork at his mouth, Gary looked too.

'They haven't gone, have they? I mean, I know Alma wouldn't. But Meryem...'

He shook his head. 'I don't think so. Where would she

have gone, Sammy? And didn't Alma's text say they were both in their rooms?'

'Yes.' And again she looked at the bags. 'Was it a stupid idea? Buying them?'

'No.' He smiled. 'It was a lovely idea, Sammy. I mean that. Nodding at her t-shirt, he said, 'It looks great. And so do the jeans.'

Sammy laughed. 'They're a bit over the top for breakfast.'

'They're not. Every day, remember? Something that sparkles, every day. That's what we said.'

'Last night. We said that last night. It's morning now and—'

'And I mean it.' Gary finished. He reached out and ran his hand up her bare arm. 'But I am worried you're cold. It's not that warm.'

Sammy looked down at her chest, at the huge letters, and as she did, she felt the familiar clumpy shadow movement of the mastectomy bra. She wasn't cold, but she was fed up with this thing, always a nano-second behind her body, never in sync. 'I'm not cold,' she started, 'but...'

'What?'

'Wait a moment, give me a moment.' Lowering her head, she reached behind her back, unclipped the bra and deft as a magician, pulled it out through an arm of the t-shirt and slapped it on the table, one pink nipple on a crumpled pile of soft polyfoam staring up at the ceiling.

'How the hell did you do that?' Gary stared at the bra, a fist at his mouth as he laughed.

And now Sammy too was laughing. 'Gary, there isn't a woman in the world that doesn't know how to take a bra off without getting undressed.'

'If you say so.'

'I do,' she said. 'And no, I'm not cold, but I am... I was fed up with that thing.'

'It's...um... It's...' He picked the bra up.

'You can borrow it whenever you want,' she said. 'In fact, you can have it because...' And she stretched her arms up. She felt lighter, freer than she had since the day of her diagnosis. And maybe that was because of the bra, and maybe it was because last night she had fallen asleep in the place she was happiest, folded within her husband's arms. 'I'm never going to wear it again,' she declared and looked down at her flat chest. 'This is me.' Looking back at Gary, she added. 'This is me, now. Take it or leave it.'

Gary leaned across the table and kissed her. 'I'll take it,' he said. 'But this? Do something with this, it's putting me off my breakfast!'

And laughing, Sammy scrunched the bra into a ball, and stuffed it into her handbag.

SHE WAS STILL SMILING when a few minutes later Alma joined them.

'I'm okay,' she said as she pulled out a chair and sat down. 'And Meryem is still here.'

Sammy nodded. 'There's tea in the pot,' she said, sliding it across the table.

Alma took it and poured. She added milk, and leaning back in her chair said, 'I gave her the letters.'

'All of them.'

'No.' Alma shook her head. 'No. She's not ready for that one yet.'

Gary leaned forward on his elbows, his hands clasped together. 'Have you spoken to her this morning?'

'By text. She's been up most of the night, but she's coming down.'

He opened his mouth to say something, but as he did his phone pinged. 'The DeLorean's ready,' he said, opening the message. And pushing his chair back, he stood up. 'I'll call a taxi. Best to get it straight away.'

Sammy nodded as he came around the table and bent to kiss the top of her head.

'See you later.'

'See you later,' she said, her fingers entwined with his.

Watching him go, Alma looked at Sammy. 'Is everything alright?'

'Everything is more than alright.' Sammy smiled. 'But...' She pressed her lips together, her head shaking as if her body was trying to refuse the words her mind had decided upon. 'I said some terrible things, Alma.'

'We all said some terrible things, Sammy. All of us.'

'Will she forgive me?'

Alma smiled. Forgiveness. It was such a precious gift to bestow, such a cruel punishment to withhold it. And didn't it go hand in hand with blame? And hadn't she, in all these long years, in one way or another, blamed herself. She had. It was there, in every decision she had ever made. The raw material she'd used to shape her life. And how constricting a material it had turned out to be. How limiting and dull and inflexible. There was no freedom to be found in such a suffocating emotion, no path forward. Meryem hadn't made that mistake. Meryem, who surely had cause, who could have wielded blame like a god wields the weather. Turning to Sammy, she said, 'Honestly, Sammy? I don't believe that Meryem will even think there is anything to forgive. I really don't.' And as she said it, she believed anew in the truth of it, and felt sandbags slip away.

'I bought her a present,' Sammy said quietly. 'They were selling them at the end of the concert. I got you one too, Alma. I'm wearing mine.' And she looked down at her t-shirt.

Across the table, Alma looked too. *'Choose Life,'* she read.

'Do you think she'll like it...? Do you?'

Alma smiled. 'I can't think of anything more appropriate.'

'Oh, that's a relief. I wasn't sure. Gary said...'

As Sammy talked, Alma held her cup at her lips, half-listening, half-hearing, her mind still stuck on that word: forgiveness. She meant what she's said to Sammy. On a scale of forgivable, or unforgivable actions, what Sammy had said last night would barely register with Meryem. Which didn't mean there wasn't forgiveness to be sought. It just meant that it couldn't come from Meryem. Couldn't, in fact, come from any of them. The forgiveness that was needed, was in the hands of people she had never met, who were so far away she didn't know where to start. Looking up at Sammy she said, 'Meryem has two children, doesn't she? Hassan and...'

' Saarah,' Sammy said. 'I'm not going to forget that, am I. Almost the same as my Sarah.'

'That's right. And Saeed was her married name. I remember her telling me. I remember that.'

Sammy nodded. 'What are you thinking, Alma?'

Trying to ignore the knot of tension tightening deep in her stomach, Alma leaned forward and put her cup on the table. 'I'm thinking of moving out of my comfort zone, Sammy.' She paused. 'So far out, I'm terrified.'

'Then I think you should do it,' Sammy said.

But Alma didn't answer.

Picking up her phone, Sammy swiped it open. 'Dubai is only three hours ahead.'

Alma smiled. 'They're not in Dubai. I think she said her daughter is in Singapore.'

'Either way,' Sammy said.

'Either way,' Alma echoed.

IT WAS like looking at Mery again. The face of the beautiful young woman whose Instagram profile bore the name Saarah Saeed was Meryem's double. Only younger, and slimmer of jaw, and lighter in the eyes.

'This must be her,' Sammy whispered. She'd moved across to the seat next to Alma, and was now leaning over her shoulder. 'It must be.'

Alma nodded. 'I want to be sure,' Five minutes later, a quick Google search had pulled up listings for a Saarah Saeed that showed she was a fashion designer and that she lived in Singapore, and there amongst her followers was a Hassan Saeed. Meryem's son.

'It's her,' Sammy said. 'It's definitely her.'

Heart pounding, Alma put her phone back on the table. As an idea, it had seemed achievable. Now that it was becoming action, it felt impossible. She sat back in her chair, the ceiling of the room lowering, the walls closing in, her phone out of reach. In a life dictated by caution, what she was about to do, what she wanted to do, was unimaginable. She simply could not imagine herself picking up her phone and sending the message. She closed her eyes. There were many things she had learned over the last two days that she could not have imagined, but were as real as the chair she was sitting on, the very ordinary table in front of her. She could not imagine selling her body for money, she could not imagine marrying a man twice her age, she could not imagine having parts of her body cut away. And she could not imagine discovering Sonja dead, calling her mother calmly and then sitting down, to wait. But she had. Long ago, she had done that, and if she could do that, and Meryem could choose to live without the bitter taste of blame flavouring each day, and Sammy could make her bald eyebrows dance... then she could do this.

'I'll leave you,' Sammy said, as she stood up. 'I'm going to have a quick cigarette and I promise, it will be my last. I've decided.'

Dazed, Alma looked up.

'Send the message, Alma,' Sammy said and walked away.

> Hi Saarah, You don't know me, but my name is Alma and I'm a friend of your mother's. I would very much appreciate it, if you could message me back? This is my number.

ALMA LOOKED AT THE MESSAGE. It didn't read right to her. She deleted it and re-typed.

> Hi Saarah, You don't know me, but my name is Alma and I am your mother's best friend. I would very much appreciate it, if you could message me back? This is my number.

Then she pressed send, sat back and waited.

Sammy returned. They ordered coffee and waited.

Twenty minutes passed and although she hadn't been hungry, Alma ate a full breakfast. No message had come through and she was on her second cup of coffee by the time Meryem appeared at the entrance to the dining room.

'Alma,' Sammy whispered.

Alma turned. Meryem was on her way to the table. She was wearing a lemon-coloured blouse and tight jeans, her hair was styled and curled, her eyelashes on, her lips glossed. And seeing her, Alma felt an unexpected and immense relief. Meryem was back. She was back and she was still standing and why, she thought, was she even surprised.

Sammy stood. 'I'm sorry,' she blurted. 'Meryem I'm sorry about last night. I feel so guilty. The things I—'

But Meryem held her hand up.

'I need to—'

'No more apologies, Sammy. No more guilt.' And looking at Alma, Meryem smiled. 'That's right, isn't it, Alma?'

'Definitely right,' Alma whispered. 'Definitely.'

Alma inched her phone closer. 'Are you having breakfast,' she said, then, 'you should eat.' Because closer now, she could see the fine lines around Meryem's mouth, the way they pulled it down and despite the layer of make-up, the hollows under her eyes were deep.

'I'll take some tea.'

The waitress came and drinks were ordered. And five minutes later as she came back, bearing a loaded tray, Alma's phone flashed.

She pulled it towards her, acutely aware of Sammy watching her closely, of Meryem, pouring herself tea. Elbow crooked round the screen, she opened the message.

Hello, Alma, Is there a problem? Is my mother ok?

She typed out a response, without pausing, without allowing herself a moment to think.

> She is fine. She's with me now, in the UK. I also knew your grandmother, Sonja, and I would very much like to talk to you. Would that be possible?

Meryem glanced across.

'Work,' Alma said.

'On a Sunday?' Sammy said, her voice light.

'Even on a Sunday,' Alma replied.

Another message pinged through.

> If you think it's necessary.

> I do, are you free now?

And then Alma was on her feet, phone at her ear, walking away from the table towards the door.

Sammy watched her go. 'I told you,' she said. 'She gets these calls from all over the world.'

Meryem smiled. 'She's done well.'

'We all have,' Sammy said and her voice was thick with emotion. 'We've all done the best we could.'

Cup at her lips, Meryem nodded and her eyes were glassy with tears that she blinked away.

Shyly, Sammy reached for the plastic bag. 'I hope you don't mind,' she said, 'but I bought something for you. There's one in there for Alma too.'

'For me?' Meryem put her cup down and took the bag. 'Sammy, you didn't—'

'Oh I did,' Sammy nodded. 'I really did, Meryem. It's not your usual style, but there isn't anyone in the world I can think of who could wear it better.'

Meryem smiled. 'Shall I open it.' And without waiting for an answer, she pulled from the bag a white t-shirt, identical to the one Sammy wore.

'*Choose Life,*' she read as she held the t-shirt up.

'You have,' Sammy whispered. 'You already have.'

'I…' Meryem shook her head. She was blinking furiously, but it was no good. Tears streamed down her face. 'Can I put it on?' she said and again, didn't wait for an answer, stretching her arms and pulling the t-shirt over her blouse, looking down at her chest and laughing and looking across at Sammy's chest, her eyes opening in shock as Sammy grinned and pulled out her mastectomy bra from her handbag, and nodded. 'You too,' Meryem said. 'You've chosen life too.'

'Yes I have,' Sammy said. 'I definitely have.'

And then suddenly Alma was back at the table, and Sammy wasn't smiling.

Meryem turned.

'I have someone who would like to talk to you,' Alma said, and stretched out her phone.

Meryem stared at it.

'It's Saarah, Meryem. It's your daughter.'

Meryem's face drained. If she hadn't been sitting, she would, Alma was sure, have fallen.

Slowly, silently, Sammy eased her chair back and stood.

And pressing the phone into Meryem's hand, Alma whispered. 'We'll be here. Sammy and I will both be here.'

25

FAITH

B*lackpool, present day*

MERYEM SAT in the passenger seat of Alma's Corsa, her phone in her hands. Beyond the low wall of the car park stretched the sands of Fleetwood beach. She could see a row of birds queued at the waterline, black specks, orderly as monks. Dogs ran in joyously wide circles, their people walking behind, slow and calm, heads bowed to the wind.

Alma wasn't in the car. She was a few feet away, talking to Sammy and Gary.

Meryem leaned forward to see. Gary was leaning against the DeLorean, Alma, hands in her pockets, was nodding and nodding, as Sammy talked. Easing back in her seat, she opened the messenger app on her phone again.

It was still there.

> Mamma, this is my new number. I will be in Dubai next week. It's difficult with work, we have a show this week, but as soon as I have the flight booked I'll let you know.

It was real. Pressing back against the headrest, she closed her eyes, tears leaking as once again her mother's words floated up.

... you might become a teacher, or you might become a nurse like Kathy. Or you might even become a doctor. I had met several women in England by then who were doctors... I was understanding, in a way I never had before, how you had the chance to be anything you wanted to be.

She had read each letter through so many times the words were etched on her bones. Nothing could separate them from her, they would die now only when she did, and even then they would lie together, and the truth of that, as she opened her eyes and looked out at the wide expanse of beach, was the wind lifting her, the sun warming her.

You would be proud, Mamma, she whispered, *so proud.*

THE SOFT THUD of a door closing made her turn. Gary was handing something to Sammy, who, although she had a sweater underneath, was still wearing her *Choose Life* t-shirt. Alma had hers on too. She looked down at her chest, she was also still wearing hers and the sight of it made her smile. When had she ever left the house in anything as casual? When had she ever walked out the door without noticing what she was wearing? But she had. How did she pack? How long had the drive here taken, with Alma asking again and again if she was alright. Would she be alright, waiting? This was something she had long promised Sammy, and... *Everything is alright, Alma.* This was all she had been able to say. Because it was. Saarah had said she was coming to visit. There wasn't much more she remembered from the call, except that Saarah had said she would visit. *She's coming, Mamma,* she whispered. *My daughter is coming to see me.*

She didn't hear the footsteps approaching, nor Sammy calling her name. It was only the soft tap against the window that broke her reverie. When she turned, she saw how Sammy was holding something, wrapped in blue cloth, and she opened the window.

'Meryem,' she started, 'you never got the chance to say goodbye to your mother, so I want to ask... I wanted to... ' Sammy's head dipped and as it did, the wind picked up the tail of her headscarf, flipping it like a leaf on the breeze. 'I wanted to ask,' she said looking at Meryem now, 'if you would please come and help me say goodbye to mine. It...' Her voice broke and it was a titan effort to put it back together. 'You might... you might even think of it as your mother.'

Meryem couldn't speak. Breathing was hard, so hard it hurt as she pulled in air, swallowed hard and said, 'I would like that very much, Sammy. Very much.'

AND ALTHOUGH GREY clouds punched across the sky, the threat of rain had never been real. Winds that were too high to be felt, but had always been present, were already clearing the skies, and shards of silver sunlight, like forked lightening, lit the beach end to end.

Sitting on the bonnet of the DeLorean, his feet on the wall, Gary put his hand up to shield his eyes, to be able to see better the three small figures approaching the shoreline. 'There you go,' he said quietly, as the first figure stopped, bent over and straightened up, turning slow circles, arms outstretched. 'There you go,' he whispered, as the second figure repeated the action. *There you go.* He watched, as the third figure did the same.

ALSO BY CARY J HANSSON

The hugely successful *Midlife Series* is available to order through my website: www.caryjhansson.com

Or at any good bookshop.

A Midlife Holiday ISBN: 978 91 987 5873 3

A Midlife Baby ISBN: 978 91 9875 8795

A Midlife Gamble ISBN: 978 91 9875 8771

ALSO BY CARY J HANSSON

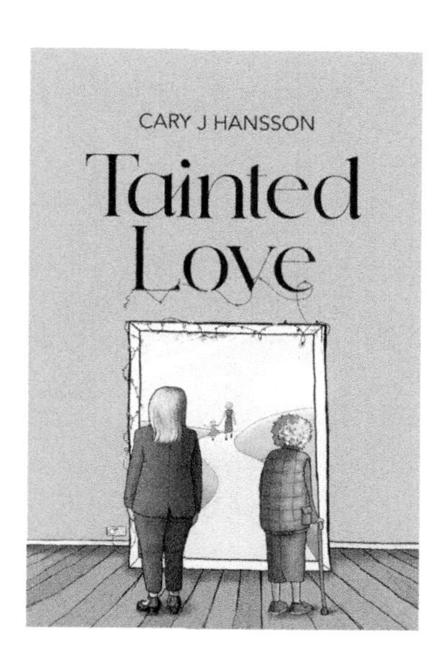

'Years ago, watching a late night movie in which a mother had turned to her son and said, I have never loved you, Toby had yawned, declared the script unbelievable and taken himself off to bed. But Jo had watched to the end, a morbid curiosity carrying her through, because she'd known. It wasn't unbelievable. Sometimes, parents didn't love their children.'

Tainted Love, is the second novel in *The Gen X* Series of women's contemporary fiction.

Available through all good bookshops. Or my website.

Use ISBN: 978-91-527-8603-1

A NOTE FROM THE AUTHOR

Thank you for reading.

Gaining exposure as an author relies upon word-of-mouth, so if you have enjoyed the book do tell your friends. Or gift them a copy! And please do consider leaving a review or rating at the site you purchased from. It really helps.

If you're interested in having me participate in your reading group, drop me a line through social media. (Instagram)

If you're interested in Writing for Wellness you can find out more on my website:

www.caryjhansson.com

If you want a more regular fix of my writing, you can sign up for my digital newsletter: *5 Minute Reads From a 50Something Woman* at:

caryjhansson.substack.com

Printed in Great Britain
by Amazon